LOVE LETTERS

LOVE LETTERS

A HIDDEN SPRINGS NOVEL

LISA MCLUCKIE

Love Letters
A Hidden Springs Novel
© 2021 by Lisa McLuckie

Discounts are available for bulk purchases. Book excerpts or customized printings can also be created. Subsidiary rights may be available for license.

Cover design by Sue Giroux. Formatted with Vellum.

Please direct all inquiries to:

The Betty Press LLC
PO Box 241
Williams Bay, WI 53191
www.thebettypress.com
(262) 729-3231

ISBN-13: 978-1-941744-06-2

≈

For my mom, who never meddled (as far as I know).

≈

CHAPTER ONE

One week ago

Dearest Dora,

Early this morning we lost Lauren. She slipped away just before sunrise. I'm thankful that both the kids had a chance to say goodbye, and so grateful that I chose to stay at the hospital last night to be with her in those final moments.

She asked for you. She was confused at the end, remembering that you had been here but not that you had left. I hope you'll come back to New York to join us for the memorial service. You must be curious to see the twins again, now that they are all grown up. I would like you to know them.

Lauren shared something with me before she died that I can't quite bring myself to believe. You are the only one who will know the truth of it. Although you avoided me during your visits this summer, you cannot avoid me forever. We have much to discuss.

Yours,

Barrett

Today

DORA HAD STARTED AND DISCARDED A DOZEN REPLIES TO Barrett's letter, but she couldn't decide what to say. Too many emotions battled for her attention. Impatience with herself for waffling. Irritation that she didn't know her own mind. Fierce protectiveness of both his family and hers. What was he thinking, bringing her into the mix when the children were still reeling from the loss of their mother? Anger, old and deep, that he would try to control her life again. But beneath it all was fear, and she hated that it still lurked after all these years.

Of course, Luke had to be away this week, so he wasn't here to talk her through the problem. Husbands were supposed to be your rock during tough times, but Luke was falling down on the job. She could wait until he came home, perhaps, but she wasn't some helpless neophyte. Waiting would just make her feel foolish.

As she paused, pen poised and ready for attempt number thirteen, impatience and irritation won the day and she scribbled her answer without second-guessing her words. No matter how much she and Barrett might have to discuss, now was not the time. As far as Dora was concerned, never would be a great time. Immature? Yes. Honest? Also yes.

The unsent reply would torment her until the moment she dropped it into a mailbox, so she addressed, stamped, and sealed it before she lost momentum. Even better, she had to leave immediately for the unveiling of the mural design over at the library. She would drop the letter at the post office on her way and the torture would end. She wasn't one to ruminate over things that could not be changed. Best move the letter into that category immediately.

CHAPTER TWO

Today

Mom,

~~I've been trying to tell you something important, but it never seems to be a good time, which is why I'm writing this email. Email can't be interrupted, or~~

Mom,

~~There's something I need to tell you:~~

Mom,

~~We need to talk~~

Mom,

~~I know you don't think I have a plan for my life, but I do. I just haven't told you yet.~~

MEL ZOOMED IN, TIGHTLY FRAMING THE SHOT SO THAT IT captured the intensity of the conversation. Midmorning light, filtered through a screen of reddish-brown oak leaves, illuminated her subjects without washing them out or creating awkward shadows. If she could just get them to open up... Now. She held the shutter button down and her camera took a burst of photos in rapid succession. Smiling, she lowered the camera and scanned the crowd for her next opportunity.

The unveiling of the design for the new mural had drawn a decent crowd by Hidden Springs' standards. More than forty people filled the freshly cleared area between the library building and the church that would soon become a small park. The newly uncovered cemetery adjacent to the church might deserve some of the credit for the crowd, but most of the truly curious had stopped by to see it already. Some of the attendees, like Mel, had volunteered during the first phase of the project, preparing the brick wall of the library for the mural and clearing the underbrush. Friends, family, and neighbors had come to offer support and hear all the latest gossip. If a freshly tuck-pointed wall and a newly cleared lot could draw this kind of crowd, then the big reveal of the mural itself in a few weeks should be a blowout.

From her perch on the first level of the scaffolding that covered the side of the library building, Mel had a clear view of the crowd, while most of them remained unaware of her presence. She preferred to work this way, an invisible witness to the lives of others. Maybe it made her a voyeur, but she didn't care. People were a mystery to be solved, and they were more likely to reveal their true selves when they thought themselves unobserved.

The creak of the ladder pulled her attention away from the scene below. Instead of the teenager she had expected, the head that popped up through the square opening in the floor belonged to her sister, Tessa, blond hair pulled back in a knot that was looser these days than it used to be. Callie, their other sister, followed on Tessa's heels. She had tamed her own long blond hair into a messy braid today. Mel wondered if she would ever lose the habit of differentiating herself from her sisters by dyeing her hair. She never ditched the blond completely, and she didn't like the idea of cutting it short, but she had always played with color and style. Right now, for example, her hair featured a bright pink streak and matching tips. It had always been important to Mel that people could tell the triplets apart.

"You ladies lost?" she asked.

Ignoring the question, Tessa asked, "What did we miss?"

"Pretty much everything," said Mel, still irritated that her sisters had sidestepped the guilt trip that had roped Mel into helping. Who cared if Mel had enjoyed the work so far, or made new friends, or met a hot muralist? What mattered was that her sisters had weaseled out of it.

"And by everything you mean..."

"Well, let's see," said Mel, letting exasperation color her voice. "You've both managed to avoid more than a month's worth of weed-whacking and tuck-pointing."

The innocent expressions on her sisters' faces fooled no one.

"The end of the sailing season has been really busy," said Tessa.

"And things are crazy for me working on the new album," added Callie. "There was no way to fit it in."

"You two also missed the excitement last weekend."

"Mom told us all about it," said Tessa. "Runaway girls, found safe. Do you know them?"

"The older sister was working on the project, so yes, I know one of them. You would know her, too, if only you had squeezed in an hour to help."

Matching grins were their only reply. Callie sank down onto the floor of the scaffolding and dangled her feet over the side. Tessa followed suit, patting the spot next to her for Mel, who took her time accepting the invitation.

How many times had they sat like this down on the pier,

dipping their toes into the water and kicking up spray? Far too many to count. In this case, they had to be more careful, or they might brain someone walking below. The cool October air reminded Mel that there wouldn't be many good days left to get out on the lake. Before she could suggest a paddle-boarding session to her sisters, Tessa spoke.

"So which one is the hot muralist?" she asked.

Thanks to a great publicity photo, Fitz had been dubbed "Hot Muralist" long before he arrived on the scene. Mel had been the first to meet him in person, happily reporting that the reality more than justified the hype. However, hearing Tessa use the nickname roused Mel's protective instincts. The hint of a spark between herself and Fitz would need shelter to achieve flame status. It did not need interference from her sisters.

At Tessa's questioning glance, Mel realized she hadn't answered the question. She scanned the crowd and picked him out with embarrassing ease.

"He's over by the bulletin board," said Mel as she lifted her camera. "Dark green polo shirt, khaki pants, crouched down by a small girl. It looks like he's explaining the mural design to her."

The angle couldn't be better. Focusing on the energy in Fitz's delivery and the rapt expression on the girl's face, Mel took a burst of photos just as the girl broke into a wide smile.

"I see him," said Callie. "Nice shoulders."

"Interesting," murmured Tessa. Mel felt her own shoulders tense at her sister's deliberately neutral tone. Anytime Tessa used her therapist voice, the sisters knew to be wary.

"What's interesting?" Mel couldn't help asking.

"He's much more clean cut than I would have expected. Less artsy." Tessa turned to Mel and cocked her head. "Not your preferred type."

It's hard to argue with facts, so Mel kept her mouth shut.

"Like I said, it's interesting."

Tessa's slow smile made Mel nervous.

"Is he a good kisser?"

Callie's question caught Mel by surprise and she choked on a laugh. "Seriously?"

"You seem to like him a lot." Her grin was pure mischief. "I thought you might know."

Mel had forgotten the joy and pain of hanging out with both her sisters at the same time.

"Well, I don't. There has been no kissing."

Callie's grin grew even wider. "Yet."

"Are we twelve?" asked Mel. "I can't believe we're having this conversation."

"We are mature adults, and it was a simple question." Callie seemed to know exactly which buttons to push. "No need to get all huffy, especially since nothing happened."

"Yet," said Tessa with a high-five for Callie.

"We're here whenever you're ready to talk about your boyfriend," said Tessa.

"He's not my boyfriend." Mel clapped a hand over her mouth, but the words had already tumbled out, and Tessa was all over it.

"Maybe you wouldn't call it that," she said in that irritatingly superior voice, "but he could be, right?"

"I'm not interested in a boyfriend right now."

"Why not?" Callie asked.

This was it, the perfect moment to tell her sisters about her plans. Maybe not perfect, because she couldn't tell the whole family at the same time, but close enough.

"It's complicated," Mel began. "I've got this gig in the works that will require some travel—"

"Mom, incoming, ten o'clock." Callie's alert derailed Mel's big news. Their mother was headed their way, and she was on a mission.

"She has 'the look,'" Tessa stage-whispered.

Mel groaned. "Is it too late to hide?"

"Way too late," said Callie.

Dora came to a stop directly below them, hands on hips, looking very displeased. Mel suddenly felt seven instead of twenty-seven.

"Girls, get down here. You're going to kick someone in the head sitting like that."

She was right, of course, so the three of them clambered down the ladder to meet their fate. As it turned out, their fate was hugs from their mother.

"Mel, honey, I'm glad I found you. Of course, I'm happy to see all my girls, but Mel, I was looking for you particularly. I've got some leads on commercial spaces that might work as a photography studio for you. We need to see them this week, because they'll go quickly. We don't want to miss the perfect one."

"Mom, I really don't think this is the time...."

"Why not? You're in between apartments, your work hours are flexible, and we're living in the same house for the first time in years. When could it possibly be more convenient?"

Her mother had a point. Even her sisters looked at her curiously.

In every other aspect of her life, Mel would describe herself as bold, assertive, and confident. Those qualities had led to success in her career as a photojournalist, turbulence in romantic relationships, and lots of fun along the way. Within the family, she was the mischief-maker—the one who could make everybody laugh. What her family didn't know, and what she herself hadn't realized until recently, was that her family was her kryptonite. She wasn't happy unless her family was happy, and she found it physically painful to let her family down. This was information that she would never, ever share, of course. Her mother couldn't be trusted with that kind of power. It was a weakness she needed to manage, now that she had figured it out.

In this moment, despite the fact that her future plans did not include a photography studio in Hidden Springs, Mel couldn't bring herself to crush her mother's enthusiasm. That would come soon enough. Maybe she could buy herself some time instead.

"But I said I would help with the mural." Even to her own ears, the excuse sounded weak.

"It's a volunteer project. If you need to take a morning off to focus on your professional future, I think Fitz will understand. Right, Fitz?" The question was directed at someone standing behind Mel.

"Of course," replied Fitz.

Mel spun around and tried to catch his eye, but he was too busy looking from sister to sister. Maybe she should have given him a heads up that she was an identical triplet. When his gaze finally rested on Mel, he registered the plea in her eyes.

"What did I just agree to?" he asked.

"I was telling Mel that if she needs to take the occasional morning off from mural painting, you won't object."

Fitz looked from Mel to Dora and back to Mel. His expression clearly said, *How can I object to that?*

Mel tried to telegraph *Find a way!* with angry eyebrows and a tiny shake of the head, but it was too late.

"Well, actually," began Fitz. Mel could tell that he was scrambling for an excuse, anything that would help her out.

"I knew you would understand," said Dora before Fitz could come up with a plausible reason to say no. "Don't worry. I'll set up all the appointments for the same day so that you don't lose too much work time. How about Thursday morning?"

Mel opened and closed her mouth, then gave Fitz a shrug. If she couldn't delay, then she might as well enjoy the outing with her mother. Maybe it would help make up for the fact that she would miss both Thanksgiving and Christmas this year.

Dora took Mel's silence for agreement. "Excellent. Now, Fitz, I need you to come with me. There's someone you need to meet."

Fitz allowed himself to be led away, his rueful smile the only hint that he was going under duress. As soon as he was out of earshot, Callie said, "I totally get the nickname."

"Was that a tattoo I saw in the shadow of his collar?" asked Tessa.

"We'll have to get to know him better if Mel is going to date him."

"I'm right here, you know," said Mel, crossing her arms.

Tessa slung an arm around Mel's shoulders and gave her a squeeze. "Maybe it's a good thing that you're exploring your options here in Hidden Springs instead of down in Chicago. With a guy like that on the line, at least Mom will ease off on the blind dates."

Leaving the country would also solve that problem, although it wasn't the only reason she was going. All her life, Mel had wanted to explore the world, and if she didn't go now, it might never happen. The longer she stayed here in Hidden Springs, the more she could feel invisible vines creeping up out of the earth and winding themselves around her feet, trying to tie her down. For years, she had tried to be here for her parents, with Callie off chasing fame, and Tessa absorbed in grad school and then work. Someone needed to check in on Mom and Dad and make sure that they were doing okay. Now that Callie and Tessa planned on spending more time here, Mel could finally explore the world without the tether of worry. It was Mel's turn to fly.

CHAPTER THREE

After introducing Fitz to a potential donor to the project, Dora scanned the crowd for her friend Lucy, finally spotting her on the sidewalk heading away from the gathering. Lucy was hard to miss. Her short gray hair was trimmed close to her head, the tips dyed a vivid purple. Next week it would probably be a different color. Lucy was easily bored.

"Leaving so soon?" Dora's question caught Lucy as she was about to put on her motorcycle helmet. She turned, resting the helmet on her hip.

"I made an appearance. My mother is happy and my work here is done. I need a ride before the lunch rush."

Lucy and her husband owned Harleys and had a habit of disappearing on sunny days for hours at a time, exploring the back roads of southeastern Wisconsin. Lucy had taken Dora on a ride once, years ago—an experience Dora had no desire to repeat. Too much noise, and you can't feel the wind on your face. Lucy had felt equally uncomfortable when Dora had taken her sailing. Too exposed, and too much at the mercy of Mother Nature. Since then they had agreed to disagree on their preferred forms of recreational transportation.

"Before you go, I have a question. Mel agreed to look at commercial spaces with me this week. Could you give me the details on that space you were talking about the other day? It sounded perfect."

The slow smile that spread across Lucy's face put Dora on her guard.

"Why, of course, I'd be happy to give you that information —on one condition."

"Which is...?"

"I've met a gentleman I think you would like. You will meet him for lunch."

"Lucy, I am not prepared to enter the dating world. For goodness' sake, I'm still married."

"Technically."

"Yes, technically, and it seems very wrong to go on a date when I'm not available."

"Yet. Not available *yet*. And it's not a date. It's a meeting."

Dora huffed out a laugh. "Don't get technical with me."

"Why not? You're getting technical with me."

"Lunch is a date."

"I say it's not a date. It doesn't even have to be lunch. It can be coffee. All I'm saying is that you have to take a teeny tiny baby step toward having a life."

"I have a life! I like my life just fine."

"If you had a life, you wouldn't be so obsessed with your daughter's life. Mel can sort herself out. You, on the other hand, will need some help."

Crossing her arms, Dora said, "Not from you."

"Fine." Lucy made a move to put on her helmet. "See you later."

"Wait."

Pausing with her helmet in midair, Lucy waited. When Dora didn't immediately speak, Lucy raised an impatient eyebrow.

"Just coffee."

Lucy lowered the helmet. "Coffee. Nothing else."

"At a time that's convenient for me."

Narrowing her eyes, Lucy clarified, "Within the next month."

"Agreed."

Lucy's satisfied expression did not make Dora feel any better.

"You're going to love him."

Dora shook her head. "The information on the commercial space?"

"Of course." Lucy pulled out her phone and texted Dora an address and some contact information. "Don't tell Mel that I'm involved."

"Why not?"

At that, Lucy laughed. "Because she'll kill me if she finds out I'm enabling your interference. You girls have fun looking at real estate. Let me know how it goes."

With that, Lucy mounted the bike, secured her helmet, and rumbled away down the street.

Twenty-nine years ago, August

Dear Barrett,

I'm sorry I didn't say goodbye in person. Things between us are too complicated, and I suspect you would have made leaving difficult, if not impossible.

These past two years have been life-changing in so many ways. Thank you for bringing me into your world and making me a part of your family. I wish that I could stay, and that things could continue as they are, but we both know it won't work.

The time has come for me to live my own life and—I hope— one day have a family of my own. Please let me go.

Farewell,
Dora

The polished black granite floor of the foyer reflected none of the heartache and doubt roiling Dora's stomach, only the cool poise she had learned from Lauren. The last two years, spent within the sumptuous walls of Barrett and Lauren's Upper West Side co-op, had been a finishing school of sorts, an education in the kind of wealth and privilege that Dora had only glimpsed growing up.

A part of her desperately wanted to stay. Even this half-life was so much better than anything she could have imagined before meeting Barrett. And really, was it so bad? In many ways, she was the glue that made Barrett and Lauren's marriage work. She would always come second in his affections, but first in his bed—and with Lauren's blessing. Far better for him to have a live-in playmate than a high-maintenance mistress with a life of her own. Dora had never truly expected to come first in any man's heart, so in her mind she hadn't settled for second place. She was lucky to have won it.

And while she would always come second in the children's affections, she still had snuggles and giggles and endless hours with them, which eased her ache for a family of her own. It was this ache, more than anything else, that had prompted her decision to leave. No matter how easy or tempting it might be to stay, her own dreams of life and love and family would be forever out of reach if she did. The longer she stayed, the stronger the ties that bound her to this life. The time to leave was now, while she could still imagine it.

"You will always have a home here."

Lauren's face only hinted at the emotion beneath the surface. Dora had learned many lessons from her friend, including the ability to hide even the most violent of feelings. She would carry that vital skill into her new life. Swallowing the knot in her throat, Dora embraced Lauren and inhaled her elegant scent one last time.

"Thank you for everything. Thank you for the chance at a fresh start."

"You've spent the last two years supporting my dreams. At the very least you should be able to follow your own." As she released Dora, Lauren said, "Are you sure you want to leave without talking to Barrett?"

Dora nodded. He would try to talk her into staying, and she would give in. He was her greatest weakness.

"I left him a letter."

She didn't kid herself. He would still try to talk her into coming back, but she would be stronger if she was already established in her new life.

She tried to soak in all the details as she left, locking them away in her memory so she would never lose them. The elevator, a relic of an earlier era with its delicate wood inlays and uniformed operator. The doorman whose wife packed his lunch every day. The light spilling through the stained glass windows of the lobby, painting the creamy marble walls in vivid jewel tones. The punch of humidity as she stepped out of the air-conditioned building onto the city sidewalk. The town car, ready and waiting with her luggage already stowed, smelling of leather and today's newspaper.

During the drive to LaGuardia, Dora studied the view out the tinted window, knowing it might be years before she saw New York City again. She loved the energy, the contrasts, and the ubiquitous food trucks selling doughnuts and strong coffee. The potent combination of sugar and caffeine had fueled her on many early-morning walks with the babies.

Don't think about the babies.

Missing them was already a weight on her chest, and she'd only been away from them for fifteen minutes. After focusing on little else for more than a year, she needed to turn her attention to something else. Anything else, really, or the tears would start and never stop.

She grimaced. The driver was heading toward the Midtown Tunnel, probably to avoid traffic. Under normal circumstances, she wouldn't care, but today was different. She didn't want her last memories of the city to be dark.

"Would you mind taking one of the bridges?" she asked.

The driver glanced at her in the rearview mirror, then nodded. "Of course, ma'am."

He smoothly changed course and headed toward FDR Drive instead. It was too bad the Brooklyn Bridge wasn't on the way to LaGuardia. Now *that* would be a beautiful farewell. She leaned her head back and watched the city pass by, hoping she would have the strength to stay the course, no matter how persuasive Barrett might be.

CHAPTER FOUR

Today

"HOW DID YOUR FAMILY TAKE THE NEWS?"

Kat's question didn't come as a surprise, but her timing wasn't great. A quick visual scan confirmed that Mel's sisters and mother were on the far side of the crowd, well out of earshot.

"You didn't tell them yet?" Kat's incredulous expression would have been comical if Mel were in any frame of mind to find things funny right now.

"I keep trying, but I always get interrupted."

"Then you're not trying very hard."

"I know. I don't know why this is so difficult."

"You know you can't run away, right?"

"Of course!"

Okay, so the idea might be tempting. It would be so much easier to slip away in the night, leaving behind only a letter by way of explanation. She could skip over the family freakout, the guilt, and her own compulsion to make sure everyone was okay before she left.

"There must be a way to break the news gently. I just need to find the right time, when everyone is all together."

"And if the right time never presents itself?" Kat's skepticism could not have been more obvious.

"It will." As Kat had so helpfully pointed out, running away in the nighttime was not a viable option.

"Are you going to back out of the gig if your family can't handle it?"

"What? No. No way."

"Then tell them. There's no such thing as a perfect moment, and you're not going to change your plan. The biggest gift you can give them right now is time to get used to the idea."

Sighing, Mel said, "You're right, of course."

Kat tipped her head to one side, her expression intrigued. "You don't want to tell them."

"Yes, I do," said Mel, insulted by the idea.

"Are you worried they'll talk you out of it?"

The startling insight caught Mel by surprise. Their long-standing acquaintance but recent friendship seemed unlikely to produce such insights. However, in much the same way that Mel had learned to read Kat's inscrutable facial expressions over the last few months, Kat had apparently learned to read Mel. It was not a comfortable feeling.

Even more disconcerting than Kat's perceptiveness was Mel's vulnerability when it came to her family. The bonds of love and duty, reinforced with guilt, might very well keep her here. Mel would do just about anything for her family, and that included locking her dreams inside a tiny box and throwing away the key.

Swallowing hard, she said, "I'll tell them."

"Good," said Kat. "Afterward, we'll go have a beer down at the Beach to celebrate."

· · ·

"So how much longer will this boondoggle last?"

Fitz almost wished his parents hadn't come to the unveiling. Between his mother's matchmaking and his father's judgment, things were not going well.

"A couple more weeks, if the weather cooperates." This wasn't the first time Fitz had told his father the details of the project. They just never seemed to stick.

"And your firm pays you while you're playing around on these side projects?"

"As we've discussed," said Fitz, "this kind of pro bono work is good for the firm's public image. So yes, they pay me."

In the interest of maintaining his sanity, Fitz had recently begun treating his father's deliberate obtuseness as a game. If you lose your cool, you lose the game. Fitz hadn't lost yet.

"But you're an architect. This…" Fitz's father waved his arms vaguely toward the wall of the library building.

"Mural design and installation," supplied Fitz, trying not to let his annoyance creep into his voice. Mom would get upset if the conversation devolved into fighting.

"Whatever. It's not architecture. It doesn't generate revenue for the firm, and a break from real project work certainly can't help your career."

"You'd be surprised." Fitz kept the remark as bland as possible because defensiveness only made things worse. Maybe he could bore his father into ending the conversation.

Sensing the rising tension, his mother tried to smooth things over. "Well, I for one think the design is beautiful, sweetheart. Turning the library itself into a bookshelf full of children's books—brilliant. The grandchildren are going to love it. And speaking of grandchildren…"

He recognized the gleam in her eye, the one that signaled her singular desire for more grandchildren. His sister had declined to provide more than the current three.

"Mom, please."

Her expression dared him to say more. "Speaking of grand-children," she continued, "there are several young women I'd like you to meet. They all live close to the city, of course, so we'll have to schedule a few dinners when you're back downtown."

It wasn't a question. He had learned long ago that his moth-er's matchmaking efforts could only be delayed, never avoided. As he was scrambling for delay tactics, he saw Mel heading his way and waved her over. The perfect distraction.

"Mom, have you met Mel James? I think you know her mother, Dora."

Mel's eyes widened when she realized she was meeting his parents, but thankfully she didn't run.

"It's a pleasure to meet you, dear. I've heard so much about you from your mother."

After polite handshakes with both of his parents, Mel took a half step back. He could sense that she was preparing to make a break for it, which would be the perfect opportunity to make his escape as well.

"Mel will be helping me with the mural," he said as he slung an arm around her shoulder. No way was he letting her slip away without him. "In fact, if you'll excuse us, we need to decide on our schedule for the coming weeks and find out how many helping hands we'll have."

"Of course, dear." His mother was more than pleased to shoo them off together, likely gauging the adorability of their future offspring, possibly planning the wedding. "You kids do your thing. Your dad and I will head home."

His father's relief at this news was not exactly flattering, but Fitz tried to shrug it off. He had stopped actively seeking his father's approval years ago, once he realized that he would never have it.

When he and Mel were out of earshot, he said, "Thank you. That conversation needed to end."

"I'm a little nervous about how happy your mom looked as she sent us off together. Is she a matchmaker as well?"

"Pretty sure she's envisioning our future babies right now."

"We'll have to keep her away from my mom."

Dora had been upfront about her matchmaking hopes where Fitz was concerned, but Mel hadn't worried too much about it, hoping distraction would buy her some time. However, if Dora was in cahoots with Fitz's mom, things could get complicated. They would need to plan their exit strategy early. Maybe some fake dating followed by a fake breakup? Mel wouldn't mind a few public displays of affection to make their cover story believable.

"Did you really need to talk with me about the schedule?" asked Mel.

"Not really. Are you still open for the next few weeks?"

"Yep. I can do my photo editing at night, or whenever."

"I'm planning to be here all day every day as long as it's above fifty degrees and not raining. You are welcome to join me for any or all of it."

"I'm not going to get up at six in the morning for you, but I can be here Monday morning at nine."

"Perfect."

CHAPTER FIVE

MEL GOT HERSELF TO THE LIBRARY BY NINE ON MONDAY MORNING, but she couldn't claim to be completely awake after a late night of photo editing. At least she was here, in body if not in mind, and that's what mattered. The oversized travel mug full of coffee would help, but until the caffeine kicked in, she probably shouldn't operate any heavy machinery.

Fall had arrived, bringing a bite in the air and a fresh sprinkling of fallen leaves. Mel's ratty jeans, long-sleeved tee, and paint-streaked sweatshirt would keep her warm enough for the moment, but she was going to have to add layers if it got any colder in the next few days. They weren't the only ones hustling to stay ahead of the cold weather. Mel noticed four or five newly planted shrubs that had appeared since the unveiling of the design only two days ago.

Fitz stood in front of the bulletin board with the mural design, his arms crossed, studying it intently. She joined him, crossing her arms to match his, and waited for him to say something. The overall composition of the mural fit the proportions of the building and incorporated all the windows and doors, the gutter downspouts, and even the tree whose leaves would obscure the top corner of the wall for most of the year.

Her gaze drifted over the design, snagging on clever details she had missed on first viewing. Damn, he was good. Throughout the design, he had made subtle nods to M.C. Escher by way of flat design elements that morphed into three-dimensional creatures. Storybook characters emerged from the pages of their books to play. That theme would extend into the real world as actual children visited the small park beside the wall and played on and around the storybook sculptures.

"So," he said, breaking the long silence, "are you ready to get to work?"

"I am yours to command," she said, pairing the suggestive remark with a cheeky grin so he couldn't possibly miss the double entendre. He opened his mouth to reply, closed it again, then shook his head. Her grin widened. This was going to be fun.

"We'll start by priming the wall with an acrylic gesso. It's more durable than a latex-based primer. If you've ever done any house painting, you might be surprised by how thick we need to lay it on to cover all the rough spots and fill the tiny pinholes."

"Thick, juicy coat. Got it." The words were impossible to say without sounding suggestive, so Mel went with the theme for the day, but again Fitz didn't take the bait.

"Once the primer is dry," he continued, "we'll use a grid system to transfer the design up onto the wall. Then we paint like crazy until we're finished."

"Do we seal it at the end?"

Nodding, he said, "We'll use a clear matte acrylic spray to lock it in."

"And if it rains?"

"That's actually my biggest worry. If the weather turns against us, we might need to finish in the spring."

"What? Why?" She got the sense that leaving the project unfinished would really bother him.

"We really shouldn't paint if temperatures drop below fifty. It won't adhere well to the surface. Sixty would be ideal, but I'll take anything above fifty. As long as the paint has at least an hour to dry, a little rain won't cause any trouble, but we'll need to be sure the wall is completely dry before painting again."

"You do know it's October, right?" asked Mel. "The weather is going to suck at some point."

"I know, but the weather forecast for the next ten days looks good. If we stay focused, we can get it done in that timeframe."

"Yes, sir!" she said, pairing her words with a military-style salute. "Awaiting orders, sir."

He gave her a long look before handing her a roll of light plastic and some tape.

"Right. Let's mask this wall."

Fitz's air of unflappable professionalism made Mel itch to get under his skin. Though she had never been to London, this must be how the tourists react upon seeing the stone-faced palace guards. The temptation to break their concentration must be overwhelming. Glancing at Fitz out of the corner of her eye, Mel decided this was exactly her type of game. She gave in to the tiny devil on her shoulder and started humming "Fever."

Was it wrong to spy on one's adult children? Dora was debating the ethics of this question when Lucy called.

"Can you come down to the library?"

After twenty-five years, Dora knew her friend's voice. Something was up.

"Are you okay? Is your mom okay?"

Lucy didn't bother to answer the questions. "I need your opinion as an artist. Can you come? Now?"

"Of course. Something to do with the mural-in-progress? Give me twenty minutes."

"I'll explain when you get here. Hurry up!"

Lucy hung up before Dora could ask more questions. Curious, Dora went in search of her shoes. She had a tendency to toe them off in random locations around the house. She couldn't help but feel flattered. The only artistic project going on down at the library was the mural. The idea that a talented muralist like Fitz would ask for her input—well, she'd be happy to assist in any way she could. This would also give her a perfectly valid reason to spy on Mel and Fitz together. She could assess their chemistry without creating any awkward ethical dilemmas. Everybody wins.

Dora's shoes had landed in front of the utility sink where she had been washing her paintbrushes earlier. Slipping them on, she grabbed her battered macrame purse and headed out the door.

At the library, Lucy sat on the bench outside the main door. When Dora's bright yellow Honda pulled into a parking space, Lucy jumped up and paced impatiently until Dora joined her. Before Dora could even peek around the corner of the building to catch the painters at work, Lucy grabbed her by the elbow and tugged her inside.

The library was snug and cozy after the crisp fall air outside. The musty smell of books plus a hint of floral air freshener welcomed them, triggering a cascade of memories for Dora. She had brought the girls here so many times when they were little, settling them into story time and then escaping to browse the aisles blissfully alone. Parenting triplets wasn't for the faint of heart.

"I thought you needed my opinion on the mural?"

Lucy shook her head without offering further explanation,

then motioned for Dora to follow her to the circulation desk.
Once there, she leaned casually against it and positioned Dora
to face her.

"Lucy, what am I doing here? Why aren't you at the diner?"

A mischievous smile spread across Lucy's face.

"Angie has things under control at the diner. I needed to
pop over here for a few minutes and visit my mom. Look over
my shoulder," she instructed.

With a teen-worthy roll of the eyes, Dora complied.

"What do you see?"

"Your mom is talking to someone over by the art display."

"Who?"

"I have no idea. His back doesn't give me much of a clue."

Lucy gave a long-suffering sigh. "We'll just hang out here
until he turns around then."

"Seriously?"

"I need your opinion."

"As an artist." Dora's voice was laced with skepticism.

"Yes. I think he's the most beautiful man I've ever seen, but I
need your professional opinion."

Lucy's remark surprised a laugh out of Dora, which in turn
caught the attention of Lucy's mother and her companion. The
two glanced over toward the circulation desk, and Dora's breath
caught in her throat.

"Hah!" crowed Lucy. "I knew it. He *is* the most beautiful
man in the world."

"Shhh!" Realizing that her shushing of Lucy might have
been louder than Lucy's remark, Dora dialed it back. "They're
looking this way."

With a chuckle, Lucy said, "I knew you'd like him. He's your
coffee date."

This news caused Dora to suck in a breath, which caused
her to inhale some of her own saliva, which led to a coughing
fit, which Dora tried to keep as quiet as possible. The last thing

she needed was to choke to death in front of the Most Beautiful Man in the World.

Damn it, she needed to come up with a different title before this one stuck. She narrowed her eyes at Lucy.

"He is not the most beautiful man in the world."

Lucy lowered her voice to a conspiratorial whisper. "What should we call him? McDreamy? McSteamy?"

"Of course not. Those are taken," snapped Dora. "And this nickname habit of yours has got to stop."

"But why? It's so much fun."

"We shouldn't be nicknaming him at all. There will be no need to refer to him in the future once my single coffee date obligation has been fulfilled."

"Still, I love nicknames. Coffee Boy?"

Dora couldn't believe she was getting sucked into this discussion.

"He is *definitely* not a boy."

The gentleman in question had shifted position as his conversation with Lucy's mother, Mary Evelyn, progressed to the next painting in the reading area. This gave Dora an excellent view of his chiseled profile, broad shoulders, and thick black hair. The hint of silver at his temples underscored the natural authority in his bearing. No paunch here. No resting on laurels. Definitely no boyish charm. This was a man in his prime, full of energy and intensity. He belonged on a movie set or in a magazine, not on a coffee date with Dora. What was Lucy thinking?

Dora dragged her attention back to her friend, who now had a smug smile on her face.

"I couldn't agree with you more," said Lucy. "Definitely a fully grown man."

"Not the kind of man who should be nicknamed, I think," said Dora.

Lucy immediately shot down her attempt to take the high

road. "Oh, I think anyone can be nicknamed. Let me think.... Mount Rushmore? I love a chiseled profile. No, maybe Mount Gushmore."

"Please, stop before you embarrass yourself."

"I can do this. Mythology? How about Apollo?"

"He was blond."

"Right. Adonis?"

He did have a hint of the Mediterranean about him, and the reference to the handsome Greek god wasn't entirely off base. The stories about Adonis typically focused on his youth, but maybe this was what grown-up Adonis would have looked like —if he were real, of course, and not a creature of myth.

"Adonis it is," murmured Lucy. "I win."

Lips pressed together, Dora gave her friend the evil eye. "One coffee date."

CHAPTER SIX

ON CUE, MARY EVELYN BEGAN TO LEAD HER GUEST BACK TOWARD the circulation desk where Lucy and Dora waited.

"Well, speak of the devil," said Mary Evelyn to Dora. "David was just asking about you." She pronounced his name the Spanish way, dah-VEED, as if she hung out with gorgeous foreign gentlemen every day. Dora suppressed the urge to laugh. Mary Evelyn and Lucy were clearly in cahoots on this.

"Dora James." She offered her hand, more than ready to get this over with.

Instead of shaking her hand like a normal person, David clasped it with both hands and didn't let go right away. "Dora James," he echoed. "Such a pleasure to finally meet you in person. You are a difficult woman to track down."

She realized several things simultaneously. One, his voice was as beautiful as his face, low and musical and shiver-inducing. Two, he seemed to know a lot more about her than she knew about him. And three, given the flutters racing through her stomach, she was in deep, deep trouble.

"And you are...?"

Lucy and Mary Evelyn were too caught up in their smug

triumph to give her any kind of help. Dora didn't like being at a disadvantage, no matter how attractive the stranger.

"My apologies. I am David Ignacio Lozano Campoverde. My family owns the Arte del Alma galleries, and we have been interested in your work for a long time."

Dora shot Lucy a glare as she accepted his business card. She showed her work only in the local gallery at the far end of the lake, and Lucy knew it. This wasn't a romantic setup. It was a business setup. Lucy had been harping on her for years to show her work more widely, to "spread her wings." Apparently, she had tired of waiting for Dora to listen to her advice and had taken matters into her own hands.

"My apologies," he said when she turned her attention back to him. "I understood that you were willing to meet with me at last, but I see this is not the case. Please forgive the intrusion."

The temptation to accept his graceful escape hatch almost overwhelmed Dora's good manners—almost being the key word. Lucy had counted on this, and Dora vowed to kill her friend later.

"No apology necessary," said Dora. "My friend has long encouraged me to expand my horizons. Perhaps it's time to give that a try. Would you like to join me for a cup of coffee?"

"That would be lovely," said David.

"You can come to the diner!" suggested Lucy, the picture of helpful innocence.

Dora shot her a quelling look. "There's a great little coffee shop down the street from the gallery. On the *other* end of the lake."

"I know the coffee shop you mean, and I would be honored to meet you there."

Dora couldn't help but smile at the formality. She could easily survive an hour in this man's company. Maybe more, if he turned out to be interesting as well as charming.

"I'll be there in half an hour," said Dora.

"Until then," he replied. "Ladies." He made his farewell with a nod, the formality smoothing over the tension that simmered beneath the surface. Only when the library door had softly closed behind him did Dora turn to Lucy, who started talking before Dora could even open her mouth.

"You should absolutely yell at me for the setup, but I swear, I have only your best interests at heart. Your work is good. Really, really good, and Ansel doesn't ask nearly as much for it as he could. He likes that it sells."

Dora grimaced because she knew Lucy was right. Ansel, the local gallery owner, kept his prices low, well within reach for most tourists. Hers were the most expensive paintings he displayed, but this wasn't New York or even Chicago and his prices reflected that.

Lucy wasn't finished. "I was in the gallery the other day shopping for a birthday present for Mom. You didn't hear that, by the way," she said to her mother. "David came in and of course I eavesdropped on his conversation with Ansel. He's gorgeous. I had to learn more. And then he asked about you, and it was clear this wasn't the first time he's tried to get Ansel to put him in touch with you. Ansel was great. Very protective—didn't say a word. But I couldn't let him walk away, not when he talked about your work that way. So I followed him out and said that I might be able to arrange a meeting."

"And then you tried to convince me that you were setting me up on a date."

Ignoring Dora's irritation, Lucy grinned. "Weirdly, it was easier to convince you to go on a date than to meet with someone who might be able to help you in your career." She paused, studied Dora's face more closely, and then burst out laughing. "You're pissed that it's not a date."

"Of course she's disappointed." Mary Evelyn marched around the circulation desk to take her usual post. "That man is

delicious, and you just told her that he's only interested in her
for her art. Not nice, Lucy. Not nice."

"I'm sorry, sweetie." Lucy pulled Dora into a fierce hug. "I
didn't realize you were ready, but now that I know, I'll get to
work. We'll find you someone amazing."

Dora extracted herself from Lucy's embrace and stepped
back. "You are not off the hook for this, and you are not to begin
some kind of boyfriend search. I will find my own man in my
own time, thank you very much. Now, I have a coffee date to
attend, and you have some brainstorming to do about how you
will make this up to me. I recommend you start with groveling
and chocolate, but I leave the rest up to you. Understood?"

"Yes, ma'am."

"That's weird," said Mel, as she watched her mother's car drive
away.

After hauling several five-gallon buckets of primer up to the
top level of the scaffolding, she and Fitz were painting their way
back down. The temperature had risen above fifty, but the
nippy breeze up here made Mel wish she had thought to bring
work gloves, if only to keep her hands warm. The view allowed
them to see all the comings and goings, including the arrival of
Dora's distinctive yellow Honda. Her mother had disappeared
into the library, but Mel had assumed she would merit at least a
greeting before her mother left. Apparently not.

"What?"

"I figured my mom was here to spy on our budding relationship, but she didn't even say hi."

Over the past few years, Dora's matchmaking efforts had
been conducted remotely, and this arrangement had suited Mel
just fine. She went about her business down in Chicago and
occasionally agreed to a blind date. These blind dates always
took place at Antonio's, a restaurant owned by an old friend of

Dora's. Tony got a steady stream of business. Mel got a lot of free meals. Dora got eyewitness accounts of each date. Everybody won. Here in Hidden Springs, Mel had expected her mother to spy on her matchmaking efforts in person, now that she had the opportunity. Apparently not.

Fitz's raised eyebrows were the tiniest bit insulting. "Our...relationship?"

"My mom is shipping us hard, and I think I'm going to play along."

Fitz looked completely confused.

"Well, the obvious benefit is that it gives me an excuse to hit on you."

Apart from a choking noise, he didn't respond.

"Also, the illusion of a relationship will get my mother to hold off on more blind dates. It's a favorite hobby of hers."

"That works?" He looked intrigued.

"It has in the past. She's skeptical, though, so we'll have to make it convincing."

Fitz studied her face for a moment, looking fairly skeptical himself. "You know I'm leaving town after this project, right?"

Aw, that's sweet. He thinks I'm trying to trick him into dating.

"Can I let you in on a little secret?" she whispered.

He nodded.

"I'm leaving town, too."

Mel found his surprised expression oddly satisfying.

"Really?" he asked.

"Yep."

"Where are you going?"

"South America. Please don't mention it in front of my family, though. I haven't broken the news to them yet."

"When do you leave?"

"Right before Thanksgiving."

"And you haven't told them?"

Everyone was a critic these days. Yes, time was running out, but this was a delicate matter that needed to be handled...delicately.

"Stop judging, Mr. Perfect. I'm working on it. In the meantime, it would be great if my mother wasn't trying to set me up on dates. I got the sense, when I had the unexpected pleasure of meeting your parents, that you would also appreciate some breathing room."

"That's very true."

"So why not help each other out? Then we'll each head off to our separate destinations, and sadly our attempt at keeping the relationship going long-distance will fail. If we're lucky, their concern over our broken hearts will give us an extra six months of freedom from matchmaking. What do you think? Are you in?"

His slow smile kicked off the flutters in her belly, and she smiled in return.

"I'm in."

She held out a hand and they shook on the deal, but he didn't let go.

"You know," he said, his voice soft and low, "this seems like the kind of deal we should seal with a kiss."

Well, this was a pleasant surprise. The buttoned-up muralist had not only agreed to her suggestion, but he was also on the same wavelength regarding the benefits of the arrangement. Looking up at him from beneath her eyelashes, she stepped closer, pulling her hand free from his and sliding her hands up around the back of his neck. The front of her body skimmed his, warming her all over, and her breathing quickened, filling her lungs with a potent mix of paint and Fitz.

"I completely agree."

He dipped his head as she rose on her tiptoes and their lips met on a shared exhale. He pressed her close, deepening the kiss. The rest of the world fell away, leaving only Mel and Fitz and the heat between them. His hands anchored her hips while his mouth traced a path across her jaw to her ear, then down her neck. Eyes closed and breath choppy, she leaned her head back while he explored.

The slam of a car door yanked them back to reality. They stood for a moment, forehead to forehead, while their breathing slowly returning to normal.

She leaned forward and bit his lip, startling him.

"Not bad," she whispered, "but we may need more practice if we're going to convince the parents."

He kissed her again, a promise of more to come. "Practice makes perfect."

She nodded in agreement and then slowly withdrew from his arms.

"Maybe we should go on a date," she suggested, "to build the illusion. Do you want to go paddle boarding in the morning? It's probably the last good day of the season."

"I've never tried it."

"Don't worry," she said. "You'll be great."

Hopefully he had decent balance, or his initiation into paddle boarding was going to be a chilly one.

CHAPTER SEVEN

Twenty-nine years ago, November

DORA TUCKED THE MAIL INTO THE SIDE POCKET OF HER ART portfolio as she stepped into the freight elevator. Dragging the accordion gates closed, she pressed the button for the fourth floor. Each day, that simple act reminded her of the stark contrast between her old and new lives. Her apartment, a warehouse conversion in Chicago's old meatpacking district, might be rough around the edges but it was hers alone. No granite or marble here, only concrete and exposed brick. No doorman or elevator operator, and nobody in her space, just her art and some of the best indirect light in the world. There were times when she missed the luxury and comfort of her Manhattan existence, but she would never give up her newfound independence.

Once inside the apartment, she set her portfolio on the kitchen counter before scrounging in the fridge for a snack. Supplies were running low and she would need to make a grocery run soon. After finding a yogurt in the back corner behind some wilting lettuce, Dora slid onto a seat at the counter and began plotting her afternoon. Homework could wait. Laundry could wait. The light this afternoon would be perfect for painting, and inspiration had struck during her line drawing class this morning. The question was, could she transfer that inspiration to canvas before she lost the light? Tossing her empty yogurt container in the garbage, she got to work.

Hours later, Dora set down her brush and, massaging her cramped fingers, took a step back to assess her progress. Not bad for a single afternoon. Not bad at all. The bones were there, but she'd have to leave the detail work until tomorrow. The sun had set, leaving behind only a glow in the sky, and she didn't want to continue under electric lighting. Her colors would shift, which would ruin today's foundational work.

After cleaning her brushes and refueling, Dora remembered the mail and fished it out of her portfolio. Phone bill. Bank statement. Letter from New York.

She studied the letter for a long time before finally opening it. The handwriting on the front did not belong to Lauren, although the stationery did, which could mean only one thing.

Barrett had found her.

Loneliness, denied for so long, broke free from its restraints and grabbed her in a chokehold. The transition from life at the heart of a family to life on her own had been abrupt and painful, and she had made it this far only by locking away all memories of her old life. Now unleashed, the memories swarmed back into consciousness with a vengeance. Days filled with the babies. Family dinners around the formal dining table. Nightly visits from Barrett.

Dora,

    These last few months have been the hardest of my life. At first, Lauren refused to tell me where you'd gone. It has taken me this long to persuade her to change her mind. We need to talk. I'll be at the Drake Hotel, room 1404, from Friday evening until Monday morning.

Please let me see you.
Yours,
Barrett

Placing the letter carefully on the counter, as if the ink might contain the same kryptonite as his touch, Dora backed away slowly, unaware of her reaction until she bumped into the refrigerator. Its cold, solid bulk held her upright for a moment, but then her knees softened and she slid to the floor. He had come for her, and already she could feel herself weakening.

He knew he held the upper hand, had forged every link in the chain that bound them together. If only she had found the courage to say goodbye to him in New York, this would not be happening, this slow burn low in her abdomen that flared whenever he was within reach.

It had always been like this with Barrett. From the moment they met, the chemistry between them had overwhelmed rational thought. She had crossed so many lines with him that she couldn't remember where her boundaries had once been. It was pathetic, really, that after so much work to build a new life, here she was, ready to melt back into his arms.

Temper rising, she pulled herself to her feet, unsure if the anger should be directed at herself or at Barrett. In fairness, probably both. There would be no more melting, no more submission. The time had come to end it.

Dora dressed with power and confidence in mind, ignoring the weather. The crisp November air would touch her only briefly. She chose tall boots, a very short skirt, and sexy under-wear—for confidence. On top, a silk camisole, suede jacket, and light scarf became her armor. When he saw her, he would feel the force of her anger, and when she walked away, he would feel the sting.

· · ·

Walking into the Drake felt like stepping into her old life. The plush carpets and muted lighting exuded class, while the musty undertones reminded you that old money was better than new. Dora's temper had cooled into a cold knot of anger in her gut, one that fueled her confident stride to the elevator bank. She punched the "up" button with more force than necessary and then stepped back to wait. And wait. Why was this taking so long? As her foot tapped silently on the carpet, Dora realized that her knot of anger had begun to unravel.

The ding of the elevator startled Dora out of her growing anxiety. She hurried inside and pressed the button for the four-teenth floor before she lost her nerve. Staring resolutely at the wood paneling as the doors slid shut, she repeated the mantra that had carried her here: *My life is my own.* She was no longer the naive country mouse who had fallen for the older, cynical city mouse. She shook her head. Barrett couldn't really be compared to a mouse. A wolf, maybe, or— Never mind. The metaphor didn't matter. She would see him in moments and she needed to figure out what to say.

As the elevator rose, so did her body temperature, her body's betrayal not entirely unexpected but still irritating. Yes, the chemistry between them had been amazing, but the throb-bing between her legs didn't exactly strengthen her willpower. She would not give in to the heat. She would not even take off her jacket.

Belatedly, it occurred to her that she could have called, or even ignored the letter completely, but neither option would have been as satisfying as telling him to his face that it was over. The elevator stopped, the doors slid open, and she stepped into the hallway.

Her courage wavered again when she reached his room, her hand poised to knock but frozen in mid-air. Had she made a

mistake in coming here? Did she have the strength to
resist him?

A swift mental kick was all it took to spur her to action. She
was here to say goodbye, not to offer herself on a platter. No
more delays. She knocked firmly on the door. A voice called
out, muffled, and then the door opened.

He stood before her, as compelling and irresistible as ever.
"You came."

His voice sounded hoarse and he looked tired, as if he
hadn't slept well—and that was her last coherent thought.

He hauled her through the open doorway, slammed it shut,
and pinned her against it, his mouth claiming hers before she
could say a word. Her suede jacket slid to the floor, the scarf
disappeared from around her neck, and his mouth lifted from
hers for barely a breath as he peeled the camisole over her
head. Then she was lost again as his hands covered her breasts
and his mouth reclaimed hers. His body pressed against hers
and she moaned, wrapping her arms around his neck. She had
known her body would betray her. She hadn't thought it would
happen so fast.

Later, Dora woke from a doze to find herself sprawled on the
bed wearing only her tall boots. Barrett was nowhere to be
seen, but the sound of running water from the bathroom
suggested he hadn't gone far. Rolling onto her back, she stared
at the ceiling and wondered what the hell to do now. She could
leave, perhaps not as triumphantly as she had originally
planned, but the point would be made. There were two prob-
lems with that scenario. First, Barrett would likely come after
her. He did have her address, after all. Second, she didn't really
want to go. All their previous encounters, sanctioned though
they may have been by Lauren, had been stolen moments,
squeezed into the cracks and crevices of an already full life. For

the next couple of days, she had him all to herself, and she found the temptation irresistible.

Perhaps they could negotiate a new normal. She would continue her new life here in Chicago. He would continue his old life in New York. And sometimes—not too often—he would come to Chicago for a visit. A no-holds-barred, naked-all-the-time kind of visit. She could work with that.

Early Monday morning, Dora woke with the dawn. Disoriented at first, she blinked the sleep away and realized that she faced the window of the hotel room, the sky outside pale gray with the light of a cold November morning. Barrett snored lightly behind her, solid and warm against her back.

She slid from the bed, gathered her clothing, and slipped into the bathroom. Barrett would wake when he heard the shower, so she locked the door, making it clear that their interlude had come to an end.

When she emerged half an hour later, she found Barrett fully dressed and drinking coffee in the dining area of the suite. Room service had been and gone. Taking a seat across from him, she accepted the coffee he offered and took a sip. He didn't wait for her to speak first.

"You're leaving." It was an accusation, delivered in the most civil of tones.

She nodded, equally civilized. "I have class this morning."

"And how long will this go on?"

"My degree program?" she asked with a smile. He might as well have called it "this nonsense." Barrett had always seen her in a supporting role, never the lead in her own movie. This must be a difficult adjustment for him.

In response to his sharp nod, she replied, "Several years, as it happens."

He snorted in irritation. "Too long."

"Not for me."

"The children miss you. Lauren misses you." He paused before admitting the truth. "I miss you."

He knew her too well, playing on every weakness to try to change her mind. What he didn't seem to understand was how painful leaving had been in the first place. The only thing more painful would be to go back, and then leave again.

"We need you at home," he continued. "This is ridiculous. You can study art in New York City."

She could never go back. Somehow she needed to make him understand that simple fact.

"No."

The word hung in the air between them, a word she couldn't remember ever saying to him before. He didn't seem to know how to respond.

"I can't go back. Please don't ask me again."

While she waited for him to respond, she set down her coffee and rose from the table to put on her scarf and jacket. Now that the weekend's sensual haze had cleared, leaving turned out to be easy. She gave him a sweet goodbye kiss, pulling away only when he tried to draw her into his arms.

"Let me know if you'll be back in town," she said as she walked to the door. "I'd love to see you again."

CHAPTER EIGHT

Today

DORA CAUGHT HERSELF CHECKING HER REFLECTION IN THE rearview mirror for what must have been the tenth time, and that was ten times too many. Shifting firmly into park, she unbuckled, grabbed her purse, and hopped out of the car before the mirror could tempt her again. This was a business meeting, not a date, and for that reason she had deliberately denied herself the time to change clothes or fuss over her appearance. She might appreciate the masculine beauty of this David, but she would not allow her appreciation to distract from the purpose of their meeting, and she would not let it send her into a weird spiral of teenage nerves.

Now her stomach needed to get the message.

The short walk to the coffee shop helped. By the time she arrived, she almost felt like herself again. After fifty years in this world one would think she'd have a better hold on her equilibrium.

David had chosen a table in the corner and a seat that allowed him to watch the door. He rose as she entered, pulling out a chair for her. As she approached, she sternly reminded herself that this was a business meeting. The prickling of her skin needed to stop. As she sat, he eased her chair closer to the table and she made the mistake of inhaling. Of course he smelled good. It was irritating, really.

"Coffee?" he asked.

"Please. A small latte would be lovely."

While he placed the order with the barista, she gave herself a mental shake. Normal, everyday Dora did not use words like "lovely."

David reclaimed his seat, but instead of beginning a polite, business-focused conversation, he studied her with a bemused expression. She raised an eyebrow in question.

"Forgive me," he said, in that deep, liquid voice. An appreciative shiver did *not* dance down her spine. "I find myself at a loss for words, now that the hope of meeting with you has become a reality. You are not at all what I expected."

Unsure how to respond to that, she waited for him to elaborate.

"You come as a refreshing surprise. I have worked with many artists in my career, and met many more, but none as strikingly lovely as yourself."

Dora caught herself before she snorted. Apparently "lovely" was the word of the day. In her youth, perhaps, she might have been called strikingly lovely, but that was decades and babies ago. Today her long blond hair had silvered, her hips had widened, and the lines on her face spoke to the journey of her life. She didn't need flowery compliments to butter her up. In fact, he was starting to piss her off.

Some of what she was thinking must have shown on her face, because he chuckled. "I see you do not believe me, so I will wait until we know one another better to convince you otherwise."

They were interrupted by the barista, who placed their

coffees carefully on the table. The two matching foam hearts made Dora long to roll her eyes, but that would be rude. She refrained.

"Thank you." She and David said the words at the same time.

"Jinx," said the barista with a grin before heading back to her station behind the counter.

Seeing David's confusion, Dora explained the colloquialism.

"I consider myself fluent in English," he said, "but I did not learn the language as a child. Moments like this remind me that I still have much to learn."

"Where did you grow up?" asked Dora.

"Ecuador. Our first gallery was in a city called Cuenca, not far from the capital."

"And how many galleries do you own now?"

This was a business meeting, after all. She should be asking businesslike questions. David leaned back in his chair, the expression on his face suggesting that her curiosity brought him a great deal of satisfaction.

"My family now owns five galleries: the original in Cuenca, an additional gallery in Ecuador's capital, Quito, and then three galleries in the States—New York, Chicago, and Los Angeles."

A laugh of disbelief escaped before Dora could stop it. The idea that an international art dealer would be interested in her work was…incomprehensible.

"You must wonder how your work would fit into our collection. We work with artists who are not yet widely known, but who show a deep understanding of color, emotion, and above all, place. Your ability to capture water on canvas is unlike anything I've ever seen. In addition, your work displays a depth of emotion that elevates it above a basic landscape."

If David wanted to dish out compliments like that, Dora would be happy to listen all day. And while he talked, she would study that gorgeous face. She had thought him beautiful at first sight, but now, in conversation, she began to understand the phrase "poetry in motion." She asked question after question for the simple joy of watching him answer. Her fingers itched to sketch him, to see if she could capture the magic on paper.

A part of her brain stood to one side and marveled at being here, in a coffee shop, having a conversation about art with a mysterious stranger. This couldn't possibly be her life. It was like watching herself in a movie, so far removed from reality that it must be fiction. The pleasant routine of her real life was, she admitted to herself, more than a little boring—not that she was complaining! She loved her friends and the life that she and Luke had built in Hidden Springs. The girls had grown up happy and stable. For twenty-seven wonderful years, Dora had managed the sailing school and painted. Luke had built a career as a music teacher and songwriter. Together they had raised the girls. Twenty-seven wonderful years—and then a shift.

Dora couldn't pinpoint exactly when the seeds of change had been planted. Callie's return this past spring had set certain events in motion, but the groundwork had been laid years before. The girls had been spending less and less time at home, their horizons broadening as their adult lives started to take shape. Home had become a touchstone for them rather than their foundation. Over the last few years, Luke had spent more and more time on his songwriting as he neared retirement from teaching. His coming move to Nashville, along with their steps toward separation, might surprise the girls, but from Dora's perspective, it was all part of a natural progression. This had always been the plan: raise the girls together, then follow the next dream. Luke's heart had always been anchored in Nashville, and Dora's had been in storage for twenty-seven years.

David had paused and seemed to be waiting for a response. She scrambled to replay his last sentence, paying closer attention this time. Something about artists building their careers with his galleries. *Exclusively* with his galleries. Her eyes narrowed.

He wasn't only interested in her work. He wanted to lock her down. She would need to keep a close eye on this one. That beautiful exterior hid a shark.

"Exclusive?" She let her tone of voice speak for itself.

"We make an investment in each new artist we acquire. Naturally, we would like some guarantee of a return on that investment."

"And if an artist doesn't wish to be...acquired?"

"I would be happy to discuss terms with you in detail, and at length."

His voice had dropped into a lower register and she could feel the vibrations deep in her belly. Dear God, the man could read accounting textbooks to her and she would probably start peeling off her clothes. She blinked a few times to clear the sensual fog and took the last sip of her latte.

"I'm not sure I'm ready for that level of intimacy."

Expression innocent, she watched him consider the different possible interpretations of her words. They didn't know each other well, so he couldn't be sure if she was flirting or just making odd word choices. He clearly suspected she was toying with him, and he responded with a slow smile.

"Perhaps we should meet again, to continue the discussion."

A half shrug was her only answer. She didn't trust her voice to be steady.

"May I call you later this week?"

And there it was, the fork in the proverbial road. Did Dora really want to let this stranger into her life? She could shut him down right now. He had delivered his pitch. She could simply say no and walk away. And yet, everyone else was moving forward. Well, everyone except Mel, but Dora was working on that. And Lucy was right—she was ready. Ready for a change. Ready for the rest of her life to finally begin. Maybe David offered a *lovely* transition to the next phase of her life. If she played her cards right, she could enjoy his voice and his charm and his outrageous good looks several more times before she cut him loose, or took him up on his offer, or talked her way into his bed.

!!!

Which she would never do, because she wasn't nineteen anymore. The idea of getting naked in front of David was just the cold shower she needed to shut off her overactive imagination. If anybody would be getting naked, it would be David, when she talked him into posing for her.

Stop it!

"You may," she answered, yanking her attention to the present moment and the fully clothed man in front of her. Pulling out the business card he had handed her at the library, she wrote her cell number on the back and handed it back to him, careful not to let their skin touch. His voice had already weakened her defenses. If he touched her skin, she might melt into a puddle on the floor.

He stood when she rose to leave.

"Thank you so much for the coffee. You've given me a lot to think about."

"Until we meet again."

Walking away, she could feel his eyes on her back, but only after the door of the coffee shop closed behind her did she release the laughter bubbling up from inside. It was ridiculous to feel this way at her age. Fun, though. She would enjoy it while it lasted.

CHAPTER NINE

MEL GROANED WHEN HER ALARM CLOCK WENT OFF, GROPING THE nightstand until she hit the snooze button. Why in the world had she suggested meeting Fitz at this painfully early hour of the morning? For goodness' sake, it was still dark outside and much too cold. The shrill beep of the alarm yanked her awake again nine minutes later, and she fought the urge to re-snooze. Fitz didn't seem like the type to be late, and reckless snoozing might lead her to accidentally blow him off. She shut the alarm off properly and stumbled to the bathroom, where a splash of cold water shocked her fully awake.

A quick check of the weather app had Mel rethinking her bikini plans. Pulling on leggings instead, she spied the compass tattoo on her ankle. Maybe this morning she would finally get a good look at Fitz's mystery tattoo. She'd seen only a glimpse of it, enough to fuel her curiosity. Had he gone for something cliché, like a dragon? Maybe something architectural? One way or another, she was going to find out, and after that kiss the other day, she certainly wouldn't object to peeling off his clothes. This morning could be her chance. In fact, perhaps seeing the tattoo should be her goal for the day.

By the time Mel made it down to the water, Fitz was waiting. Not only was he early, but he looked alert, which suggested that he might be one of those insufferable morning people. Then he yawned, and she decided she might be able to put up with him, at least for a few more weeks. It was too bad she hadn't suggested kayaking. They would have at least been in the same boat, within touching distance. Unfortunately, paddle boards and sexytimes did not mix. Not a mistake she would make again.

"Morning, sunshine," she said by way of greeting.

"Is it morning yet?"

The sun had cleared the trees on the far side of the lake, highlighting water as smooth as glass. Mist rose over the lake, cool air teasing warm water into a kind of dance. She might consider waking up early more often if she could be guaranteed a view like this.

"So how does this paddle boarding thing work?" he asked.

She led the way over to the rack that held her family's collection of paddle boards and pulled out her board and paddle, tucking the board under her arm and gripping it by the deep indentation in the center.

"They're lighter than they look," she said. "Why don't you grab the one on the bottom? That's the one my dad uses, and you're about the same size."

He pulled it out and, after some fumbling, managed to mirror her grip on the board. They walked out to the end of the pier, where she pulled a life vest for each of them out of a long storage locker. Dropping her board into the water with a splash, she said, "Let the lesson begin."

For a guy who had never tried paddle boarding, Fitz thought he was doing pretty well. And by "well" he meant that he was still dry. Given the shaky state of his balance, he assumed he would fall in eventually. His goal was to delay that moment for as long as possible. After a while he felt steadier on his feet. He had seen people doing this on busy summer days, when motorboats buzzed around pulling skiers and creating giant waves. To his relief, the lake was perfectly calm this morning, giving him a fighting chance to stay upright.

After showing him the basics, Mel led the way as they followed the shoreline. They paddled in silence for about fifteen minutes, long enough for Fitz to gain confidence and possibly get a little cocky. Mel slowed her strokes, allowing him to catch up, and for a while they glided side by side. He jumped when she spoke and almost tumbled over backward. It was all he could do to keep his balance without worrying about conversation.

"So," she said, "are you staying with your parents?"

Her quiet voice carried surprisingly well over the calm water. He glanced briefly her way, but even that small movement was enough to throw off his balance. She might have smothered a laugh, but he didn't dare look in her direction again. Too risky.

"Yes," he answered when he had his board back under control. "It seemed crazy to rent a hotel room or look for a short-term rental when I could stay right nearby for free. This is also a great chance to spend some time with them before I leave."

"Where are you going?"

"I don't know yet. It depends on where I'm staffed. I've been applying for international assignments, and I'm cautiously optimistic that I'll be selected for one that starts in November, but no official word yet."

"What country?"

He opened his mouth to answer, but changed his mind. "I don't want to jinx it. I'll tell you if it comes through."

"Superstitious," she said. "Interesting."

He would have liked to respond to the amusement in her voice by splashing her with his paddle, but he didn't dare make any unnecessary movements.

"What do your parents think about this plan?"

At his silence, she laughed.

"Let me guess. We're both keeping international travel plans a secret from our parents. Seriously?"

Risking another quick glance over at Mel, Fitz smiled sheepishly.

"Why haven't you told your family?" he asked.

She didn't answer right away, finally saying, "I don't know. My mom has been so caught up in this idea that I'm going to move back here permanently, and I haven't figured out how to tell her without crushing that dream." She paddled a few strokes without saying anything, pulling slightly ahead, then coasted while he caught up. "I don't want to be a dream-crusher."

"Well," said Fitz, "I think you're going to be a dream-crusher either way—hers or yours." His words probably sounded harsh, but they needed to be said.

Her shoulders slumped and she turned his question back on him. "What about you? Why haven't you told your family?"

He almost lost his balance again, and took a minute to steady himself before answering. "My mom had treatment for cancer last year. Non-Hodgkin's lymphoma. She's still fragile, but one of the things that really lights her up is planning my life, setting me up on dates. The last thing I want to do is take that joy away from her."

"That's hard."

He nodded. "My dad gets really wound up about my career and not wasting my potential. He retired last year when my mom got sick so that he could take care of her. Now that she's mostly recovered, he has way too much time on his hands."

"Time to focus on you."

"Exactly."

"So you, too, live in fear of being a dream-crusher?"

Nothing like hearing your own wise words reflected back at you.

"I do."

They paddled in silence for a while. Mel found it oddly comforting that she wasn't the only one trying to balance her family's happiness and her own. Most of her friends in Chicago didn't get along all that well with their families, so her conflicted feelings were simply incomprehensible to them. Her sisters might understand, to a certain extent, but they hadn't let family get in the way of pursuing their goals, even if it meant being away from home for extended periods of time. Only Mel seemed to have this compulsive need to know that her family was okay before spreading her wings. If only there were a way to turn it off.

"Maybe we can help each other with this problem," she said.

"How?"

"We could practice our 'we need to talk' speeches on each other, and then we could report back when we've actually told them. Think of it as mutual accountability and moral support for the dream-crushers of the world."

"Not a bad idea," he said, then chuckled. "You go first."

Before she could answer, she heard the sound of a boat starting up behind them, followed by the thumping bass of party music.

"Get ready," warned Mel. "That's a wakeboarding boat. They make the biggest waves of all the boats on the lake, and by the sound of it, this one's heading our way."

"I'm good." Fitz bent his knees a bit and continued paddling.

Rookie. Mel hid a smile and let Fitz pull ahead. This was going to be fun to watch.

A moment later, the boat cruised past them. Even at a moderate speed, the wake was enormous. For Mel, staying upright was a matter of hitting the right hula rhythm on her board. She'd been battling these waves all summer. For the newbie, Fitz, it was a question of whether he would follow Mel's advice for beginners and crouch down on his board or to demonstrate his manliness by staying on his feet.

Fitz did not disappoint.

He almost made it. He really tried. Following most of her advice, he kept his knees bent and paddled like his life depended on it, a great strategy for tackling small waves. These waves were not small, and the final one hit him hard. With a grand windmill of his arms, he tumbled off the board and into the water.

Unlike the air, the water still retained some of the summer heat. Fitz popped back up and shook his head like a wet dog. Mel circled around to retrieve his paddle, which was floating toward shore. He caught his breath before pulling himself onto the board and into a sitting position.

Mel returned with the lost paddle, approaching him from behind and appreciating the way his wet T-shirt outlined the muscles of his back and arms. The shadow of his tattoo showed through the white fabric, not so much that she could tell what it was, only that it stretched from his neck diagonally down his back. More curious than ever, she wondered if he would take his shirt off if she asked nicely.

She glided up beside him and handed him the paddle. When he looked up at her, all dripping and bedraggled, she couldn't help it. She giggled.

"You think this is funny? Laughing at the expense of the newbie?"

She nodded.

"Figures," he said.

Then he grabbed the side of her board and tipped her right over into the water.

CHAPTER TEN

NOTHING HAD CHANGED SINCE LUKE'S DEPARTURE A COUPLE OF weeks earlier, but Dora felt different, even a little nervous. He would arrive home any minute, so she puttered around in the kitchen, cleaning things that didn't need to be cleaned and keeping an eye out the window over the sink. He would ask how she was doing, and she honestly had no idea how she would answer. The foundations of her life were shifting beneath her feet, and she had nothing to hold on to—no way to keep her balance.

The "strictly business" coffee date with David had left her feeling prickly all over. She had spent the last two days wondering if he would call, then annoyed at herself for wondering, then irritated that he hadn't bothered to call, and then angry all over again that she was obsessing over whether or not a boy was going to call her on the phone. She was an adult, for Pete's sake, not a middle schooler.

When Luke finally walked through the back door, she ambushed him with a giant hug and held on to him. He had been her rock for so long that she couldn't wrap her head around the idea of life without him.

"Sweetheart, what's the matter?"

"Nothing," she said, swallowing hard and trying to sound completely normal. "I just missed you, and I hate change. That's all."

He laughed and gave her shoulders a squeeze as he let her go. "Change can be good. You'll see."

Dora followed him upstairs and sat on the bed while he unpacked. How many more times would she do his laundry? Who would change the oil in her car after he left? She didn't know anything about cars or the computer or the pilot light on the water heater. The list multiplied in her head as she sat there watching him toss his dirty clothes into the laundry basket and ramble on about all the things he had done with Zeke in Nashville. There were so many ways they had divided the responsibilities of life. If—no, *when* he left, she would need to learn a whole new set of skills. She fought to slow her breathing as her anxiety spiraled into panic, but Luke knew her too well.

He stopped everything and sat beside her on the bed.

"Dora, honey, tell me what's going on."

"I don't—" Her breath hitched, and the tears started to slide down her face. "I don't know how to change the oil."

Luke folded her into his arms and held her while she cried, trying to explain through her tears that she wanted him to be happy but she didn't want to learn how to light the ancient gas grill. He didn't tell her it was going to be okay. He didn't shush her. He stroked her back and waited for the storm to pass.

Who would hold her when she needed to cry? Who would be smart enough not to try to fix everything?

Later, when the sobs had subsided and the tears had dried, Luke pulled away and met her eyes squarely.

"I won't leave until you're ready."

She sniffled.

"What if I'm never ready?"

At that he laughed, a big belly laugh that made her smile in spite of herself.

"You, my dear, are going to surprise yourself." He kissed her smack in the middle of her forehead, then rose from the bed to finish unpacking. "Now, tell me what's got you so worked up."

"I went on a date." The minute the words were out of her mouth, she realized that it couldn't even technically be called a date. She was that pathetic.

"Oh, really?"

Apparently they *were* in middle school, and Luke looked ready to trade his Cheetos for some good gossip. Dora threw a pillow at him.

"Not like that," she backtracked. "As if. At my age." She huffed about it for a minute before explaining. "Lucy tricked me into meeting a gallery owner for coffee. He wants to sell my work in his galleries. Exclusively."

Luke's grin widened at her horrified tone of voice.

"That's amazing. How are his terms? Is it a good deal?"

"I don't know," she muttered.

"Why not?"

"We didn't get to that part yet."

Luke studied her face for a minute. "You like him."

"I do not!" Her words might have been more convincing without the heat creeping up her neck.

"I bet he's good-looking. Hot, even."

Dora's sputtering was answer enough, and Luke laughed again.

"I like him already. When can I meet him?"

"There will be no meeting, or chatting, or...or..."

Luke closed up his now-empty suitcase and carried it out to the hall closet. He came back to the bedroom and leaned against the doorframe.

"Fine," he said. "I'll leave you to your negotiations and try to avoid meeting him—for now. But you need to tell me if things get interesting, okay?"

She nodded.

"Anything else going on?"

"It's all happening so fast. I want to see Mel stable and happy and then, maybe, I'll feel ready for my own life to start again. All this with the gallery owner is too much. It's not happening in the right order."

"We've never really lived our lives in the right order, have we?"

Shaking her head on a watery laugh, Dora scrambled off the bed and over to Luke. "Thanks for putting up with me all these years." She wrapped her arms around him in another hug.

"Thanks for giving me the family I always wanted," he answered, giving her a big squeeze before letting her go. "Now go find out what kind of terms this gallery owner is offering you. They had better be good."

"Yes, sir." She started down the stairs.

"Next time you see him, sneak a picture, so I can check him out."

"I'll do better than that," called Dora over her shoulder. "I'm going to paint him."

28 years ago, January

The suitcase latched with a snick. A part of her didn't want to leave. This getaway to the sunshine and white sand beaches of Turks and Caicos had been an unexpected treat over the winter break. Barrett had sent the airplane ticket in the mail with no other explanation. She had debated the wisdom of meeting him away from her home turf, but subzero temperatures in Chicago had tipped the decision in his favor.

His sensual assault had begun in the limo on the way from the airport to the beach house and had continued throughout the week. She'd had more orgasms in the last seven days than she'd had in her entire life, and that was saying something. Barrett had claimed her at every opportunity. The private beach at sunset. The cabana. The bed, of course, but also the kitchen, living room, and laundry room. Even the dark hallway of the nightclub where they'd gone out dancing. She wouldn't be able to look at a picture of Turks and Caicos ever again without getting turned on. They'd had some wild times over the last few years, but always in stolen moments, nothing like this. This week was the longest stretch of uninterrupted time they had ever spent together.

Of course his beach house was amazing. Barrett enjoyed every advantage that wealth could offer. She could enjoy those advantages, too, if she were willing to live in the odd space Barrett and Lauren had carved out for her in their lives. Times like this made her wonder. They made her weak. It was too easy to forget the reality of everyday life when you were naked in the sunshine, but her reasons for refusing him remained the same. She would always come second to Lauren, and second with the children, and eventually it would grind her heart to dust. Better to keep Barrett at arm's length and set the terms of engagement.

The timing of Barrett's first visit to Chicago in mid-November had meant that he couldn't jet out to see her the following weekend, or the weekend after that. Between holiday parties and charity galas, Barrett's social calendar had been booked solid through the new year. Hopefully, amid all the public obligations, he had remembered to set aside private time for the family. She suspected that her vision of family life did not line up well with Barrett's.

Dora's holiday experience had been lonely, but also an important milestone. Her family had cut ties with her years ago, when she had gone to work for Lauren and Barrett. All her new school friends scattered to their various hometowns for comfort food and family bonding, so Dora had spent Christmas alone. She had filled the time with long walks on Michigan Avenue and lots of window shopping. Most of her friends returned to the city for New Year's Eve, so at least she celebrated that milestone with some company. Building a new life takes time, and she wasn't going to give up this early in the game.

Dora looked around the room for any items she'd missed. No stray items of clothing. No toiletries left in the bathroom. The limo would arrive any minute. She double checked her purse. Money, drivers license...passport? She looked again, more slowly this time. Then again. No passport.

Not good.

She heard footsteps behind her and then Barrett's arms wrapped around her waist, pulling her back against him.

"Don't go," he whispered in her ear.

She ignored her body's response and slipped out of his arms, suspicion darkening her mood.

"I can't go," she said. "You've made sure of that, haven't you?"

She didn't care for his smug smile, nor the way he grabbed her by the hips and pulled her close again.

"You're my prisoner."

"Give me my passport, Barrett." She didn't back away this time, but made her anger clear. Her life wasn't a game to be played and won.

"And if I don't?"

"Do we really need to do this?" Now she pulled away, and put enough distance between them that he couldn't grab her again.

He changed tactics. "Why won't you come back to New York with me?"

"I have a life of my own."

As usual, he had no response to that.

"Let me make this simple for you," said Dora. "If you would like to enjoy my company again, then you will get your head out of your ass and give me my passport. If you do that right now, without any more games, I might even let you ride with me to the airport." She paused to give him a hard stare. "If you don't immediately bring me my passport, then our arrangement is over. I will never agree to see you again."

He made a grumpy face, but she could tell he was paying attention. "You don't have to be so difficult, you know." Sighing in defeat, he turned around and walked into his study. He removed her passport from the safe and handed it to her.

"Thank you," she said, keeping her voice even despite the fact that she wanted to punch him. No matter how strong their chemistry, she would not allow him to control her life. She had little patience for his struggle with their new dynamic. If he couldn't handle it, she would end it. It was that simple.

"When is the limo coming?" he asked.

She checked the clock. "Five minutes."

He looped his arm through hers and led her toward the bedroom. "I love a challenge."

CHAPTER ELEVEN

Today

DORA COULDN'T IMAGINE WHY MEL RESISTED MAKING PLANS FOR her own future, but she planned to find out. Instead of asking Mel directly, Dora had a more subtle approach in mind. Her daughters might question the use of "subtle" and "Dora" in the same sentence, but it was worth a try. Mel had never been much of a morning person, so if the subject came up over breakfast, while Mel was still fuzzy with sleep, maybe they would get some answers.

Mel typically drifted into the kitchen around eight-thirty looking for food, and for the past few days she had been driving over to the library right before nine. With this schedule in mind, Dora had put together a French toast bake last night and popped it into the oven at seven-thirty this morning. By the time Mel got out of the shower, the whole house should smell like butter and cinnamon. Dora had chosen this particular recipe first because it was one of Mel's favorites, and second because even the worst cook in the world (aka Dora) could not screw up.

Dora had also invited Mel's sisters, who should have been here by now. Seriously, those girls could never get anywhere on time. Callie had come up from Nashville with Luke the day before, but she was staying at Adam's house. Now that the two of them were engaged, she had basically moved in with him—at least when she wasn't in Nashville. Tessa might as well be living with RJ, although neither of them would admit to being that serious. Dora couldn't quite tell what their status was, but they seemed happy and she didn't want to jinx it.

Dora paced the kitchen, peering out the back window every thirty seconds to see if Callie was cutting through the hedge yet, then checking the baked French toast again to see if it was still warm. Why was everyone taking so long?

Luke shot her an irritated look over the top of the newspaper.

"Dora, for the love of Pete, will you please sit down? What in the world has gotten into you this morning?"

She sat down with a huff. Luke would be no help this morning. His mantra had always been "Let the girls live their lives." Well, she'd given them each a chance to do that and it hadn't gone well. Callie had finally gotten herself straightened out this summer, and Tessa seemed to be on a better track, but Mel was still drifting, and Dora's window of opportunity to intervene was closing. If Mel didn't want to be the captain of her own ship, then Dora would have to take the helm and steer her in a new direction. The right direction.

A creaky floorboard alerted Dora to Mel's arrival. She had stopped in the doorway of the kitchen, her brow wrinkled and her eyes still sleepy.

"Are we having special breakfast?"

"It's your favorite. I made French toast bake."

A subtle narrowing of Mel's eyes alerted Dora that she needed to strengthen her cover story.

"I wanted to do a welcome back dinner for your dad last

night, but your sisters couldn't make it. They're coming over for breakfast instead. I thought I'd make a something nice."

Mel's face brightened and Dora relaxed.

"That's cool. I didn't realize they were coming over." She shuffled over to the coffee pot and poured herself a cup. Leaning over the still-warm baking pan on the counter, she inhaled deeply. "Can we start without them?"

With a broad smile, Dora popped out of her seat. "Of course, dear. Why don't you sit down and I'll get you a plate. Syrup?"

"Sure. That would be great."

Dora could hear the edge of suspicion again in Mel's voice. She needed to play it cool, so she kept her mouth shut as she pulled a stack of plates out of the cupboard and set them on the counter. Taking her time, she pulled the bowl of cut-up fruit from the fridge and set it on the impromptu buffet. The plate she delivered to Mel with a flourish had a nice, fat square of baked French toast swimming in a puddle of syrup, with a brightly colored pile of fruit beside it. Honestly, it would make a great still life. Maybe she should take a quick picture of it for later. If she only knew where her phone was.

"Mom, what's going on?"

Dora stopped patting her pockets looking for her phone. Both Luke and Mel were staring at her as if she'd lost her mind.

"Nothing. Why?"

Mel's expression turned skeptical. Instead of saying something helpful, Luke got up to hit the buffet. *Someone* was not displaying his supportive husband skills this morning. Dora plunked herself back into her chair at the table, trying to look innocent.

"Just looking for my phone. And I'm happy that we're all going to have breakfast together."

Had Mel's face softened? Yes, it definitely had.

"Or we will be when your sisters get here. Why are they

always late? Oh, and I'm very excited about our real estate tour. We have some great options to check out."

Mel choked on her French toast. "Our what?"

There was a commotion at the back door as both Callie and Tessa arrived at the same time. Finally.

"Come on in, girls," said Dora. "I was about to tell your sister about the cool places we're going to see tomorrow morning."

"Ooh, tell us all about it," said Tessa as she made a beeline for the French toast and fruit. After loading up a plate, she claimed her usual spot at the table, completely ignoring the "change the subject" look that Mel shot her way. Callie wasn't as vocal as Tessa, but Mel could tell that she was curious. Her sisters were going to be no help at all in avoiding this discussion.

If Dora's deep inhale was any indicator, they were in for a long story.

"Well, you wouldn't believe our luck. There are three places on the market right now that all sound amazing. Nice big space for a photo studio, storage for all your equipment. We'll need to assess the light in each space of course, and you'll want to think about what's most important in terms of location. Are you hoping for a central location with a lot of foot traffic? Do you want a lot of space for parking? I can't really decide that for you."

Mel stifled a snort. *Really?* Her mother had charted an entirely new course for Mel's career, but she didn't feel comfortable choosing the photo studio?

"How's the rent?" asked Tessa.

"I don't remember," said Dora, "but I know it's cheaper than Chicago, and that's what matters."

"Mel, what's your budget?"

Mel shrugged, her mouth full. Tessa seemed ready to negotiate a deal on her behalf, but the last thing Mel needed was to rush this process. She had only agreed to this outing because her mother had been so excited, and really, what was the harm in a little real estate shopping? The harm, she now realized, was in raising her mother's hopes. The higher the hope, the harder the fall.

"It doesn't matter," said Dora. "We can certainly help out with the rent until the business is up and running."

"Mom, I don't think—"

"Let us help you, honey. We're family, and we stick together. You shouldn't have to do this on your own."

Mel met her father's eyes across the table and she did her best "help me" look, but he just smiled and shook his head. There was no stopping Dora when she got on a roll.

"It will be awesome to have you here all the time," said Tessa. "Maybe we could start a book club!"

Callie began wriggling out of the proposed commitment immediately. "That sounds fun," she said, "but my schedule is really up in the air, so I won't be very reliable."

Dora, however, was totally on board. "What a great idea! I'm sure we can find some other young people to join. I'll start asking around to see if anyone has books to recommend. Oh, I bet Mary Evelyn would be happy to help get things started. Always good to have a librarian on your side."

The conversation flowed around the table, but Mel tuned it out, letting her sleepy brain focus on the last bites of French toast. Maybe, after this last bite, she could fake a bathroom break and then sneak over to the library with her family none the wiser. Or maybe she should choose the nuclear option and tell the whole family about her actual future plans right now. But Mom was so excited about the real estate showings and had gone to a lot of trouble to set them up. It seemed cruel to yank the carpet out from under her now. Maybe after the showings.

And maybe she could change the subject. Surely there must

be a topic of conversation that would make her sisters as uncomfortable as she was. Mel tuned back in to the conversation, looking for any opportunity to turn it in a new direction. Dora was in the middle of giving Tessa a rundown of the properties they would see tomorrow, including Dora's first impression based on the real estate photos. It seemed that Mel could evaporate from the table and they'd never notice her absence.

As she sat there watching the Tessa-Dora show and sipping her coffee, Mel thought about what Kat had said. She needed to give her family the gift of time to get used to the idea of Mel being away. Over the past ten years, Mel had been the only one of the sisters to make it home for every holiday and most of the summer weekends. Now, her plans included leaving the country before Thanksgiving, and visiting home no more than once every six months for at least two years. No matter how much time they had to get used to the idea, the first holiday apart would be difficult, for Mel maybe even more than the rest of the family. To miss the entire holiday season was almost unimaginable.

The alternative, however, was almost as unimaginable. The idea of giving up her work and her life in the city to settle down here—alone—in Hidden Springs...it made her heart hurt. Some people called it putting down roots, but to Mel it felt more like accepting shackles and chains. She loved her family, but she wouldn't squeeze herself into a tiny box for them. And that's what she would tell her mother after tomorrow's outing.

CHAPTER TWELVE

AFTER BREAKFAST, FEELING AWFULLY PLEASED WITH HERSELF, Dora retreated upstairs to the attic to paint. This morning's get-together had gone exactly as planned, with conversation centering around the real estate search and Mel's future plans. Dora frowned to herself as she reached the top of the first flight of stairs. Now that she thought about it, Tessa had led the conversation, asking lots of questions and freely sharing her thoughts. Even Callie had seemed interested in the proceedings. Of all the girls, though, Mel had seemed the least engaged, and Dora couldn't remember if she'd asked a question or offered an opinion. Climbing the second set of stairs to the attic, Dora shook off any lingering concern. Mel might be able to coast through a conversation with her sisters, but tomorrow it would be just Dora and Mel alone in the car, following the real estate agent around. Eventually Mel would have to say something.

Fall was Dora's favorite time of year in the studio. Opening the windows one by one, she invited crisp air to fill her workspace. The leaves on the oaks were just beginning to turn, changing the sound of the wind from summer's whisper to the rustle of fall. She curled up in her creaky, overstuffed armchair with a sketchbook and charcoal pencil, letting the images flow from her brain onto the page. This had been one of her favorite exercises from art school. Not only could this stream of consciousness be a source of great ideas, but it was also a great way to clear her mind and settle down—something she sorely needed.

She and Luke had talked about the coming transition for years, starting on the day they decided to build a family together. But now that the turning point had arrived, Dora felt only confusion. Luke found it so easy to leave, probably because he was moving *toward* something. Callie's regular visits to Nashville would ease any homesickness he might feel. But from Dora's perspective, he was leaving—and he was taking one of the girls with him.

During Dora's visits to New York this past summer, Tessa had stepped in at the sailing school, handling the day-to-day emergencies that needed a level head. If Dora wanted to take an extended leave of absence at some point in the future, Tessa was perfectly capable of filling her shoes. It couldn't be any easier for Dora to spread her wings and fly.

But to where? Given the perfect circumstances to start a new chapter in her life, Dora found herself without inspiration. The dreams of her youth—to explore faraway places, to meet the people, taste the food—seemed silly now. Impractical. Did she plan to set off alone, leaving behind her home and the people she loved? The life of the lonely nomad might appeal to some, but for Dora, the joy of a new experience came from sharing it with someone else.

Not Luke, of course. He had plans of his own.

Not Callie or Tessa. They had barely begun their adult lives. It wasn't the time for detours.

Not Mel. She needed direction, not distraction.

That left Dora. Alone.

She could always sign up for a group tour and meet other retirees with time on their hands and a love of travel, but instead of anticipation, the idea left her deflated. She wanted something to do. A purpose, not a pastime. She might live for another fifty years, and she wasn't going to spend it reflecting on the first fifty years.

She wasn't finished yet.

Blinking, she focused on the images that had flowed from brain to pencil and felt a flush creep up her cheeks. There was a chiseled profile. Thick, black hair with silver at the temples. Strong muscles clearly defining a set of broad shoulders, narrow waist—

Apparently her subconscious had plenty of inspiration. It was beyond embarrassing for a woman her age to have these fluttery feelings in her belly. They were not unwelcome, exactly, but she had learned long ago that good chemistry leads to bad decisions, and that it is all too easy to lose yourself in someone else. The question was, in the last twenty-seven years, had she learned anything about finding a balance?

Her phone buzzed with a number she recognized as David's. Stretching languidly, the newly awakened siren within her whispered, *There's only one way to find out.*

Fitz and Mel had spent Monday masking the side of the building. On Tuesday, they had begun spraying and rolling a thick coat of primer. Fitz had focused on the spraying, having a better sense of how thick to lay down the gesso. Mel had followed behind with a roller, smoothing the thick layer of acrylic and making sure to fill any lingering pinholes. Now, as lunchtime approached on Wednesday, they neared the finish line, at least as far as primer was concerned. Fitz had finished spraying at ground level and Mel lagged behind with the roller. He suspected her arms were killing her, although she was too stubborn to admit it.

"Need a hand?" he asked as he finished cleaning out the sprayer.

"I'm fine."

Her answer was more grunt than spoken word, and he hid a smile.

"I really enjoyed paddle boarding yesterday," he said. What he said was true, but adding an arm workout to an already brutal day of paint rolling might not have been the best idea. If he was feeling his arms today, she must be in serious pain.

"Glad to hear it."

Drying his wet hands on his pants, he waited until Mel had finished rolling the very last corner. She let the roller drop to rest on the plastic sheeting. Walking up behind her, Fitz placed his hands on her shoulders and began to knead her overworked muscles. She moaned softly and let the roller handle fall to the ground. He stopped kneading briefly and she made a disappointed sound in the back of her throat, but he was only moving the roller off the top of her feet and resting it in the paint pan. He resumed the impromptu back rub, and she let her head loll forward.

"You're awfully tight." He murmured the words in her ear, and was pleased to see the goosebumps rise on her neck.

"Stop and I'll kill you."

"I wouldn't dream of it."

The first few days on a new project were always tough, but he had learned to increase his arm workouts in the weeks leading up to a project start. Photography probably gave her a good base of arm strength, but not the kind of endurance she needed for multiple days of roller work.

Pausing briefly, he led her over to the bench and nudged her to sit down, which she did without protest. The sun warmed them through the thinning screen of oak leaves. It was hard to believe that they had been out on the water only yester-day. The weather had tipped toward fall, and this morning was noticeably cooler, barely warm enough to paint. He worked his way from her neck down to the middle of her back, and then down each arm. Her hands, in particular, needed attention, after gripping the roller all morning.

"You seem a little...cranky this morning," ventured Fitz as he worked on one of her hands.

She answered without opening her eyes. "My family is ganging up on me."

"About?"

"They've planned out my new career as a wedding photographer, and everyone is very excited about the tour of potential commercial properties tomorrow morning." She dragged her eyelids open to look over at him. "By the way, I need tomorrow morning off."

"So you're going to stay here?" he asked, confused. "I thought—"

"I'm not staying. I just haven't told them yet."

If his own conflict avoidance was borderline dysfunctional, Mel was taking it to new levels. At least he didn't have an official assignment or travel plans yet.

"How long do you have to sort this out?"

"I leave November fifteenth."

He didn't catch his laugh in time, and she scowled at him.

"Have you ever thought of just throwing it out there and seeing what happens?"

"Right. I'm sure that'll be great," she muttered, her eyes closed again. "'Hey, Mom, by the way, I can't rent a commercial property because I'm leaving the country.' That will go over really well."

He gave her hand one last squeeze and then placed it on her leg. "Seriously, what's stopping you from telling them?"

Pinching the bridge of her nose, Mel grimaced. "I don't

know. Every time I open my mouth to say the words, I freeze. I literally can't make myself say it out loud. The plane ticket is booked, I know where I'll be staying. It's all set. I'm sure there's a name for this kind of paralysis, and I'm sure my sister Tessa— a licensed professional counselor—will be happy to tell me exactly what it is when I finally drop the bomb on the family." Mel gave him a wry glance. "She won't be able to resist."

"Every day you wait makes it worse." He winced even as he said it. Not the right thing to say at all.

"Thanks, Captain Obvious. And how's that working for you? Have you told your family yet?" She was watching him closely when she asked the question. Some of his guilt must have shown on his face, because she said, "Ah hah!"

"How can I tell them when there's nothing to tell? I didn't get the assignment yet. I could tell them, and deal with all the related drama, and set back my mom's recovery—all for nothing. Better to wait until I know for sure."

"Mm-hmm." Mel's bland response made her skepticism quite clear.

"How can I bring my mom down from the high of watching me go on a paddle boarding date?"

"She liked that, did she?" asked Mel as she stood and stretched. "Let's see how she likes it when I break your heart by leaving the country."

Fitz stood as well, and they headed back to close up shop for the day.

"I was thinking about that, actually...."

Picking up her roller, Mel walked over to their makeshift cleaning station. "I already know I'm not going to like this."

"Oh, I think you will."

She paused and looked at him over her shoulder. "You're going to explain to my family where I've gone so that I don't have to do it?"

"Ah...no."

She resumed walking. "Bummer."

"I was thinking that my mom is unlikely to believe we're attempting a long-distance relationship. We're going to have to sell it."

"Sell it how?"

"A convincing number of dates. Maybe a family dinner." Keeping his expression innocent, he added, "A *lot* of public displays of affection."

CHAPTER THIRTEEN

Fitz had a point. A self-interested point, but a valid one, nonetheless. If they wanted to get the full benefit of a fake relationship, with the additional cover provided by an attempt at long-distance and subsequent breakup, they would have to make it look good.

"I'm on board with this plan," she said. Taking a step toward him, she wrapped her arms around his neck and leaned closer. "I certainly hope you can be convincing. Maybe we should schedule some practice sessions."

He leaned forward until his lips brushed her earlobe. The caress sent shivers down her neck.

"Be sure to let me know if there's anything I can do to improve the quality of my work," he murmured, right before his teeth closed around her earlobe and tugged, surprising a gasp from her. "I respond very well to feedback."

Her eyes drifted shut and she slid her hands up into his hair, which was surprisingly soft. She moved slowly so as not to interrupt the lovely things he was doing with his mouth on her neck. Leaning forward, she kissed his skin inside the collar of his shirt, inhaling the scent and warmth of him. He took his time, lazily exploring the contours of her neck, and she let herself float in the moment, oblivious to the world around them.

The sound of voices around the corner brought her back to reality, and she slowly pulled away. Stolen moments with Fitz would not be enough. He deserved her full attention, somewhere away from his family, her family, and random strangers who happened to be strolling down the street. Looking into his eyes, she was relieved to see a mix of vulnerability and need. It would be awkward if she were the only one affected by the chemistry between them.

"We need to get a room," she said.

His laugh helped to break the spell. "Agreed."

"So what are we going to do while the paint dries?" she asked.

"Well," said Fitz, "my top choice is not a possibility because we both have parents at home."

"This is going to become a serious problem."

"I know," said Fitz. "And while we're figuring out a solution, I should make a run to Milwaukee for supplies."

"That would be the responsible choice."

"Want to join me?" he asked.

"Only if we stop somewhere on the way home to make out." Mel was only kind of joking.

"Deal."

As they closed up for the day, Mel couldn't help but wonder what they might have become, if only they had better timing.

Dora stood in front of the gallery tapping her foot. She had just dropped off a painting with Ansel, and—even better—picked up a check, but her good mood was being ruined, second by second, as she waited for David. They had agreed to meet at noon in front of the art gallery.

"You're late," she said when she finally saw him walking toward her down the sidewalk.

He smiled and reached for her hand, bringing it to his mouth for a kiss. She steeled herself to resist the old-world charm, but it was the zing of electricity that got past her defenses, arrowing from her knuckles to her palm and lighting up her body from there.

"Perhaps you are early," he replied, holding on to her hand a few seconds longer than necessary before letting go.

She refused to check her watch because he was probably right, damn it, and now she looked too eager to see him.

"Shall we have our coffee?" he asked.

"I'd like to walk."

David made her restless. She would be more comfortable if they could stay on the move.

He offered his arm. "In that case, we shall walk."

Accepting the offered arm, Dora led the way down the street. If she also noticed that he had a nice, strong bicep, well, that couldn't be helped. She hadn't taken anyone's arm but Luke's in forever, so it was only logical that she'd notice any differences. She had walked through life with Luke as her partner for so many years that he had become her definition of normal. David, of course, was not Luke. He was very different. Taller, for one. Luke only stood a couple of inches taller than Dora. David must be a good six inches taller, because each time she snuck a glance at his profile, she had to look up. He was also broader in the shoulders. The bicep beneath her fingers felt stronger and thicker than "normal," and she didn't think it could be attributed to his coat. She could feel him beneath the wool, warm and solid.

She waited to see if he would open the conversation, but he seemed content to walk in silence, and that irritated her for some reason. Everything about David made her prickly, even the fact that he made her prickly.

"Tell me more about this deal you're proposing," she said abruptly. "What are your terms?"

As he explained, over the course of several blocks, Dora made a mental note to check in with some of her friends from art school to see what was considered fair these days. She had been out of the game for too long. Technically, she supposed that selling her work through the gallery here still counted as being "in the game," but this tiny gallery was a long way from the center of the art world, and she had never navigated those waters.

"What other questions can I answer for you?" he asked.

"Those are all my questions, for now."

"And your answer?"

They had stopped walking, and to her surprise she realized that they had reached the end of the sidewalk at the lakefront park. She had been so caught up in his mesmerizing voice that she hadn't really paid attention to her surroundings. His eyes threatened to pull her even deeper under his spell, so she looked out over the lake instead.

"I'll need to think about it."

"While you are thinking, I hope you'll allow me to take you to dinner."

It wasn't the response she had expected. They walked a tightrope separating business and pleasure, and Dora couldn't quite find her balance. Every time she thought his interest in her might be personal, he would talk business, and every time she thought he was all business, suddenly he would do something that sent shivers up her spine. It was time to bring clarity to their interactions, so rather than trying to keep her balance, Dora stepped off the tightrope.

"Actually..." she began.

"Yes?"

It had been a long time, but she remembered what interest looked like in a man's eyes. David was *definitely* interested.

"I'd like to paint you."

He opened his mouth but no words came out, and Dora laughed.

Cocking his head to one side, he said, "Perhaps I do not fully understand your meaning. When you say you want to paint me..."

"I mean that I want to paint you," she repeated. "You would come to my studio, sit for me, and I would paint you. Well, actually, I would sketch you first, but then I would paint you."

It was David's turn to laugh, and she couldn't help her answering smile. This was no chuckle, but a full belly laugh, the kind that lights up a room.

"Never in all my years of working with artists has anyone asked to paint me. You cannot be serious."

Dora raised an eyebrow. "I wouldn't ask if I wasn't serious. You're a beautiful man and you know it. That beauty should be captured on canvas."

David, of course, zeroed in on the compliment buried in the request. "So you think I am beautiful?"

"I just said so, didn't I?" The brisk wind off the lake had already reddened her cheeks, hiding the blush. "Don't pretend you don't know. Beautiful people always know."

"As you do?"

She shook her head. "I used to be quite pretty, and I remember what it was like to capture the attention of others so easily, but that was years ago."

"And yet, I am captivated."

"Don't be absurd."

"I believe you have disproved your theory that beautiful people always know their own beauty, and have instead supported the truism that beauty is in the eye of the beholder."

She had no answer for that, only a skeptical shake of the head.

"I must ask you a question first."

He waited for her nod to continue.

"Your friend Lucy mentioned that you are separated from your husband, and yet you still wear a ring. I will not intrude on a marriage."

"But you'll flirt with a married lady?" she asked with a smile.

"Only a little."

Dora had loved the flirting, but she appreciated his respect for marriage even more.

"Lucy had it right. My husband and I are in the process of getting a divorce. We've always had a strong friendship, and that will continue, but the time has come for us to take separate paths." She looked down at her hand and twisted her rings around her finger. "I suppose I wear the rings out of habit, or maybe nostalgia."

He studied her face for a moment before nodding. "To answer your original question: Yes, you may paint me."

"Excellent." Hopefully her red cheeks would also hide the flare of panic at his easy agreement.

"When would you like to begin this collaboration?" he asked.

It was so tempting to suggest next week, to give her time to build up her courage, but she knew herself well. The longer she waited, the more her courage would slip away. If she was really going to do this, she needed to dive in before she talked herself out of it.

"How about this afternoon?" she replied. Luke was out for the day, and Mel had called a few minutes ago to say she and Fitz were making a run to Milwaukee. Dora had the house to herself for the afternoon.

"It would be my pleasure."

CHAPTER FOURTEEN

28 years ago, June

WHEN THE AIRLINE TICKET ARRIVED IN THE MAIL, DORA couldn't figure out whether she should laugh or cry. Barrett was nothing if not persistent. She had told him, repeatedly, that she would not be joining them in the Hamptons this summer, but he hadn't accepted defeat.

Summer in the Hamptons might as well be subtitled "Dora's Favorite Things." They would spend endless hours on the beach, sail whenever the mood struck, and roast marshmallows around a bonfire at night. The babies, now officially toddlers, had grown in her absence. A summer together would bring an opportunity to get to know them all over again. She and Lauren could catch up, she and Barrett steal some alone time, and she could paint the ever-changing ocean whenever she wanted.

It would be a perfect summer, and that was exactly why she couldn't go. Reclaiming her place in their lives would be absurdly easy. Finding the strength to leave again would be impossible.

So instead of the Hamptons, Dora would spend her summer here in Chicago, taking a summer class and working part-time at the yacht club. Sailing on Lake Michigan would offer an escape from the oppressive heat of the city. No matter how tempting Barrett's offer, she would choose Chicago.

She hadn't seen Barrett since their get-together in Aspen over spring break. (There had been no actual skiing involved.) Before that, they had managed two weekend getaways in addition to the winter break in Turks and Caicos. Physically, their interludes had been amazing, but Dora had slowly come to the realization that very little connected them other than chemistry. Even sailing, which had initially brought them together, was no more than an occasional amusement for Barrett, not a true passion. She wondered how long their fire would burn, and, other than ashes, what would remain.

Five days after Dora did *not* fly to the Hamptons, Barrett showed up in Chicago—not exactly on her doorstep, but close. The buzzer announced the arrival of a courier with a hand-written note from Barrett inviting her to his suite at the Palmer House. She thanked the courier for the delivery and scrounged up a tip, but told him he didn't need to wait for a reply.

Tapping the heavy stationery absently on the counter, Dora weighed her options, wondering if their odd arrangement could or should continue. Her body voted in favor, but her mind had reservations—lots of them. Still, the sun was shining. A lake breeze cooled the city. She was finally feeling back to herself after a nasty sinus infection and a round of powerful antibiotics. The prospect of a leisurely walk followed by great sex was awfully appealing.

One last time.

She chose the sundress for Barrett. He liked the buttons that ran all the way down the front. The sandals she chose for comfort, because the hotel was at least a half hour walk away.

She threw a light cardigan around her shoulders, expecting frigid hotel air conditioning, and set out.

Barrett would never have walked. The city streets would damage the soles of his Italian dress shoes, and he hated getting sweaty. She knew these odd facts about him for the same reason that she knew Lauren didn't own sweatpants and their babies could sleep through almost anything. They were her family, the only one she had left, and the thought of severing that connection terrified her. Logic couldn't fight the bone-deep fear of losing her one and only chance to be part of a family.

As she entered the cool, dim interior of the Palmer House, she left her fear behind, giving herself permission to live in the moment one last time.

"You should come back with me."

Barrett's words roused Dora from a massage- and sex-induced stupor. Morning sunlight streamed through the window, illuminating not only the rumpled sheets but also the growing distance between them. She knew him well, knew that he was about to put on the hard sell. He had shown impressive restraint in waiting so long to bring up the subject. As he traced delicate patterns on her back, he spoke in a low, persuasive voice.

"The kids have a new nanny, and I'm sure Lauren will be very busy with social engagements. We could have a lot of time to ourselves." Translation: they could have sex all the time. "We could go sailing, or walk the beach, or just hang out at the house."

He seemed to be waiting for an answer, or at least a comment, so Dora made a noncommittal noise, her face nuzzled into the sheets and her muscles too relaxed to move.

"There will be lots of parties, and playtime with the kids.

They're growing so fast you wouldn't believe it. Bonfires on the beach. You could even paint if you want."

Interesting that her art came at the very tail end of his list.

"And if I meet someone at one of these parties?" she asked, unable to stop herself from needling him.

"What do you mean?"

"What if I meet someone and I want to date them? Or sleep with them?"

His hand stilled on her back. Curious to see his face, she rolled over beneath him and looked up at his face. Jaw set, he took her wrists and pinned them above her head.

"You belong to me."

"I see." She said it calmly. Barrett wasn't usually so direct in sharing his view of their relationship.

"What do you see?"

She shrugged, which was actually kind of tricky with her hands pinned above her head. It was more of a twitch. "I see that I belong to you, but I doubt the reverse is true. Do you abstain between our visits, or do you find comfort closer to home?"

"They mean nothing."

She smiled, more surprised by her own disappointment than by his response.

"So comfort is permitted for you, but not for me."

"You wouldn't need comfort if you gave up this fucking nonsense and came to live with us again. You belong in my bed, not with a stranger you met at a party."

She considered his words as he grew impatient for her response.

"I don't think this is going to work anymore."

"What?"

"Our arrangement."

"That's ridiculous."

"Funny how my needs are ridiculous, whereas your needs are completely reasonable."

"Dora. Please."

"We have three hours left before checkout, Barrett. Let's not waste it talking. I'm going to miss this."

Dora walked home the long way, waiting for tears that never fell. Leaving Manhattan had been hard. This final cut was harder still. Barrett had tried to change her mind using every trick in his arsenal, but she had held firm. No more visits. No more contact. She had to give him up if she hoped to have a life of her own.

Today

Dora had only an hour to prepare for David's arrival. What in the world had she been thinking? She barely knew him. He could be an axe murderer, or a playboy, or into something kinky that she knew nothing about because she had never gotten around to reading *Fifty Shades*, which now seemed like a giant oversight. There was so much she didn't know. At fifty, Dora suspected she was more naive than the average fifteen-year-old. Even a teenager would know better than to invite a stranger over for the afternoon.

Frantically tidying the house (or at least the parts David was likely to see), Dora worked her way up to the second floor, where she stopped in her bedroom, thinking she should probably change clothes. Into what, she had no idea. After staring into her closet for a full five minutes, she gave up and went to splash water on her face. There would be no sketching this afternoon if she couldn't calm down.

CHAPTER FIFTEEN

AFTER THE LONGEST HOUR OF HER LIFE, DAVID APPEARED AT HER door and Dora welcomed him inside. The moment he stepped across the threshold, she went on autopilot, offering him coffee, water, a snack—all of which he declined. The rest of their journey from the kitchen to her studio was something of an out-of-body experience, with half of Dora's consciousness hovering off to the side and offering a critique of her attempt at normal behavior. Flushed cheeks gave away her nerves, as did the excessive fluttering of the hands when she talked. He lingered in the hallway by the family photo gallery, and Dora found she was self-conscious about the utter normalcy of her life. Her relationship with Luke might not be conventional, but it certainly looked that way from the outside. She did what she could to usher him along, short of dragging him upstairs, all the while reminding herself to breathe.

Gesturing for him to take a seat in the armchair, she opened all the windows and hunted down her sketch pad and charcoal pencil. The familiar routine grounded her, helping her to settle back into her skin. David's masculine presence was enough to change the entire vibe of the studio. She wasn't sure why this came as a surprise. People rarely visited her studio. Even Luke treated it as a private space, and the girls hadn't been up here in years.

When everything was ready, Dora perched on her painting stool and took her first deep breath since David's arrival.

"Relax," she said, speaking as much to herself as to him. To her surprise, he did, leaning back in the chair and resting his hands on the carved wooden scrollwork at the end of each chair ram. He should have looked out of place or uncomfortable on the soft, feminine chair, but he didn't. The contrast between his dark slacks, dark sweater, sharp white collar, and the faded fabric of the floral upholstery only emphasized his masculinity. Cradling her sketchbook, she did a series of quick studies, exploring in reality the images that had leaked out of her subconscious earlier this morning.

Having David here, in reality rather than shrouded in her imagination, overwhelmed the senses. He was intense, a panther resting on the limb of a tree watching her every move. She avoided the heat of his gaze as she worked, instead sketching his hands, the broad strength of them, and the dark hairs on his forearms that disappeared beneath the rolled-up cuffs of his shirt.

A stolen glance at his face turned out to be a big mistake. She couldn't breathe again. Nobody had looked at her like that in...well, ever. Maybe Barrett, in the beginning, but she could scarcely remember, it was so long ago.

"Look out the window," she ordered. She couldn't work with him staring at her.

He complied, but the half smile on his face suggested he knew perfectly well why she was avoiding his gaze. She distracted herself by sketching his profile. Dear God, the man was beautiful. The planes and angles of his face practically begged her to trace them with her pencil. Without the sketchbook to keep her busy, it would be tempting to take a more hands-on approach.

She didn't realize she had stopped sketching until he glanced over.

Busted.

"Shall I take another pose?"

She licked her lips, considering. Would it be wrong to ask him to take his shirt off? The challenge in his eyes dared her to do it, and—feeling like a teenager—she did.

"Would you please remove your sweater and shirt?"

The boyish grin took her by surprise. She'd been so busy processing her own reaction to him that she'd missed the spark of mischief in his eyes—the boy hidden within the man. Over the years, watching her friends' children grow up, she'd realized that all men hide the boy within. Glimpse it, and you can understand the man in an instant. Some hide their true selves better than others. In this case, she hadn't even been looking for it, too caught up in the swirl of newly awakened hormones.

She had his number now. The mischief-maker. The tree-climber. The "let's see what happens when you press this button" explorer.

He didn't hesitate. "Yes, of course."

Peeling off the charcoal-gray cashmere sweater, he tossed it into the corner of the room. Before today, she would have pegged him as a fold-the-sweater kind of guy. Then he began to unbutton the starched white dress shirt. Earlier, she had admired the cosmopolitan look of the spread collar. No boring oxford buttons here. But with each button unfastened, he became less cosmopolitan and more...primal. And naked. Not completely naked, of course, but suddenly there was a shirtless man reclining in her chair, staring at her with a challenge in his eyes.

She swallowed.

"Thank you. Now if you could put your right hand on

your knee and look out the window again..." If he kept looking at her like that, she was likely to do something she shouldn't.

He complied with that half smile again. She tucked away the memory of his earlier grin, knowing she would sketch it. Now, as she traced the contours of his form with her pencil, he talked.

"Do you often bring strange men to your studio and ask them to remove their clothing?"

She pressed her lips together to keep from smiling. "I'm tempted to say 'Yes, I do this all the time,' but in fact you are the first."

"I am honored."

"As you should be."

Dora knew she was objectifying the man in front of her, but in a sense, that's what artists do. He was her subject, and she absorbed every detail. So much muscle, and so little belly fat for someone his age. She wasn't sure whether to be impressed or intimidated. Maybe he had simply won the genetic lottery. Regardless, there was no way he would be seeing her belly anytime soon. She sketched the planes and angles of his chest, adding the salt and pepper hair that led southward in a vee pointing directly where she shouldn't be looking. Those muscles didn't come from good genes. He must exercise religiously. She sketched his shoulders, carefully tracing the lines and shadows of each muscle.

"Would you like me to change position?"

Her pencil had slowed again, and he had noticed. Worse, he had caught her staring at his chest, daydreaming.

"No. You're perfect just as you are."

He responded with a slow smile. "I am yours to command."

She found herself longing for a glass of water. Was it warm in here?

As she sketched her way down his body, she noticed that

the line of his slacks had changed across his pelvis. He wasn't...
He couldn't possibly be...

Eyes up, missy.

She sketched, frantic, trying to clear the inappropriate
thoughts from her mind. There was no way in hell that
anything was going to happen between this muscled specimen
and her own squishy self.

"Choose a new position, please." The words came out
sounding more curt than she had intended.

"Any position?"

She couldn't miss the suggestive tone in his voice.

"It's your choice," she replied, keeping her eyes on her
sketchpad. "I don't want you to be...uncomfortable."

"Never." He leaned forward, forearms on his knees, hands
clasped, and looked directly at her. "What are your plans for
this new chapter in your life?"

Looking up, Dora sucked in a breath. This was how she
would paint him. Ignoring his question, she sketched intensely
for a few minutes, then slowed. Stopped. She had it.

She set down her pencil and looked back up at him.

"I'm not sure. When Luke and I married, we promised each
other that after we had raised our family we would set each
other free. That time has come, and to my surprise, I find I'm
not ready."

"How long have you been married?"

"Twenty-eight years."

Nodding slowly, he said, "My wife and I were married for
twenty-nine years when I lost her. We had built a life together,
one that I had to rebuild after she was gone."

"The next chapter of my life needs to be written, but I'm not
ready to turn the page." She couldn't think of a better way to
explain it, but he seemed to understand.

"You are in the in-between space. Much can happen when
you are in between."

"I suppose I should open myself up to new experiences."

"Like this one?"

"Exactly."

She was caught by his gaze again, mesmerized, and who knew what she might have done next. Before she could find out, the slam of a door downstairs jolted her out of his spell.

"Hi, Mom. I'm home."

Dora shot to her feet, blushing furiously. David leaned back in the chair again, unperturbed.

"Your daughter?"

"One of them."

He smiled, and there was that hint of mischief again. "And would she be shocked to find a half-naked man in your studio?"

"Definitely."

He didn't move. "Would you like to shock her?"

Dora's laugh broke through the tension, and she sat back down on her stool.

"Not today. Not yet."

At her response, he looked disappointed, but reached for his shirt, covering that beautiful chest. She fidgeted, not sure what to do, half an ear open for Mel's footsteps on the stairs.

"Would you like to help?" he asked, daring her to come closer.

She nodded, and they both stood. Before she lost her nerve, Dora stepped closer and began buttoning his shirt. His skin was hot where she brushed it with her fingers. Burning, even, making her flushed and nervous. Halfway up his chest, she realized that she was off by one button and made a sound of frustration before undoing her work. He placed his hands gently over her own.

"Take your time."

"You don't understand."

"I think perhaps I do. I have children as well, and no matter how old they are, they are never ready to see their parents as anything other than parents."

He held her hands still so that she couldn't do the buttons.

"You have a right to your own life," he continued. "It may not feel like it right now, but you do."

She could feel tears pricking at the back of her eyes and looked down, trying to blink them away. He released her hands and made quick work of the buttons, then tucked in his shirt. She stepped back, her hands shaking.

He retrieved his sweater from the corner of the room and pulled it on over his head. He was rolling his cuffs, looking perfectly composed, when Dora heard Mel's feet on the stairs to the second floor. Dora grabbed her sketchbook and snapped it closed, tucking it on a side table under some other papers. She ignored David's raised eyebrow. Normally, Mel wouldn't interrupt her mother in the studio, but with David's car parked beside Dora's in the drive, the usual rules might not apply.

Before Mel could reach the attic stairs, Dora asked, "Would you like to go sailing with me on Friday afternoon?"

"Yes."

Dora had a feeling she was going to like being in between.

"Hey Mom, who's here? I—"

Mel stopped short at the turn in the stairs, surprised to see anyone, let alone a stranger, here in Mom's studio. Nobody went into the studio, not even Dad. Of course, they had come up here when they were little, but the older they got, the more off-limits the space became. And yet, here was Mom with someone in her space.

"Sweetheart, let me introduce you to my friend, David. He owns a number of art galleries and he's interested in my work."

Mel managed to come up with a reply, but it wasn't very smooth. "Um, hi. Nice to meet you."

"The pleasure is mine," he said.

Mel suddenly felt the vibe in the room. The tension between the two of them—sexy tension, not angry tension—was so strong that it was almost visible to the naked eye. And now she had thought about nakedness and this guy and her mom at the same time, and she couldn't unthink it. Mom's paintings were still stacked against the wall. What exactly had they been doing up here?

"We'll be finished up here in a few minutes." Dora's subtext was clear: time for Mel to leave.

"Great," said Mel. "I'll be downstairs. Actually, I need to find Tessa. Pretty sure she's at RJ's. Back in a bit."

It wasn't the most graceful exit, and in fact Mel almost tumbled down the stairs when she tried to walk backward, but at least it was an exit.

"Nice to meet you," she called over her shoulder as she turned and fled.

She really, really needed to talk to Tessa.

CHAPTER SIXTEEN

M EL BANGED ON THE BACK DOOR OF RJ'S HOUSE, HOPING THAT Tessa and RJ weren't out sailing. Both their cars were here. Chances were good her sister was inside. Eventually, a rumpled RJ pulled the door open, while an equally rumpled Tessa walked into the kitchen.

"Your timing sucks," said Tessa, but then she got a good look at Mel's face. "What's wrong?"

Mel was practically shaking as she walked inside and slumped into a chair at the kitchen table.

"Have you met this guy, David?"

"I have no idea what you're talking about," said Tessa as she sank into a chair opposite Mel.

"Apparently he owns a bunch of art galleries. Mom had him up in the studio."

"So?"

"She never has *anybody* up in the studio. When I went looking for her, the vibe between them was very...strong."

Tessa looked over at RJ, who rubbed his face and said, "I'm going to watch TV."

When he was gone, Tessa asked, "Were you weird about it?"

"What?" Mel couldn't have been more insulted. "No. Of course I wasn't. I was perfectly normal."

Her sister didn't look convinced.

"I was!"

"Was he hot?" she asked.

Tessa's question sent Mel right back to the headspace where thoughts of her mother and David and nakedness all swirled together.

"Ugh. No," said Mel. "He's at least fifty."

"You know Mom is fifty, right?" Tessa smiled her super-aggravating calm smile, as if nothing could bother or shock her. Mel hated that smile. She scowled at her sister.

"Okay, fine. He was good-looking for an old guy."

"And why does that bother you?"

Mel sputtered before regrouping. "Why *doesn't* it bother *you*? Our family is crumbling, and all you can think about is getting laid."

Mel must have pierced the therapist veil, because Tessa's eyes narrowed and when she spoke, it wasn't in her calm, soothing voice anymore. She sounded pissed.

"Are you listening to yourself? Our family is fine. We all still love each other. You didn't freak out like this when Dad came out, or when he started spending time in Nashville. Why are you having so much trouble with the idea that Mom might want to have a life, too? What did you think she was going to do? Sit around all day and wait for a chance to be a cheerleader for everyone else?"

Mel was so taken aback that her mind went blank. Tessa rarely went on the attack, and now that she had, Mel felt like a pouty child.

"Of course not," she said at last, chastened. "Mom can have a life."

"Even if that life involves dating hot older men?" Tessa was not letting Mel off the hook.

Mel mumbled her response. "Yes, even if she wants to date some random guy she just met."

"And what if she decides to date a bunch of different men, see what she missed by getting married so young? What if she starts having overnight guests?"

Mel covered her face. "Why are you torturing me?"

"Maybe Mom just wants to get laid," said Tessa, leaning back and crossing her arms.

Okay, so Mel understood why Tessa would want to echo Mel's earlier words, but did she have to do it in reference to their mother?

"I'm not ready to go there," said Mel.

"And that's the hard part—for you, not for Mom. This has absolutely nothing to do with you, and you need to give Mom some room to figure out what she wants. If you so much as *hint* that you can't handle her exploring her options, she's going to shut it down, just to spare her baby some uncomfortable feelings. That's not fair, and I won't let you do it."

"Jeez. What ever happened to the therapist thing about staying neutral and asking questions?"

"I'm not your therapist. I'm your sister, and this is my family, too. Don't screw it up."

Now that Mel's initial freakout had subsided, she could admit that Tessa might possibly be right. She would never admit that out loud—no need to feed Tessa's bossy streak—but she could admit it to herself. If her mother wanted to get up to some mischief with a sexy (gag) art gallery owner, then Mel wasn't going to stop her. No more freakouts, either. And, come to think of it, her mother might need some dating advice. It would be irresponsible to throw her to the wolves with no preparation. Maybe they could talk about that at dinner tonight.

. . .

"Sweetheart, it's such a treat to have you stay with us," said Fitz's mother. "You haven't spent this much time at home since the summer after your freshman year of college."

Fitz took a sip of his Malbec, wondering how to respond. She had conveniently forgotten the month he had spent at home last year helping to take care of her during the worst of her cancer treatments. As a group, the family had a tendency to gloss over that time, and to be honest Fitz wasn't really sure how clear her memories were.

It was really too bad that Mel hadn't come over for dinner tonight. She was dealing with some kind of family drama that he would probably hear about tomorrow. He had survived on his own thus far by asking a lot of questions about his sister and her kids. How were they doing? (Not great. After all, it had only been six months since the divorce.) How was Pippa coping? (Also not great. These things take time.) Fitz's father had a lot of opinions about Pip's ex-husband, and he didn't mind sharing those opinions. At length. Perhaps he'd used up his judgment quota on Pippa's evil ex, making him more mellow when it came to Fitz and his career. He certainly hoped so, because he was waiting for the right moment to tell his parents about his interest in international work.

"Enough about your sister," said his mother. "I want to hear about you. What comes next for you when the mural is finished?"

This was exactly the opening Fitz had been waiting for, but before he could take it, his father jumped in, earning himself irritated looks from mother and son. He either didn't notice or didn't care, because he certainly didn't stop talking.

"I'll tell you what comes next," said his father. "It's time to get serious about your career. For chrissakes, you're almost thirty, and you haven't made partner yet. I was talking to Chip the other day at the club—you know Chip, his son works over at Jones-Henderson—"

Fitz had only met Chip once, but having heard about him and his superstar son on any number of occasions, he felt like they were honorary members of the family.

"—and his son, the same age as you, made junior partner two years ago."

"Darling, I hardly think it makes sense to compare—"

"These firms are 'up or out,' Margot, and if you're not moving up you're in trouble. Fitz is not moving up. It's not something to take lightly. If you're not careful, you'll find yourself out of a job and starting all over again at another firm, if you can even get your foot in the door."

"Dad, I—"

"I don't want to hear a bunch of excuses. This is your life we're talking about."

"Well then, why don't I clear the table," said Fitz, pushing back his chair and rising to his feet.

"Don't run from me. This is a serious discussion."

"It's hardly a discussion," replied Fitz in what he considered an impressively calm tone of voice. "My role here is to say, 'Yes, sir,' and to promise to do whatever you want. Other than that, there's nothing I could possibly say that would make you happy right now."

"That's for damn sure."

Fitz ignored his father and began gathering up his dishes. There was no need to rehash the same discussion for the thousandth time. It only upset his mother. Glancing over to check on her, he resigned himself to the fact that Dad was going to be even more pissed off. They had managed to make her cry, or at least get teary.

"Why can't you two make it through a single meal without fighting? I hate it. You know I hate it."

Fitz started toward the kitchen, pausing on the way to kiss his mom on the forehead.

"No more work talk, Mom. Let's talk about Thanksgiving instead. Are you hosting, or Pip?"

Fitz escaped into the kitchen, giving his father a smile in response to his dark look. Any discussion of his actual future plans would have to wait until they were out of earshot of his mother. Tackling his parents separately was probably the smart move, given his dad's intransigence. His mom, he had no doubt, would be excited and supportive, even if it would complicate her matchmaking efforts. His dad, on the other hand, would blow a gasket.

He would talk to his mom first.

CHAPTER SEVENTEEN

28 years ago, July

FOR THE HUNDREDTH TIME, DORA WONDERED WHY SHE HAD bothered to come out tonight. Ever since she had sent Barrett on his way, she hadn't been herself, as if he had infected her with some kind of malaise that she couldn't shake. It had been more than a month without a word from him, which either meant that he had accepted her decision (unlikely), or that he was plotting to change her mind (probable). For a month she hadn't been able to sleep. Nothing tasted good anymore. She was cranky and tired and the last thing in the world she wanted to do was go out clubbing with her friends.

But she had promised herself that she would get a life. Whatever the time limit on moping, she had exceeded it. A month was way too long.

So here she was, out with friends and wondering when the fun would begin. Expecting the dark, thumping intimacy of a nightclub, she instead found herself in some kind of country and western dive bar on the west side. Waitresses in fringed tops, denim miniskirts, and cowboy boots wove between the sticky tables, carrying a never-ending supply of drinks. The smoke eventually drove Dora to a tiny table on the far side of the room, near a high window that had been cracked open. A trickle of hot and humid but thankfully fresh air provided the lifeline she needed to make it through the band's first set. The occasional sip from her watery light beer kept her stomach calm. To her surprise, the band wasn't bad, if country music was your thing.

Sitting alone, she must have looked like easy pickings because as soon as the band stopped playing, a wannabe cowboy strutted over, grabbed a chair from a nearby table, and straddled it, his forearms resting on the back and his suggestive smile more than she could tolerate right now. She wondered if he dressed like this in his everyday life—full-on cowboy in his boots, hat, and belt with giant, shiny buckle—or only when he went on the prowl.

As she waited for his opening line, she wondered idly if she was going to throw up on him. It would be an effective deterrent, if nothing else. The smoke was really getting to her.

"Well, hello, little lady." The hat tip matched the drawl.

"Hello."

"What do you say we make like horseshit and hit the road?"

Dora choked on a laugh before saying, "Does that really work? I mean, has anybody ever left with you when you asked that question?"

"You're sober, huh?"

She nodded.

"Never mind."

He stood and walked away, leaving only relief in his wake. Embarrassing scene avoided.

Another guy approached, less "cowboy" than the first, and he didn't take the open seat. She realized after a double take that he was one of the guys from the band.

"You okay?"

Raising an eyebrow in question, Dora waited for more information. Was this a come-on or an actual question?

"You look a little green around the edges. Walt has that effect on people, but you seem to have taken it harder than most."

Well, that was flattering—or not. Although, come to think about it, she really didn't feel good. Scanning the crowd for her friends, she couldn't see them anywhere. Their table had been taken by another group, and they didn't appear to be on the dance floor.

"I'm good. Probably should find my friends, though."

"Walt didn't give you any trouble?"

She shook her head. The humid mix of sweat and stale beer filled her lungs, triggering a wave of nausea. Her new cowboy must have sensed either her nausea or her panic.

"Bathroom?" he asked.

"Please. Fast."

He grabbed her by the hand and pulled her through the jumble of people and tables, leading her into a dark hallway. Had she not been about to throw up, she might have spared a thought for her safety, but it wasn't exactly top of mind. The second door he tried was open, and he pushed it open, clearing the way for her to lunge for the toilet.

Gripping the filthy sides of the bowl, she emptied the contents of her stomach and maybe her entire body into the toilet, vaguely aware of hands holding her long hair out of the way. When the spasms subsided, she flushed and hauled herself up to a standing position. Her low-key cowboy guided her to the sink, where she scrubbed at her shaking hands until they were pink from the friction. Only when she was sure they were clean did she splash water on her face and rinse out her mouth.

She raised her eyes and met his in the mirror. He smiled, rueful.

"I'd ask if you're feeling better, but I can see the answer."

She managed a half-hearted smile in return. "Thanks. It would have been pretty gross if I had puked at the table."

"It happens more often than you might think, but usually when people are a lot more drunk."

"I think I have the flu or food poisoning or something."

He gestured for her to follow him, but instead of leading her back into the crowded main room, he led her farther down the hall to a door at the end. It opened into a decent-sized room with two couches, a scuffed coffee table, and a dressing-room setup along one wall.

"This is the green room. The rest of the band are out at the bar getting drinks, so you can hang out in here as long as you need. There's less smoke, and you can lie down on the couch if you really feel like shit."

Tears filled her eyes, which was silly. He was being kind. Lots of people were kind. Her friends would probably be equally kind if they knew she was feeling bad. She blinked the tears away before he could see. She was probably just PMS-ing.

"Thanks." The word came out as more of a giant exhale. She plopped onto the overstuffed couch and let her head fall back. "I think I need to stay out of the smoke for a while, maybe close my eyes."

He took a seat on the other couch and put his feet up on the coffee table.

"Do you want me to find your date, or your friends, or whoever, to tell them where you are?"

"I think they already left."

"Nice."

Looking down at her hands, she said, "I was kind of a buzzkill tonight, anyway. They probably thought I left first."

"Still."

"Yeah."

She might have dozed off, because his next question startled her awake.

"Why are you out if you don't want to be here?"

She took a minute to figure out the short answer to his question. The long version would take all night. "I'm getting over a tough breakup," she finally said, "and I've been hiding out in my apartment for a month. It was time to get out and do something. I can't hibernate forever."

"Me, too," he said. "Getting over a bad breakup, I mean. It's hard."

"Do you run into her often?"

He opened his mouth to answer, but paused and seemed to change his mind, finally saying, "No. She's down in Nashville, refusing to deal with a drug problem."

"I'm so sorry."

"What about you? Do you see him?"

She shook her head. "He lives in New York City."

"We're back on for our second set in a few minutes. Want me to call you a cab before I go?"

"That would be amazing. Thank you."

He stood to leave, probably to find a phone.

"What's your name?" she asked.

"Luke." When he saw that she was also moving to stand up, he held out a hand to help her up off the couch.

"I'm Dora. It's nice to meet you, Luke."

"We play here every Saturday night. Come see us when you're feeling better."

"You know what? I will."

CHAPTER EIGHTEEN

Today

"Mel, hurry up or we'll be late."

Even with the bathroom door closed, Mel could hear her mother yelling from the bottom of the stairs.

"Coming," she yelled back, although with a mouth full of toothbrush who knew what Dora actually heard.

Mel's subconscious had tried to spare her this morning's outing, nudging her to hit the snooze button a few too many times. As a result she would be viewing these amazing, too-good-to-be-true commercial properties after rushing through the bare minimum of personal grooming.

Minutes later, Mel clattered down the stairs and into the kitchen, hoping to grab some food, maybe a banana, on the way out the door. Her mother had apparently been thinking along the same lines, because she handed Mel something warm wrapped up in a paper towel. Blinking in confusion, Mel unwrapped one side to find a toasted bagel with cream cheese.

"Thanks."

A travel mug full of coffee appeared in Mel's other hand, and then Dora was leading her out the door.

During the drive to the first listing, where they would meet the real estate agent, Dora kept up a steady stream of chatter, describing the location, parking situation, and all the other details she had gleaned from the online listing. Mel nodded along, thankful that they weren't discussing David, and chewed her bagel as slowly as possible. By the time they pulled up in front of the property, Mel had begun to wonder if her mother should consider a career in real estate.

Before she even stepped out of the car, Mel mentally rejected the property. The pictures on the real estate website had featured the interior of the space, with only a close-up of the exterior. It was located in an industrial park on the outskirts of town, and the vibe couldn't have been more utilitarian. It lacked character and charm and would not impress potential clients. And what the hell was she doing actually evaluating the property? She was only here to humor her mother, not to get sucked into the fantasy.

Luckily, one glance at her mother's face and Mel knew Dora was having the same reaction. They both listened politely as the agent showed them through the space, and truthfully, the interior wasn't bad at all. It was the first impression that was the problem, and first impressions mattered in the business of photography.

On the drive to the second property, a few strategic questions got Dora sharing the latest gossip, which meant that Mel could relax and enjoy the ride.

"...Oh, and did I tell you that Lucy said Kat and Rob have been meeting at the diner for breakfast almost every morning? She can't be sure if they're actually sleeping over at each other's places, but it's all very promising. Don't you think it's nice that they're officially dating?"

Mel murmured her assent and nodded, which was enough to keep her mother rolling.

"Don't make any plans for Saturday night. I'm trying to organize a family dinner while everyone is still in town, although Callie hasn't confirmed yet whether or not she can make it. I know she needs to spend time with Adam, but really, couldn't she split her time more evenly? When she's here, she's spending so much time with Adam and Danny that we don't really get to see her."

Callie needed to be in Nashville right now to launch her solo music career, but her heart belonged here with her new fiancé Adam and his nephew Danny. Mel couldn't blame her for spending every possible moment with them. Given their mother's interest in grandchildren, she shouldn't be complaining either.

Dora shook her head while taking a breath. "And don't even get me started on Tessa. She spends every possible minute with RJ. Although I do have to say that it's nice to have her help at the sailing school. I've been thinking about doing some traveling myself, and it's very freeing to know that I can leave the sailing school in good hands."

Mel choked on her coffee and it took her a few minutes to sort herself out, with Dora handing her tissues from the box tucked into the door of the car. Her mother was suddenly planning to travel? Alone? As a family, they had road-tripped to most of the national parks, but that wasn't exactly a solo activity. Mel couldn't help but wonder if her mother's new friend, David, had something to do with her sudden interest in exploring the world, but she wasn't ready to ask.

The second property was much better—not that Mel was seriously considering all this. An older lake cottage had been converted for commercial use, and it was the definition of charming. Parking would be a nightmare in the summer, and there wasn't much storage space for equipment and files, but it was otherwise perfect. Back in the car again, Dora dismissed the first property out of hand, but she raved about the second. Mel made some noise about the rent being high, but that was clearly the wrong tack to take. Dora wasn't having it.

"So what if the rent is a little high? Live at home until you've built up the business and can afford a place of your own. You can't keep on couch-surfing and freelancing. It's not a viable career path. You need this." Dora took a fortifying breath and glanced over at Mel before turning her eyes back to the road. "I know these things can be hard to admit, sweetheart, even to ourselves, but you need to look yourself squarely in the eye and acknowledge what your behavior is telling you."

Mel began to wonder exactly how much time her mother had been spending with Tessa. That kind of therapist-speak had to be coming from somewhere.

"You're basically living up here. You wouldn't be doing that if you didn't want to be here. There's no other logical explanation for your behavior."

And there it was, the opening she'd been hoping for. "Actually, Mom, I—"

"Let's not argue about it now," said Dora. "Take the night to think about it, and we can talk about it again tomorrow. For now, let's look at the last property with an open mind."

Years of frustration leaked out in Mel's sigh. "Mom, I—"

"We're here!"

Judging by the excess of cheer in Dora's announcement, this conversation was over. Her mother was already stepping out of the car. Mel followed suit just in time to hear her mother murmur, "Oh, this is perfect."

Mel suppressed the urge to climb right back into the car. She had agreed to see three properties, and she would see them. She would waste the agent's time and energy in a futile effort to appease her mother. And then, hopefully sooner rather than later, she would break her mother's heart.

But first, one more property.

Less than a block off Main Street, this little storefront would be quiet, but it was still close enough to the corner that people would be able to see the sign. The inside was light-filled and spacious, with more than enough storage space. The rent was the lowest of the three properties, and it had two dedicated parking spots—plenty for a photography business. You really couldn't ask for a better space.

The realtor stepped outside to take a call and Dora began to gush.

"I can see it all so easily. You would do portraits here, families and new babies and graduates. You can do location work, too, but you would always have a backup location. You can use this as your base of operations while you're building up your wedding business. You'll stand out from the crowd because of your journalistic style. You'll capture those candid moments that everyone wants to remember, not only the staged photos. It's perfect."

"Mom," said Mel softly. She really needed to tell her mother. Now.

Dora didn't seem to hear her. "I can hardly believe that I'll have all three of my girls living here, most of the time anyway. Honestly, nothing could make me happier. The place I grew up was never truly home for me, but the idea that we've built a true home here, a place you all want to spend time—it just feels good. I'm so proud of my girls!"

Her mother's monologue ended on a wail as Dora burst into tears. With an inward growl of frustration, Mel folded her mother into a hug. This was not the moment. Maybe at the family dinner on Saturday, or maybe even when they got home today, but not now.

Her mother's crying jag eventually eased, and Mel gave her one last squeeze before stepping back and opening her purse to hunt for some tissues. In moments like this, the idea of slipping away in the night and leaving behind only a note was not only tempting but also seemed like the only viable way to tell her family. She needed a better plan than "wait for the right moment." Maybe she should talk to Tessa about it and get her advice on how to break the news to the rest of the family. There had to be a better way.

CHAPTER NINETEEN

FITZ WATCHED CURIOUSLY AS MEL (AND LUNCH) WERE DROPPED off at the library by her mother, who waved enthusiastically before driving off. Dora had clearly enjoyed the morning. He wasn't so sure about Mel. Her body language was giving nothing away. Fitz opened his mouth to ask as she drew closer, but one look at her face and he closed it again without saying anything. She shoved a sandwich in his direction and marched toward the ladder. Apparently the morning had not gone well.

Fitz gave Mel a few minutes before following her up to the top level of the scaffolding. They sat side by side, eating their sandwiches and staring at the view of the lake over the trees. Fitz finished first and eased into conversation.

"Rob's been busy," he said. Landscaping seemed like a neutral topic of conversation. "He must be planting in the dark, because every morning I notice a few more shrubs. He's even marked out the location for the willow dome. I bet it will be installed by tomorrow morning."

"That seems fast," she said.

Fitz was relieved that her voice sounded normal. Her

mother might have made her angry, but she wasn't about to burst into tears.

"We're making good progress ourselves. Last night I gridded out the design, and I spent this morning working on transferring it onto the wall. You probably noticed on your way up."

She nodded but didn't say anything, just kept chewing.

"I finished the lower level. If you and I both work on it this afternoon, I think we can have the entire design on the wall by the end of the day. We don't need all the fine detail at this stage. Just the broad sweep of it, so we can block in the larger areas of color."

"What are you using to draw the design?" she asked. "I didn't look at it closely."

"Just some thinned-out acrylic," he replied. "We'll be painting over it later. This way if it rains unexpectedly, it won't wash off like charcoal would."

She nodded again and took the last bite of her sandwich. Leaning back, Fitz let the sun warm his face and he breathed deeply, soaking it all in. If the weather stayed like this, up in the sixties every day, they had a decent chance of finishing before Halloween. He really didn't want to leave the project half-finished over the winter. Not only would they lose the momentum they'd built, but he also wasn't sure when or how he would be able to finish if he got an international assignment. He couldn't control the weather, so he put that worry aside and dared to ask about Mel's day.

"So how did it go this morning?" He wondered if she would shove him off the scaffolding for asking.

"I don't want to talk about it."

Maybe Mel didn't want to talk about it, but they had agreed to help each other out, and he couldn't really do that if she didn't tell him what happened. He tried another approach.

"I saw your mom when she dropped you off and she looked awfully happy."

"Oh, she's happy all right." Mel, on the other hand, did not sound happy. "We found the perfect photography studio, and I never had the chance to tell her why I wouldn't be renting it."

"How is that possible? You were together for almost three hours."

"The real estate agent was there for some of it." She sounded like kid on the defensive.

"But not all of it," he pointed out.

"It was impossible, okay? Right when I was going to tell her, she started going on about how amazing it was going to be to have me up here, and how happy she was going to be to have me 'settled,' and how nice it would be for me to be with my sisters, and how she might be able to travel with all of us up here. It was awful. She was so happy she started crying, and I just couldn't do it."

"You know you have to find a way."

"I know!"

There might be a way for him to help more directly. "Do you need me to set it up?"

"You mean spill the beans for me?"

"Not exactly. I could refer to your big plans in front of your family, so that you're forced to explain."

She scowled, then muttered, "No. That's lame. And then they'd be sad that I told you first."

He shook his head. "You need to tell them—and soon."

Mel uncrossed her legs and let them dangle down off the scaffolding, consciously mimicking Fitz's pose. Her mood sucked. She was grumpy and irritated and probably needed a punching bag at the gym. Without one at hand, she was taking her frustration out on Fitz. Not fair, perhaps, but he seemed like he could handle it.

"What about you?"

He looked away, and she knew she had him.

"Hah. You didn't tell your family either. You were supposed to tell them last night at dinner."

"Yes, I was," he admitted.

There was something so satisfying in knowing she wasn't alone in her frustration.

"But you didn't."

"I did not."

"So, what happened?"

He was quiet for a minute. "It's hard to explain."

She didn't bother to hide her sarcasm as she gestured expansively and said, "I have all day."

He took his time in answering, but she wasn't kidding about having all day. She could wait him out.

"My dad has a lot of opinions about my career and how it should be unfolding," he finally said, his voice so defeated that she almost took pity on him. "He particularly likes to measure my progress against the offspring of his friends from the country club."

"Are all these offspring architects?"

"No—not that it matters when playing My Kid is Better than Your Kid. As it happens, *one* of these offspring, the estimable Chip Morton, Jr., is not only my age but also an architect at a big firm in Chicago. He's at a Chicago-only company, so it's not as big as my firm, which is global, but their Chicago office is roughly the same size as our Chicago office. Close enough to play the game."

"So you're not winning?"

"It's a competition among parents, so my dad's the one who is not winning, not since Chip made junior partner two years ago."

"I don't even know what that means," she said. "Partner" sounded like a big deal, but "junior" took away some of the heft.

"I haven't made partner yet. It's not something I want, but my dad doesn't want to hear that. I want to be a site supervisor and run huge construction projects all over the world. Partners spend all their time on sales. They don't actually do the work. I want to build things."

"So at dinner last night..." Mel prompted. She didn't see what all this had to do with telling his parents about his plans.

"Last night, before I could tell them, my dad went on a rant about my lack of career progress." He shrugged. "I got pissed off, so I didn't tell them."

"I see." Mel considered herself very mature for *not* pointing out that this was definitely a pot-calling-the-kettle-black situation.

"Weirdly, I think you do."

At that, she smiled and let their feet tangle together, and after a minute he smiled, too. Maybe he wasn't exactly happy, but she felt oddly proud of cheering him up. Although they would be going their separate ways all too soon, she hoped they could stay friends while they wandered around the globe. It would be nice to have someone to chat with at odd hours, or email with a random observation about how things were different so far from home—things only a fellow traveler would understand.

As they got back to work, Mel realized that Fitz was one of the few people in the world that she could stand to hang out with all day. Most people were annoying or, worse, boring— one reason she'd never had a serious relationship. If you couldn't imagine spending a weekend with someone, commitment was out of the question.

They transferred the mural design onto the wall square by square. As they worked their way up the wall, Mel imagined all the different ways she could break the news to her family. None of the scenarios was particularly appealing. Too many of them involved her yelling at them to be quiet for five seconds so she could tell them something important. After the joy of dreaming big dreams and making big plans, the difficulty in sharing those dreams and plans had come as a shock. Everybody seemed to know better than Mel when it came to planning out her career and her life. Everyone had an opinion they wanted to share. Problem was, she didn't want their opinions. She wanted their support, and then she needed them to let her go.

CHAPTER TWENTY

28 years ago, July

DORA VENTURED BACK TO THE COUNTRY AND WESTERN BAR THE
following weekend, curious to talk to the urban cowboy who
had been so kind. Maybe she would actually have fun now that
she was, for the most part, feeling better. She claimed a seat at
the same tiny table near the open window. It was just as hot
and humid inside as out, but she hoped the cooler night air
would trickle in as temperatures dropped.

"Hey, honey, what can I get you?"

The waitress wore the same belly-baring cowgirl outfit that
Dora remembered from last time, including cowboy boots that
looked well broken and really comfortable. Given the stickiness
of the floor, closed-toe shoes would have been a better choice
than Dora's strappy sandals.

"A ginger ale, please, and some fries."

The last thing Dora wanted was a watery beer like last time.

"Should I make it a Shirley Temple?"

"What's that?"

"Ginger ale with some cherry syrup and a cherry on top."

"Yes, please," said Dora.

"Pickles with your fries?"

"Absolutely."

The waitress must be psychic, because all her suggestions sounded amazing. Dora still hadn't quite shaken off whatever germs Barrett had brought from New York, but she didn't feel bad enough to go to the doctor. She'd blame her slow recovery on the heat and humidity. The only thing that seemed to sit well in her stomach lately was fried food, as if she had a permanent hangover.

"You're back."

Dora looked up to see her cowboy approaching from the back hallway.

"I am," she answered with a big smile.

Her first impression of him had been good, but it was based more on heroic behavior than looks. On second viewing, he was actually pretty cute. She didn't want to rip his clothes off or anything, but in light of her disastrously unhealthy relationship with Barrett, this was a point in his favor.

"Give me a minute to finish the sound check and then I'll have time to talk."

She waited through the endless check-one-twos, passing the time munching on her fries, until he rejoined her at the table.

"I honestly didn't think you'd come back," he said, taking the seat across from her. "Your first experience here was memorable for all the wrong reasons."

"I know," she said with a laugh, "but I figured I couldn't blame the venue when I only had a few sips of beer. And besides, you were so nice. I knew I needed to come back to thank you and listen properly to your band."

"You will not regret it."

"My memories from last week are a bit fuzzy. What instrument do you play?"

He leaned back in his chair, saying, "I'm a banjo player, and I write the songs for the band."

"You're kidding!" she said. "You write them all?"

Art had always come easily to Dora, but never music. In middle school, she had learned to lip sync in chorus rather than show off her inability to carry a tune. The idea that someone could write a song was amazing.

"Most of them. We collaborate on some, but mostly I write on my own."

"That's very cool."

"What about you? What do you do?" he asked.

"I'm in art school."

The waitress swung by to take away the empty fry basket, asking if Dora would like another. She accepted, thinking Luke might be hungry before the show.

"More pickles, too, please."

"Also very cool," said Luke, in response to her earlier comment. "What kind of art do you do?"

"I'm a painter. I like to work in watercolor or acrylics."

"What do you paint? People? Fruit?"

Laughing, she said, "No fruit for me. I really like to paint the water."

"Why is that, do you think?"

Nobody had ever asked why she liked to paint water so much. They mostly nodded and moved on.

"It's very moody," she said after some consideration. "Even if you've painted a particular view before, it will be different every time you go back."

He nodded. "I know exactly what you mean."

One of the bandmates called out to Luke, gesturing for him to join them.

"Sorry. Gotta run. I'll talk to you at the break."

Dora enjoyed the music more than last week, perhaps because she knew that Luke wrote the songs. The fries, pickles, and Shirley Temple left her feeling sated and happy. She was able to sit back, relax, and let the music wash over her. Her cowboy was a good and kind human being, and she decided she'd like to see more of him.

During the break, he stopped by as promised, but as he walked up, she yawned.

"Are we putting you to sleep?"

"No!" she said, embarrassed to be fading so soon. "Sorry. I'm so tired today. You guys sound amazing."

"Thanks."

She yawned again. There was no hiding it.

"You're not going to make it through the second set, are you?" he said.

She shook her head, feeling sheepish and hating to disappoint him.

"I don't think so."

He mimed a wound to the chest. "I'm heartbroken."

"I think you'll survive," she said.

"You'll just have to come see us again."

Given how early she'd been falling asleep lately, another attempt at a late-night outing would likely end the same way. However, she really did want to see him again, preferably in a setting where they could hang out and talk.

"How about I buy you breakfast instead?" she asked. It would be a lot easier to get to know him if he wasn't working.

"That would be awesome. When did you have in mind?"

"Is tomorrow too soon?" She didn't want to seem overeager, but she saw no point in playing it cool if she actually wanted to see him.

"Works for me," he said. "Do you have a favorite breakfast place?"

"Have you heard of Over Easy?"

He nodded.

"Let's meet there. Tomorrow at ten?"

"It's a date."

Luke headed back toward the green room and Dora waved to her waitress for the check. Anticipation bubbled inside her, happy and fizzy and innocent. No dark attraction pulled her toward Luke, only curiosity and an odd sense that they could be good for each other. This was the kind of simple happiness that she usually found on the water. Today she had found it with a person, and that definitely made him a person she wanted to know better.

Today

After dropping Mel and lunch at the library, Dora returned home for the afternoon. She kicked off her shoes in the mudroom and closed the garage door with her hip as she juggled her purse and the takeout sandwiches for herself and Luke. As she entered the kitchen, the house phone rang, catching her off guard. She set down her purse and the sandwiches and walked over to answer it.

"Hello?"

"Dora."

After almost thirty years, she still knew his voice. It tugged at her memories and they tumbled out, a cascade of images and sensations and echoes of feelings she hadn't experienced in years. This was why she had avoided him on her trips to visit Lauren in New York. A part of her had hoped to avoid him forever. She had made that clear in her letter to him, so why was he calling her now?

"Can you hear me?"

She nodded, then shook her head when she realized that, of course, he couldn't see her.

"Yes, I can hear you."

"It's good to hear your voice," he said. "I wanted to talk."

As far as Dora was concerned, they had very little to discuss, but she wasn't the one who needed convincing.

"I got your letter," he said. "I'd like you to reconsider coming out."

"For the service? No."

"Why not?"

Why not? He must not be thinking clearly, because there were a million reasons why she shouldn't come, or if not a million then at least two, which she thought she had made quite clear in her reply to his letter. Not clear enough, apparently.

"I've already said my goodbyes," she said. "There's no need to say them again."

"And what about your hellos? The kids should meet you."

"Jesus, Barrett, they've just lost their mother. This is not the time to throw me in the mix."

"Why not?"

And that, in a nutshell, was why she had broken things off. Only his perspective mattered. He wanted her there to offer him comfort because he was hurting, and he imagined that everyone else would find comfort in her presence as well, but to his grown children she would be a stranger at best, an interloper at worst. Add to this the fact that she didn't want to offer Barrett comfort, and her decision was clear.

"I'm not coming."

"Please, Dora. I need you there," he said, his voice breaking. "I can't get through this alone."

"You won't be alone. You'll have your family with you, and you'll help each other through this difficult time."

"Dora—

"Goodbye, Barrett."

Dora placed the cordless phone gently back on the receiver with a twinge of guilt. She had made her peace with leaving many years ago, but it seemed that Barrett had created an imaginary role for her in his life. Did he really think that she would intrude on the memorial service? It didn't make sense.

The pictures Lauren had chosen to send over the years had showed a happy family, four people who enjoyed spending time together. Perhaps the truth was more complicated. Lauren had been the one who wanted children so badly. Barrett had been less enthusiastic. He certainly hadn't changed any diapers during that first year, but then, he was hardly the only father to skip diaper duty. Dora could only hope that he had built strong relationships with his children, or else he really would be going through the loss of Lauren alone.

If nothing else, Dora had learned a couple of interesting facts from their conversation. His voice no longer sent shivers down her spine, nor did she feel compelled to please him. She had her own agenda now, one that did not include Barrett.

CHAPTER TWENTY-ONE

"HONEY, WHAT'S THE MATTER?"

Dora nearly jumped out of her skin at Luke's question, with no idea how long she'd been standing there with her hand still on the phone, staring out the window. She must have looked as shaken as she felt, because Luke put an arm around her shoulders and led her over to the kitchen table, then filled the kettle and put it on to boil. While he busied himself pulling out mugs and tea and honey, Dora rubbed her temples, still processing Barrett's phone call.

Luke left her alone until the kettle whistled. When he set a steaming mug in front of her, she knew her time was up. Still, she took her time selecting a tea bag and stirring honey into the hot water.

"Did someone call?"

She didn't look up from the tiny tornado in her mug.

"Barrett."

"*The* Barrett?"

She nodded. "The one and only."

"And what did he say that's got you so shaken up?"

"He wants me to come out for Lauren's memorial service."

"I thought you already declined."

"I did."

Dora looked up and caught Luke making a face, which made her smile.

"You never liked him."

"Of course I didn't. He's the center of the universe, and all that matters is what he wants. My question is, what do you want?"

Dora reached across the table and squeezed Luke's hand. He had always been her champion, especially in those early days when she was still extracting herself from Barrett's gravitational pull.

"I told him I'm not coming."

"So that's that."

She shook her head slowly. "He says he needs me. He wants me to meet the kids."

"Now?"

"That's what I said." Dora could feel some of the shock dissolving into anger, and it felt good. Barrett's request was, frankly, foolish. "They're still reeling after losing their mother. This is the worst possible time for them to meet me."

"I agree," he said. "But you've already said you're not going. I don't see the issue."

She took a sip of tea, then set down her mug and rubbed her temples.

"I'm just worried. This door has been closed for so long, and now that it's open, who knows what will happen? Barrett used to hold such power over me. What if he still does?"

Luke laughed—not the smartest move when sitting across from a badly shaken wife.

"This may seem funny to you," snapped Dora, "but it's not to me."

He reached for her hand and gave it a quick squeeze.

"It's only funny because you can't see how much you've

changed since you saw him last. That was so long ago. You are a completely different person now. Whatever hold he had over you is long gone. I have no doubt that you could see him in person and feel no connection whatsoever."

A grimace was all she could give him in response.

"What?"

"It seems very convenient for you to believe that," she said.

"What's that supposed to mean?"

The shock she'd been feeling after the call had receded and anger flowed in to take its place—anger that should be directed at Barrett, but he wasn't here right now, and Dora was itching for a fight.

"You've already got one foot out the door—two, if we're being honest," she said. "You've started building your new life, leaving me to make sure everything is settled before I move on with mine."

Luke was always so calm and rational. She needed him to share some of the chaos she was feeling, and it seemed that her words were getting under his skin.

"Now hold on, there," he said. "What exactly needs to be settled?"

"How about the house?"

"We talked about that. We're keeping it, for a few years at least, so that we have a home base for summers and holidays."

"And who's going to take care of it? An old house like this takes a lot of work." Dora set down her mug with some force, accidentally sloshing the hot liquid onto her hand.

"Why are we rehashing this?" asked Luke, his voice rising. "I suggested a service. You said that the girls could do it, since they're basically living up here now."

"And what about Mel?" Dora needed him to see, to understand all the things that were left undone in their life together.

Leaning back in his chair, Luke crossed his arms and braced

himself in for the rest of the "discussion." Dora hated it when he did that.

"What about her?" he asked, raising his eyebrow in that skeptical way that made her want to throw something at him.

"She needs to be settled," said Dora.

All Luke had to do was tilt his head, making his skepticism even more plain, and she could almost feel the steam coming out of her ears.

"She does!" Dora insisted.

"Mel is doing just fine."

"How can you say that? She's twenty-seven years old and everything she owns could fit into a suitcase. She's perpetually between apartments, lives from gig to gig, and doesn't seem to know what she wants out of life."

"Dora. Honey. It's her life."

"And we're her parents. She's stuck, and it's our job to unstick her."

"I disagree."

Dora sputtered. She knew that they had a difference of opinion about how to advise Mel on her life choices, but she hadn't thought they were this far apart.

"I can't move on with my life until I know the girls are going to be okay, and I don't think Mel's okay. My brain won't move on to the next thing until the current thing is finished. Mel's not finished."

Luke appeared to be trying not to laugh, which was going to result in his untimely death. She narrowed her eyes at him.

"Don't laugh at me."

He seemed to realize that he was in imminent danger, because the humor left his face as he leaned forward. "Have you talked about this with Mel?"

"No." Dora looked down at her tea and decided to swirl in some more honey.

"Why not?"

She chose not to answer that question, and Luke sighed.

"Talk to her. Listen to what she has to say." Her head snapped up, only to see him holding up a hand to forestall her objections. "Really listen, don't simply wait your turn to talk. Mel knows what she wants. She hasn't told you yet. Maybe you need to ask her why that is? What's stopping her from sharing her plans and dreams with her mom?"

"That's a low blow, Luke."

"Sometimes you need to hear the truth, even if it hurts."

She studied him for a minute, trying to understand how they could see the world so differently. Mel could tell her anything. Anything.

"And when were you planning to tell the girls that you're going to move to Nashville permanently?" She wasn't the only one who needed some tough love. Luke's wince told her that she had scored a hit with her question.

"Soon," he said.

"Mm-hmm." She didn't hide her skepticism.

"I will," he insisted.

"Everyone will be here Saturday night for dinner. Maybe you can tell them then."

Kat and Rob dropped by the library on Friday, bringing lunch with them. Rob quickly pulled Fitz into a walking tour of the park, the two of them eating and talking as they surveyed the landscaping progress to date. Kat and Mel claimed the bench and laid out a picnic between them.

"You look good," said Mel. "Relaxed. Should I attribute that to all the time you've been spending with Rob?"

Her smile was all the answer Mel needed.

"I should give you a heads up, then. You've caught the attention of the local gossip circuit. I hear that Rob's truck is often parked at your place overnight, and that the two of you have become regulars for breakfast at Lucy's."

Small town life had a lot to recommend it, but privacy was not on the list.

Kat pursed her lips. "I'm not sure how I feel about that, but I suppose the interest is not unexpected. Lucy's been monitoring my social life for a long time."

"Things are good?"

"They are," said Kat. "Slow, but good." At Mel's curious look, she explained. "Rob is worried that if we let things progress too quickly—physically, I mean—we might trigger some bad memories."

It wasn't an unreasonable concern. Kat had a mountain of baggage from her past and Rob wouldn't want to inadvertently shake anything loose.

"You don't share his concern?"

Shaking her head, Kat said, "The only way forward is through. It's not like it would be my first experience since everything went sideways, and I'm willing to risk a few flashbacks if it means we can...connect."

"You're going to try to change his mind?"

If Kat's mischievous smile was any indication, Rob would soon be rethinking his position. "I'm thinking a little light bondage might do the trick."

"Seriously?"

"How can he trigger any bad memories if he's tied to my bedframe?"

Mel snuck a glance at Rob, who was with Fitz down in the far corner of the small park, then burst out laughing. He had no idea what he was in for.

As the guys turned to head back their way, Kat asked, "Have you told your family yet?"

"Working on it, but sometimes I think the universe is fighting me."

"Tick tock."

"I know," said Mel with a groan. "Trust me, I know."

Kat lowered her voice as the guys drew closer. "You and Fitz seem to be getting along. Any decisions on whether or not to have a fling before you leave?"

It was Mel's turn to answer with a smile, as the guys were close enough now to hear whatever she would say.

"What's up with the community service kids?" asked Mel, her question pitched loud enough for everyone to hear. "I thought they were going to keep helping with the landscaping."

"That first group finished up their required hours, but I plan to ask future groups to help maintain the park. Anything beats picking up litter." Kat didn't ask any more questions about Fitz now that the guys had joined them, but she did note the hand that Fitz casually rested on Mel's shoulder. "Rob and I have been meeting here after work to tackle the installation one plant at a time."

"That's romantic," teased Mel.

"Nothing like getting your hands dirty," said Kat.

"I'm sure it's a 'bonding' experience." Mel couldn't help the double entendre, and when she met Kat's eyes, the two of them dissolved into laughter. Neither offered to explain, despite the guys' mystified looks. Rob would just have to find out the hard way.

CHAPTER TWENTY-TWO

"Sorry I faded so early last night. I must still be getting over that bug."

Dora wondered how long it would take to get her energy back. Between working at the yacht club and taking one art class, she was exhausted all the time.

"No worries," said Luke. "I'm more of a morning person anyway."

"But you work nights."

"I know. Crazy, right?"

Dora scooted her chair to make room for the server who was trying to get through. Over Easy was the kind of breakfast place that catered to the student budget. High volume, low prices, and not a lot of elbow room. The decor and mismatched tables and chairs had come from jumble sales. More than half the treasures on the walls were Chicago-themed in some way, from old street signs to novelty mirrors to postcards. Dora loved it. It felt homey in a way that her studio apartment didn't. Not yet, anyway.

"So how did you get into songwriting?" she asked.

"My grandfather taught me how to play guitar and banjo. He's the one who explained basic music theory to me, and I picked up more in high school. If you understand how songs work, it's not that hard to build one of your own. You just need an idea of the structure and it flows from there. For me, the hardest part is the lyrics—figuring out what it is I want to say."

Dora leaned forward and rested her elbows on the table. "It's the same with art. I mean, it's easy enough to do an assignment for class, but when you need to decide what to paint in the first place—that's hard. Once I have a subject in mind, I understand how to approach it from different angles, how to frame it, the different choices I can make and what they communicate. It's the subject itself that I have trouble choosing."

"I would love to see your work."

It didn't sound like a pickup line—not that she would mind if it was. He seemed genuinely curious.

"Maybe you could come by my apartment after breakfast."

Was she moving too fast? Flirting too hard? She really liked this guy, and they seemed compatible. Most important, she didn't completely lose her mind when he was around. That way lay danger, and she didn't want or need any more of that.

"That would be great," he said, but he didn't look like he meant it. He actually looked kind of uncomfortable.

"What?" she asked.

"Nothing," he replied, shaking his head. "Never mind."

"Well, it's not nothing. Something's bothering you. Tell me."

"Is 'no' an option?"

"No." She grinned. If they were going to hang out, he would have to get used to speaking his mind.

"You are amazing, and I love hanging out with you." He had leaned forward to match her pose, elbows resting on the table.

"I sense a 'but' coming."

"But I need to tell you something."

She waited.

"I'm gay."

"Oh."

She couldn't think of anything else to say, really. Yes, it was a bummer, having to shift gears from flirting with a potential boyfriend to hanging out with a friend, but she could do it. They hadn't known each other *that* long. And yes, it was weird to be this disappointed when they were hanging out for the third time. But still.

She realized Luke was waiting for some kind of response.

"Um...thanks for telling me?"

He leaned back and ran a hand through his hair. "It's not something I typically spring on new acquaintances, but I really like hanging out with you, and it didn't seem fair to let you think...to lead you on, if you know what I mean."

Making a face, she said, "I get it."

"Have I scared you off?"

"No. No, of course not. I just need a minute to adjust my thinking." A wave of nausea caught her by surprise as the table next to them got their food. This was becoming something of a trend when she was with Luke. "Can you excuse me for a sec? I need to use the restroom."

Dora beat a hasty retreat and locked herself into the tiny bathroom. Keeping her breaths shallow—the muggy bathroom air didn't make her feel any better—she peed, washed her hands, tugged at her itchy bra strap, and splashed some cold water on her face. The nausea was fading. What she needed to do now was squelch the irrational disappointment at Luke's announcement. She barely knew him, he didn't even get her motor running, and now she was feeling tears at the back of her eyes because he had taken himself out of the running? It was ludicrous.

She bent to splash water on her face again and as she

looked up, she caught a glimpse of her cleavage in the mirror.
Either the lighting in here sucked or she had a major rash
going on. Or both. She dried her face with a bunch of paper
hand towels and lifted up her shirt to get a closer look at the
skin under her bra strap.

"No no no no no..." she murmured, a different kind of sick
feeling settling into her stomach. That rash could mean only
one thing, and it was not good news. Winding her way back to
the table, Dora slumped down into her chair, her mind
reeling.

Luke took one look at her and said, "I'm sorry."

"For what?" she asked, confused. Then she shook her head.

"I knew I shouldn't have said anything," he continued. "It's
okay. I get it."

"No, really, it's fine."

"Dora, I can tell it's not fine."

She tried to laugh, but it sounded more like choking.
"Things are definitely not fine, but it has nothing to do with
you."

"What are you talking about?"

"I'm pregnant."

Saying it out loud only made her feel worse. She let her
head thunk down onto the table.

"What???"

"I just figured out that I'm pregnant," she muttered into the
table, "and it's a disaster."

"The ex?" he asked as she reluctantly raised her head.

"Yep."

"Oh, honey."

"I'm not sure if I can eat." Maybe it was for the best that
they hadn't ordered yet. "I'm so sorry. I have to know for sure
and I won't be able to think about anything else until I take a
pregnancy test. I need to get out of here."

"Let's go, then."

"You don't have to miss breakfast because of me. You must be starving."

She already felt stupid for not realizing it sooner. The signs had all been there, and she had completely missed them. He was sweet to stick with her, but she didn't need a witness for the confirmation of her worst fears.

"Dora, please. You're having a crisis. I'm not going to sit here and eat scrambled eggs while you're peeing on a stick and freaking out all by yourself. Let's go."

She stared at him for a long minute, realizing that she wanted him to come with her, potential boyfriend or not. He made her feel safe, and that was something she hadn't felt in a long time.

"Okay."

They walked around the corner to the pharmacy and picked up two pregnancy tests (just to be sure), then walked another block to her building. He didn't seem fazed by the industrial brick exterior or the ancient freight elevator, but that all changed when they walked into her apartment.

"Holy shit, this place is amazing. I thought you were a student."

Dora never had friends over for this very reason. Guests led to questions, and she didn't want to have to explain her past.

"Um...I got a good deal?"

Snorting inelegantly, he said, "Try again."

She stared at her toes.

"I...inherited some money, so I don't really have to worry about how much things cost."

"Must be nice."

She looked back up again, gauging his reaction. He didn't have that calculating look on his face that she had come to recognize. Relaxing, she laughed.

"It is, actually."

He handed her the pharmacy bag and said, "Go pee on the sticks."

"Do you really think we need to use both?"

"I think you'll feel better if you're extra sure."

"You're right," she said, nodding. Then she took a fortifying breath and headed for the bathroom.

After peeing on both sticks, she laid them carefully on a tissue on the counter, put the toilet seat down, and sat down to wait.

A knock on the door made her jump.

"Want some company while you stare at the sticks?" asked Luke through the closed door. "The suspense is killing me."

She didn't fight the smile. Opening the door, she waved him in.

"Standing room only."

"Fine by me." He leaned against the wall and together they stared at the sticks while the two minutes ticked down. With each second that passed, her feeling of dread intensified.

"Has it been two minutes?" she whispered. Two minutes or not, a plus sign was fading into view on both sticks.

"Close enough."

She nodded, unable to pull her eyes away from the double plus signs. They mocked her naive longing for independence. Then they blurred as the tears finally spilled over. Luke pulled her to her feet and drew her into a big hug. He rocked her gently back and forth, stroking her hair and making soothing noises.

After a while, he said, "It's going to be okay."

She shook her head, her forehead pressing against his solid chest.

"Whatever you decide to do—"

"I love babies." The words came out more forcefully than she had intended.

He pulled back so he could hold her by the shoulders and study her face.

"Really?"

Tears were still falling, but more slowly now. Nodding, she said, "I do. I know it's not a cool thing to admit, but I could cuddle them all day."

"Wow."

"Crazy, huh?"

"Not crazy, just a surprise. You don't come across as a baby-lover."

Her surprised laugh was a welcome release. She grabbed a handful of tissues from the box on the counter and began wiping off her face.

"And what exactly does a baby-lover look like?" she asked. What a strange thing for him to say.

He shrugged, looking sheepish.

"At least you have cash to spare. No need to panic on that front."

"It's not the money I'm worried about."

"What then? Your ex?"

After blowing her nose, she nodded. "I don't want to get back together with him, but he'll insist. He's very good at the guilt, and he's got plenty of money for lawyers. I don't really see a way out."

"Don't tell him," said Luke, as if the answer was obvious.

"He'll figure it out the next time he comes out to Chicago—which he will. He'll do the math, and it will be game over."

"But what if you're dating somebody else?"

"Right," she scoffed. "Like I can find a boyfriend in the next month. There are so many guys out there who want to date pregnant ladies."

He was clearly delusional. Dating was hard enough without throwing pregnancy in the mix. Maybe she could squeeze in a few dates, but then she'd start showing and no eligible male would come within forty feet. Luke was good-hearted, but he had no clue.

"I'd be happy to give it a try."

His serious expression made her want to cry all over again.

"You're very sweet, but you just told me you're not interested—"

"—in the sexy stuff, sure, but that doesn't mean we can't spend time together."

He seemed determined to play the knight in shining armor, so she took a different tack.

"This might take a while," she said. "It doesn't seem fair to lock you up for months, maybe longer..."

"Hanging out with you isn't a hardship, and if it helps you keep a toxic ex at bay, all the better."

She studied his face for a long time before asking, "Are you sure this is something you want? And do you think we could make it look real?"

He gave her a wry smile. "I've been faking being straight my whole life. This will be a piece of cake."

Maybe it was the shock of finding out, or the fear of being alone, or that crazy feeling of being safe with him—whatever it was, all her objections faded away in the face of his calm certainty.

"I can't believe I'm agreeing to this, but you are the best," she said, and threw her arms around him.

CHAPTER TWENTY-THREE

Today

ON FRIDAY AFTERNOON, DORA STOPPED BY THE LIBRARY TO return a book, which provided a convenient excuse to peek in on Mel and Fitz working on the mural. If she could watch them for a minute, without them knowing they were observed, she was confident she could assess their chemistry level. Not that she intended to interfere. She was merely curious.

This errand wasn't strictly necessary, but it provided a helpful distraction from her actual plans for the afternoon. Those plans, the reason she kept checking her makeup in the rearview mirror (just enough to look good, but not enough to look like she was trying), were her meeting with David. Putting the car in park, she shook her head at her own foolishness.

Call it what it is, Dora. A date.

They were meeting at the sailing school, because in a moment of insanity on Wednesday afternoon she had offered to take him out on the water. This afternoon's nerves, after two relatively calm days, had caught her by surprise—not so much the fact that she had them, but the reason behind them. She didn't worry that he would find her boring, or not have fun, or anything like that. She worried that *she* wouldn't like *him* out on the water. Some people could be charming on land but hopeless on the water. You never knew until it was too late.

First things first. She had parked on the far side of the library so that Mel wouldn't see her coming. Walking down the sidewalk past the main entrance, Dora slowed as she reached the end of the building and peeked around the corner as Mel burst out laughing and flicked paint on Fitz. He stalked her, seeking revenge, and punished her with one very hot kiss. Backing away slowly, Dora smiled in satisfaction. Definite chemistry, and clearly not the time to interrupt.

Well, this was an interesting development. She had noticed Mel's grudging interest in the "hot muralist" and hoped to encourage it, but she hadn't realized they were actually...what would the kids call it these days? Dating? Hanging out? Chilling? Whatever they wanted to call it, this was very promising. Very promising indeed. She needed to call Fitz's mother, Margot.

Dora had been distracted by the kiss and only had a vague sense of the progress on the mural, but she didn't want to go back for a second look. That could wait. Instead, she popped inside to say hello to Mary Evelyn and return her book. Dora found her in the children's section, surrounded by an explosion of toys and an industrial-sized tub of Clorox wipes. Dropping to the floor, Dora immediately started helping with the wipe-down.

"The mural is looking good," she said, hoping Mary Evelyn wouldn't ask for specifics.

"Is it? I haven't been out to look at it yet today. As of last night, they had the design transferred to the wall. I think they were going to start filling in with color today."

"Yes, they have," said Dora, reaching for anything else she could say that would be vague but true. "The colors are wonderful. Vibrant. I can't wait to see more."

"Fitz and Mel seem to be getting along well." Mary Evelyn's tone of voice was a request for inside information, but Dora didn't cooperate. She didn't want to jinx it.

"I suppose they are," she said mildly.

Now that Mary Evelyn mentioned it, Dora realized that Mel had said very little about Fitz on their real estate outing yesterday morning, even though she'd been spending all day every day with him. Mel wasn't one to hold back her opinions. If Fitz were annoying in any way, Dora would have heard about it. The fact that he was *not* driving Mel crazy was remarkable. Mel had a strong personality, and she didn't always gel with other people. Not only were Mel and Fitz "hanging out," but Mel seemed to enjoy spending long stretches of time with him. The possibilities got more and more interesting.

"And you?" asked Mary Evelyn. "How is the lovely David doing?"

"Fine, thank you." Dora had long ago stopped thinking of Mary Evelyn as her good friend's mother and instead considered her a friend. That said, the situation with David was very new, and she wasn't ready to talk about it yet.

"How was your coffee date?"

"It was a business meeting, and it went very well."

"So you'll be working with him? All the time? Maybe traveling with him?"

Dora was going to have to be more direct if she wanted to shut down this line of questioning. There were times that Mary Evelyn reminded Dora of a bird, with her bright, curious eyes and her tendency to pepper a person with questions, the way a bird might repeat the same trilling call over and over and over again at four thirty in the morning.

That wasn't a kind thought. Mary Evelyn certainly didn't intend to be intrusive.

"I haven't given him an answer yet, but even if I agree to work with him—" Dora emphasized the unlikelihood of that outcome with her skeptical expression. "—I certainly won't be spending time with him. He has responsibilities all over the world. I would be one of many artists that he works with. I would probably see him once or twice a year."

Mary Evelyn looked disappointed, but at least she stopped asking questions.

"Pity. I was hoping he might become a regular around here. I could stare at him all day." Mary Evelyn flashed a wicked smile. "What? I appreciate a good-looking man. 'Hot Muralist' will be done with his project soon, and I need some new eye candy. Give an old lady a break."

On the drive from the library to the sailing school, Dora found herself growing more and more nervous, and she didn't understand why. Was it because their time together had ended so abruptly the other day? Or maybe because she'd seen him half-naked and been completely unable to get the image out of her mind? No, that didn't make her feel nervous. It made her feel lots of things, but not nervous.

A more likely explanation for her nerves was the fact that the high school sailing team practiced on Fridays after school, weather permitting, as they tried to squeeze a season into September and however much of October they could get. This year the weather had been very cooperative. Today, in particular, was brisk but beautiful. The school would be crawling with parents and coaches and kids. How in the world would she explain David? Instead of the romantic outing she had envisioned, he was going to get an in-your-face introduction to the world of high school sailing.

To make things more interesting, the wind had picked up and it would be challenging out on the water. Fun, but cold and wet. They should definitely wear wetsuits. Maybe even dry suits. This meant getting his measurements so she could loan him a suit in the right size, and checking to make sure it fit. What if he didn't want to change out of his snazzy suit? Would he be wearing a suit? Would he have had the sense to wear something more casual?

Lurking below all her other panicky thoughts was the fear that charming, handsome David would turn out to be a pretentious turd who didn't know how to relax and have fun. She wanted to shake herself. This wasn't an audition for a life partner! This was a date with an attractive man. He didn't need to be perfect. She just needed to figure him out. In the same way that she had exercise friends and book club friends and mom friends, David didn't need to be amazing in all ways. Once she knew his limits, she would be able to work around them and perhaps their little experiment could continue.

Right now, however, Dora needed to relax and deal with whatever curious parents, coaches, and staff might be waiting for her at the sailing school. She was an adult. She could handle a few nosy questions.

Dora walked through the main doors to find everything in chaos. As far as she could tell, David hadn't arrived yet. The two coaches were beside themselves, talking over each other in an attempt to explain. Apparently some of the kids had rigged their boat in the warehouse, out of the wind, and had left the sail halfway up, not thinking about what would happen once they got outside. As they approached the launch ramp, a gust of wind caught the half-raised sail and knocked the boat off the trailer. One of the kids had sprained his wrist or possibly broken his arm trying to catch it. He was in the office with one of the staff, who was trying to reach his parents. The boat now blocked the ramp so nobody else could get on the water. The boat had sustained damage and would need to be repaired. By the time Dora had heard the tale from front to back, she could feel a headache coming on.

"Okay," she said. "Let's take this one problem at a time. How's Kyle? Let's check on him and see if Julie has been able to get through to his mom."

"Right. Of course."

The coaches had that shell-shocked look that meant they weren't thinking clearly. They followed her into the office, where Kyle was putting on a brave face while his arm turned purple. Julie had his parents on the phone, but they were about half an hour away. Dora listened for a minute, then asked for the phone.

After identifying herself, she said, "The coaches have brought me up to speed on what happened. Kyle is handling this all really well, but I think we'll all feel better if he sees a doctor sooner rather than later. Why don't we have one of the coaches drive him over to the urgent care and you can meet them there? It will be closer for you and no trouble for us."

Within a few minutes, Dora had everything squared away. One coach would stay and have the kids de-rig the rest of the boats and put them away. A little extra practice with the rigging never hurt anyone. They could all help lift the damaged boat back onto the trailer and haul it to the warehouse for repair. Then they could meet in the classroom to talk about race strategy and safety in a high-wind situation. The staff would close up after practice.

Dora pulled Julie aside and asked her to keep an eye out for David while she went to rig a boat for their outing. Julie didn't ask a single question about Dora's "friend," which meant that a ton of questions would be coming later. At least she had some time to come up with answers.

Ducking out of the side entrance, Dora walked around to the front of the school and headed uphill toward the building where the boats were stored, intending to rig the boat before David arrived. But as she crossed the parking lot, she saw him walking toward the main entrance, looking much sexier in athleisure than she would have guessed. It was probably some kind of designer track suit, which made her feel suddenly frumpy in her basic track pants and fleece.

She called his name, and David's answering smile melted her insides. It had been too long since she felt so deliciously off-balance, and she had missed that feeling. Maybe it wasn't smart, given her history of falling hard and asking questions a few years later, but she didn't want to hide from strong feelings. She wanted to revel in them.

He greeted her with a sophisticated kiss on the cheek. Was she actually supposed to kiss him back, or only brush her cheek against his? She let her skin slide briefly across his freshly shaved cheek and refrained from sinking her nose into the hollow of his neck. She wasn't up on the latest international etiquette rules, but she was pretty sure inhaling him would be considered bad manners.

As she pulled back, she asked, "Have you been sailing before?"

"With friends, yes, but on the ocean. There were hors d'oeuvres and champagne."

"Ah, yes. That kind of sailing." She had crewed for similar outings at the yacht club on Long Island where she met Barrett. God, that was a long time ago. "It's wonderful, but I should warn you that today's experience will be very different."

"I do not fear a challenge."

His expression of smug, sexy, affronted masculinity had her hiding a smile.

"Then follow me."

She led the way first to the side entrance of the main building, where they scrounged up dry suits in appropriate sizes. The waterproof fabric would protect them from both wind and water and fit easily over their regular clothing. From there, they headed over to boat storage to rig an M17. He followed her instructions, comfortable asking questions but letting her take the lead. By the time they arrived at the lakefront, the ramp had been cleared and they soon had their boat on the water. As she explained what David needed to do, she avoided using sailing-specific jargon. It was more important that he understand critical instructions like "tighter" and "looser."

To Dora's relief, the wind eased a bit as they headed out, giving them a chance to settle in. All her fears about today's outing now seemed silly. David behaved with as much class out on the water as he did on land. He didn't fill silences with idle chatter, but seemed genuinely curious to learn more about the mechanics of sailing, and today was a great day to learn. By the time they returned to the dock a good two hours later, it took their combined efforts to safely glide in alongside the dock. His enjoyment was obvious, and his delight in the wind and the water matched hers. Even more fun, he had responded to each of her instructions with a suggestive ¡A la orden, Capitàn!, making her wonder if he might enjoy following her instructions in other arenas as well.

But maybe she was getting ahead of herself.

The high school practice had ended, and only a few staff members remained, for which she was grateful. There would be fewer curious eyes and fewer nosy questions. It took some time to get the boat out of the water, de-rig it, and put it away. Afterward, he leaned against the frame of the oversized warehouse door and gazed down the hill at the lake.

"It is very beautiful here. Thank you for sharing your love of sailing."

She walked over to stand beside him. "It's an important part of my life."

"I can see that."

He turned to face her, taking her hand and slowly pulling her closer. Her heart began to pound, making her feel a little light-headed, but she wanted more of these feelings and didn't pull away. He placed a hand on her hip, but didn't pull her closer. She wished he would.

"Is this part of your campaign to woo me as a client?" Her voice was supposed to sound teasing, but instead came out as breathless and uncertain. His expression stayed serious.

"I prefer to separate business from pleasure. You may choose to become my client. That is business. Spending time with you is a pleasure. I would like to continue to spend time with you, regardless of whether or not we do business."

"I would like that, too."

Finally, he closed the last inch of space between them so that her body rested against his. She could feel the heat of him from her breasts to her knees, the evidence of his desire solid between them. It was a good thing that he was bearing some of her weight because her knees weren't doing much to hold her up. Other than Luke, she hadn't been this close to a man in so long that she had forgotten the feeling of fire dancing down her skin. She found it increasingly difficult to breathe.

"I'm glad we are in agreement on this."

She nodded, but her thoughts were growing muddled. She wondered if it would be very uncomfortable to have sex in a car. Or maybe a sailboat. Or what about the couch in the foyer of the sailing school?

She licked her lips and tried to draw in more oxygen. His eyes dropped to her mouth, and she sensed the moment when he decided to make a move. Her hands, resting on his chest, slid up to his shoulders, and he smiled that slow, sexy smile she was coming to love. He pulled her even closer and lowered his mouth to hers.

Their first kiss was a greeting. Their second, an exploration.

After that, she could no longer count, the kisses flowing from one to the next without pause. He kissed like he had all day and all night and nowhere else he'd rather be. She decided, with the last of her functioning brain cells, that she had all the time in the world.

CHAPTER TWENTY-FOUR

28 years ago, August

Dear Lauren,

I've met someone. His name is Luke. He's kind and smart and the most amazing musician. We're already talking about getting married! I know, I know—it's too fast, but this feels right. He's interviewing for teaching jobs, and once we know where he'll be working, we'll move in together. I'll let you know as we make our plans for the future.

Love to all and hugs to the children.

Dora

DORA SEALED THE LETTER. IT HURT—PHYSICALLY HURT—TO close the door on that chapter of her life, but she could see no other way out. If she didn't make a clean break, the pain would stretch out over the years until it snapped, and she suspected that would be much more painful.

Luke was very sweet to play the role of boyfriend. She and Luke had been spending every free moment together, and any lingering doubts about their "pretend boyfriend" plan had faded in light of their growing friendship. Hopefully their fake relationship and the cover story it provided for her pregnancy would be enough to convince Barrett that their relationship was truly over. He was a stubborn man. It might take a while, and Dora would accept Luke's protection for as long as they needed to maintain the charade. A big part of her hoped he would land a job in the city. His friendship had come to mean a lot to her, and she dreaded losing him to the suburbs. If he stayed in the city, he would have plenty of time to settle into teaching before the baby came. Maybe he would consider coming with her to the hospital. Giving birth wasn't something she wanted to do alone.

Luke had been applying to music teaching jobs not only in Chicago but also out in the suburbs and even as far away as southern Wisconsin. The idea of moving out of the city, far from the center of the gay community, was intimidating, but teaching jobs in music were hard to find, and he'd take what he could get. If being in a rural setting brought back too many bad childhood memories, he could always come back to the city. He had an interview coming up in Wisconsin, and he invited Dora to join him for the road trip north.

Dora didn't have any particular interest in exploring Wisconsin, but the heat and humidity of August made the city unbearable. An escape was just what she needed. As they left the city and suburbs behind, cows began to outnumber cars, and she wondered what it would be like to live so far out in the sticks. Growing up toward the end of Long Island, life had been quiet during the off season, but the hum of New York City could be felt even on the quietest of days. Through the car window, Wisconsin looked like a real-life version of a Grandma Moses painting, only flatter and more spread out. Maybe at lunch she would order a grilled cheese sandwich. She had heard a lot about Wisconsin and cheese.

The school was in a tiny town called Hidden Springs. If he

got the job, Luke would be teaching music to a student body of fewer than three hundred children. Dora had stopped by the library downtown to do some research, and learned that the town itself was home to barely over a thousand people, which seemed impossibly small. There were probably a thousand people living within a one-block radius of her apartment in the city.

Her first glimpse of Hidden Springs came after more than an hour of endless farmland. They rounded a curve to find themselves on a downward slope, heading into a tiny, tree-filled town with a lake that stretched into the distance. The sight took Dora's breath away.

"You didn't tell me there was a lake."

"I didn't know," said Luke. "Is this a good thing?"

"Nothing better," said Dora.

It wasn't the ocean, or Lake Michigan, but still a glorious stretch of water, more than big enough for sailing. Long and narrow, it stretched so far into the distance that she couldn't see the end. Maybe while Luke was doing his interview, she could explore the lakefront.

As it turned out, the school was only a short walk from the beach. Kicking off her shoes, Dora waded in the miniature surf, the gentle lapping of the waves tickling her feet. The water was cold and clear and nothing like the ocean surf. She visited the marina next, which catered primarily to motorboats rather than sailboats. The marina manager mentioned a yacht club halfway down the lake. Maybe they could stop there on their way home.

After a couple of hours on her own, Dora circled back to meet Luke at the little diner down the street from the school. He was there already, waiting for her, and bubbling with excitement about the job. The principal didn't mind his lack of experience, as long as Luke didn't mind the fact that he would be the only music teacher in the school, covering kindergarten through eighth grade. It seemed like the perfect job, and Dora was happy for him. Truly. She would visit him in Wisconsin whenever she could. There were a few more candidates vying for the position, and Luke would know in the next week whether or not he got the job.

Dora fell in love with the kitschy, lake-themed decor of the diner. They found a booth in the back. The spiky-haired girl working the counter made Dora wonder if there might be room for misfits in this postcard-perfect town. Growing up, she had never fit in, but maybe in a place like this things could be different.

On the long drive home, Luke shared the story of why he left Nashville, unwilling to watch his friend Zeke sink deeper into drugs. They had already lost too many friends that way. His current band was a nice enough group of guys, but one would be leaving in the fall to move to LA. Another was about to have a baby and get a day job. Their days were numbered. Change was coming whether Luke wanted it or not, and while the shine had faded from his dream of making it in the music business, his other dreams seemed even further out of reach. At heart, he wanted to settle down and live a normal life. But how? Dating in the gay community was a nightmare right now thanks to AIDS. To complicate matters, Luke had always loved kids. In his hazy vision of the future, he had imagined working with kids as a music teacher while raising a family of his own. Obviously, these daydreams had little to do with logic or reality. How was a gay man supposed to pull off a life like that?

Change was coming for Dora, too, ready or not. Babies had a tendency to disrupt pretty much everything. She would need to baby-proof the apartment, find a nanny, and break the news to her art school friends. The idea of juggling art school and a baby at the same time was intimidating, and she toyed with the idea of taking some time off. She had learned so much this past school year, but at a certain point you just needed to paint.

As the tall buildings of Chicago came into view, Dora hoped
that her friendship with Luke would survive the changes of the
coming year. She had lost so much already. She really didn't
want to lose him, too.

Today

Mel and her sisters headed down to the shore on Saturday
morning to sneak in one last round of paddle boarding. Some
of the docks had already been removed for the season and were
now stacked neatly along the water's edge. Mel loved this time
of year, when Mother Nature reclaimed the lake and the
humans eased off for a while. The naked shoreline captured
her imagination in a way that the crowded version never could.

"Did Mom not want to join us this morning?" asked Callie.
As the only daughter actually sleeping in the house, Mel had
been assigned to invite her.

Mel shook her head. "She said something about us girls
enjoying ourselves, and to bring the boards and paddles back
up to the garage when we're done. It's time to put them away for
the season."

"That's weird. I thought she wanted to get out on the water
one last time," said Tessa as they reached the dock and began
pulling their boards off the storage rack.

The fall had been very kind, offering more unseasonably
warm days than usual. Today would be the grand finale, with
temperatures in the sixties and little to no wind. Barely a week
out from Halloween, the chance of another gorgeous day like
today might as well be zero.

They had the lake to themselves. As they had hoped, the
water was like glass, so calm that you could see the seaweed
reaching up toward the sun from the rocky bottom of the lake.
In some spots, it brushed the surface. Mel tried to avoid falling

off her board in those places. There was nothing she hated more than the slimy feeling of seaweed tangling with her legs. Heading toward the quiet lakefront, Mel was curious to see how many boats were still in their slips. This time of year, most people started pulling their boats out for winter storage.

It had only been a few days since Mel had taken Fitz paddle boarding, but the water felt significantly colder, from brisk to bone-chilling in less than a week. She should have worn water socks. Her feet were already starting to go numb. At this rate, it wouldn't be a long paddle boarding session.

After all the failed attempts to share her plans, this morning Mel had decided on a new strategy. It would be much easier to tell her mother with her sisters' help, so once they reached the lakefront, Mel was going to tell her sisters and together they could tell Mom and Dad. But as Mel opened her mouth to speak, Tessa broke the silence.

"RJ and I are thinking about moving to California."

Mel's mouth snapped shut as she reeled from the bombshell.

"What brought this on?" asked Callie. "I thought RJ hated California."

"He loved California. He hated working for his dad. He's got a buddy out there who started a small law practice and he's invited RJ to join him. The practice is growing. We could live near the beach and he could surf all year round. We'd come back in the summers, of course, but probably not for the whole summer."

After a beat of silence, Callie asked, "What about Christmas?" Interesting question coming from the girl who had missed any number of Christmases over the last ten years.

"We could come back for that, too...or you guys could come out to California."

Mel's board flowed over a patch of particularly tall seaweed. In her imagination it crept up over the edges of the board and snaked toward her ankles. If Callie and Dad shifted their base to Nashville, and Tessa and RJ ran away to California, that left only Mel behind to support Mom through the divorce and the transition into a new normal.

"So how firm is this plan?" asked Mel.

Tessa shrugged, which almost unbalanced her. After recovering, she said, "We're brainstorming. I mean, the offer to become a partner in a small law firm out there is real, so it's more than just talk, but no decisions yet."

"And how do you feel about the idea?" asked Callie.

Tessa was quiet for a few strokes.

"I'm not sure yet. On the one hand, it sounds like an amazing adventure, and as the weather gets colder, the Southern California sunshine sounds better and better. But I'd miss the lake. I've really enjoyed helping Mom with the sailing school this summer, and I've loved being able to split my time between counseling and sailing. California is an expensive place to live, especially if we want to be close to the beach, so I'd probably have to go back to counseling full time."

"And RJ?" Mel thought her question was a good one. RJ seemed to thrive on his current part-time work schedule.

"He'd have to work more, too."

"Huh." Mel didn't know what to say. It's not like she could forbid her sister to leave.

"I know, it sounds crazy, but I've never lived outside the orbit of Chicago. I'd like to try living somewhere else—even if it's only for a few years."

You and me both, sister. Mel couldn't argue with her because she wanted to explore the world, too. The key difference here seemed to be that Mel couldn't bring herself to leave unless she knew her family would be okay without her—specifically her mom. Tessa's plans changed everything for Mel, and it made her want to throw something at the wall, if only there were a wall nearby and she wouldn't fall off her board. Mel couldn't abandon her mom to a long winter alone.

"I'm so glad you're spending more time here at the lake," said Tessa, blissfully unaware of her sister's growing frustration. "Knowing you'll be here for Mom makes it easier to imagine going away. With Callie down in Nashville to support Dad, nobody will be lonely. I know sometimes Mom drives you crazy, but having somebody nudge you toward your goals is not a bad thing. Sometimes you need that external push to make things happen."

Mel kept her mouth shut because if she opened it she might scream. Damn it, that was *her* speech. This was *her* plan. She was supposed to be the one to say, *I'm only comfortable leaving because you all are here for Mom and Dad.* Clenching her jaw, Mel stayed silent and kept paddling. Nothing good would come of saying anything right now, but she couldn't just paddle along as if everything were fine.

"You okay, Mel?" asked Callie. Tessa might be clueless, but Callie could always sense when Mel neared the breaking point.

"My feet are numb," said Mel, her voice tight. "I'm going to head back."

Turning the board before they could respond, she headed for home. Later, when the urge to lash out had faded, she would talk to her sisters about this. They would be surprised, but they would listen, and together they would figure it out. Later.

CHAPTER TWENTY-FIVE

28 years ago, August

THE BLINKING LIGHT ON THE ANSWERING MACHINE WELCOMED Dora home. Pressing "play," she walked into the kitchen to get a glass of water. The weather outside was like a steam room. She stilled when Barrett's voice cut the silence.

> *Lauren told me. I'm coming to see you. I get in this afternoon, and I'll be staying at the Hilton and Towers again. We need to talk.*

She drank the entire glass of water before walking back over to the answering machine and deleting his message. Had it been too much to hope that he would let her go?

This time, she would make sure he couldn't sex her into submission. Pregnancy aside, sex would be a step in the wrong direction. Add the pregnancy to the picture and sex would effectively end her bid for independence. He would know the instant he touched her. Already her clothes were tight and nothing about her body was working quite right. She craved food and sleep above all things, and sex at the most awkward moments, which had come as a surprise. Hunger seemed to take precedence over everything else and she worried about gaining too much weight. Some of the magazine articles she had read said that if you ate too much, the baby would be too big, which makes for a difficult delivery. In no way did she want to make this delivery any harder than it needed to be.

He had left the message this morning, probably before leaving for the airport, meaning he might already be at the hotel. She wouldn't put it past him to come looking for her if she ignored him, so she called the hotel and left a message for him with the front desk suggesting they meet in the hotel bar at seven. She would have proposed a later meeting time, but these days she was sound asleep by nine most nights, and she would need to be at least semi-alert in order to deal with him.

Meeting in the bar was definitely the right call. It wouldn't matter how much he tempted her as long as she didn't go back to his room.

Dora arrived early at the hotel and ordered club soda with lime. Better that she order her drink now rather than face questions later about why she wasn't drinking alcohol. Sitting at the curved end of the bar with a view of the entrance, she was mid-sip when he walked in. He looked like hell warmed over, and a small, vindictive part of her took satisfaction in his pain. The life he envisioned for her in New York would cause her pain on many levels, and still he was relentless in his quest. It only seemed fair that he should suffer as well.

Holding off his attempted embrace with two hands firmly on his chest, she allowed him to kiss her cheek, then slipped back onto the barstool, patting the seat beside her.

"What's this I hear about a wedding?" he demanded.

"I'm getting married." She kept her voice mild and took a sip of her "vodka soda."

"Do I get to meet him?"

"No, thank you."

"Why not? Don't want the comparison?"

She cocked her head to one side and gave him a cool stare. "Are you planning to divorce Lauren so you can marry me?"

That shocked him into silence—not that she had expected an answer. His reaction reinforced her decision to keep the pregnancy a secret. He would use it to compel her return to New York. He had an army of lawyers at his disposal, and far greater resources. They would battle. He would win, and she would never be free.

"I didn't think so," she said when it became clear he had no answer. "My marriage has nothing to do with you. My life and yours will no longer intersect. I'm going to be part of a family and I'm going to be happy."

"But you could have all those things with us."

She snorted. His lost puppy look was wasted on her. "I will no longer eat the crumbs from your table, Barrett."

He reared back as if she had slapped him, and she realized that she'd never been quite so blunt with him before.

"But the connection between us—"

"No matter how amazing the sex, it's not enough for me anymore. For you, I'm sure it enhances your enjoyment of life. Perhaps it even makes your life complete. For me, it's far less than the full life I deserve."

"Dora, I—"

"I want a husband who will put me first and who will be a true partner in life," she said, waiting a moment to see if or how he would respond. He was silent. "I want a home of my own full of children to love, and they'll love me back and call me Mama." Her voice almost broke on the last word, but she caught it in time, swallowing hard to try to keep from breaking down. She couldn't show weakness in front of Barrett.

When the twins had started talking, when they had first called Lauren "Mama," Dora had realized how very, very much she wanted that for herself. It wasn't enough to care for children or to be a part of their lives. Maybe it was selfish, but she wanted to claim a husband and children as her own, to love them fiercely, and to create the family she had never had but always wanted. Barrett could never give her this dream, and the longer she remained entwined in their lives, the smaller her chances of making the dream come true.

He still hadn't said anything, so she continued, her voice calm but unyielding. "I'm sure you'll find plenty of women in New York who are willing to see to your needs."

The bartender slid Barrett's drink in front of him, and he studied her as he took his first sip.

"You're different," he said at last.

"I hope so."

"Cold."

She smiled at that. Barrett had never liked it when he didn't get his way.

"I'm sorry I can't be what you need."

His expression shifted from confusion to determination. Apparently he had taken her refusal as a personal challenge.

"Come up to my room," he said, the heat in his eyes coaxing a response from her off-kilter body. "Just for tonight, for old time's sake."

She took a sip of her drink before answering. "No, thank you."

"No? That's it?" His determination was starting to look more like anger and frustration.

She nodded because there wasn't much else to say. Walking away from Barrett and Lauren and the twins would leave a hole in her heart, it was true, but it would be equally painful to stay. She would miss their chemistry, and Lauren's friendship, but most of all she would miss watching the twins grow into the people they were meant to be. That journey wasn't hers to take, so she had to let it go.

"After all we've been through together?"

She took one last pull on her soda, drowning out his words with loud bubbles in her straw because she knew he would hate it. Then she put her empty glass on the bar and grabbed her purse. Slipping off the barstool, she took two steps toward the lobby, before pausing and turning back to him.

"Enjoy your family, Barrett."

"Dora—"

"Goodbye."

And she left.

Today

"Hey, Mom."

Fitz always seemed to find his mother in the kitchen. She truly loved to cook. Growing up, he had been one of the lucky kids with an amazing packed lunch every day for school. Of course, kids are idiots, and he had traded his mom's homemade treats for bags of Cheetos and the occasional candy bar. This morning she was chopping vegetables, which would likely end up in tonight's dinner.

"Hey, Bertie. You need some breakfast?"

Flinching at the sound of his childhood nickname, he walked over and gave her a quick kiss on the cheek.

"It's Fitz, Mom. Please don't call me Bertie. Where's Dad?"

"He's out running errands. Come eat something and tell me how the project is going."

He scrounged up a bagel and updated his mom while it was toasting.

"It's going really well. We should finish with the color blocking today and can start on the detail work tomorrow. Rob Murray, the landscaper, stops by at the end of every day to install another few shrubs or plants. The forecast looks good, so as long as the weather holds, we should finish the project by next weekend."

"That's great, sweetheart. And how is Mel doing? I haven't talked to Dora lately."

The ding of the toaster saved Fitz from answering. He took his time putting cream cheese on the bagel and then took a big bite as he sat down at the counter, buying himself time to formulate an answer. Too much enthusiasm and his mom would know that something was up. Too little, and she'd keep setting him up on dates.

"She's good. Great, really. I'm not sure I would have been able to get the project done without her help."

He took another bite of bagel, trying to look innocent.

"I'm glad to hear you two are getting along so well. She's awfully good-looking, don't you think? I mean, if the pink hair doesn't bother you."

"It doesn't."

His mother smiled but didn't say anything, which led him to believe she would soon be in contact with Dora and match-making would commence. He'd have to report back to Mel that he had laid the groundwork for their budding "relationship."

"But enough about the project," he said. This was the perfect time to tell her about his plans.

"Yes, enough about that," said his mother. "I have some very interesting news for you."

"What news?" asked Fitz. He could be patient and wait his turn.

"Well, my friend June's daughter Marcy recently moved back to Chicago after grad school. She got a job downtown but is going to live in Wilmette, which is wonderful, don't you think? She'll be close to home but she'll have her own space."

"Um, yeah, Mom. That's great." He vaguely remembered Marcy—braces, dark hair, freckles, and significantly younger than him—and he didn't want to speculate on why she would choose to live in the suburbs instead of downtown.

"I know you haven't seen Marcy since you were in high school, but I've been getting regular updates from her mother, and it sounds like she's grown into an amazing young woman. She's a graphic designer who specializes in typography, and she's going to work at an ad agency. I told her mother that you could meet her for coffee, show her the ropes."

"Wait, Mom. What?"

"Well, you're really good at the train, and you know all the tricks for getting around without a car. She doesn't have a car right now, and apparently doesn't want to get one—which is odd given that she's going to live in the suburbs, but whatever—and you know what the young people like to do these days."

"Mom," he said, not bothering to stifle a sigh. "I'm turning thirty next year. I haven't been to a club since...I have no idea. Maybe since I was twenty-two. This girl sounds very nice, but I'm not the one to show her around."

"Look, Bertie—I mean Fitz—I know you've been spending time with Dora's daughter, but I'm not trying to set you up on a date here. It's coffee, as a favor to a friend. It shouldn't be too painful. I really think you and Marcy would get along. Besides, I promised her mother, and you wouldn't leave me hanging, would you?"

They had a bit of a staring contest, but he caved first. At some point in his life, he would need to learn to say no to his mother. Not today, apparently, but someday.

"If you give me her number, I would be happy to reach out and see if she wants to get together for coffee." His tone made it clear that he was accepting this mission under duress, but his mother didn't seem to care either way.

"Excellent! I'll get her number from June."

The sound of a car pulling into the garage closed the door

firmly on this opportunity to tell his mom about his plans. Dad was home.

"Oh, and before I forget, your sister and the kids are on their way up from the city, so we'll be doing a special dinner tonight. Don't make any other plans."

"Of course not. There's no place I'd rather be on a Saturday night."

CHAPTER TWENTY-SIX

FITZ'S DAD WALKED INTO THE KITCHEN.

"Good," he said. "You're awake. I could use a hand in the garage."

"I have to head over to the library—"

"That's a volunteer effort. It can wait. Come on."

Fitz took the last bite of his bagel and followed his dad to the garage. Some battles were better conceded than won.

In the garage, he learned that his dad had purchased an air compressor and needed Fitz's help to get it out of the back of the Suburban. His dad had back issues, so Fitz made sure to take the bulk of the weight. Together, they wrestled it out of the truck and found a spot for it in the corner of the garage. Then his dad got the box of accessories from the back of the truck and started opening it.

Fitz had missed his chance to tell his mom, but maybe he should bite the bullet and tell his dad first. It wouldn't be a great way to start the day, but at least it would be done. Best to start with flattery, and let his dad think he was getting what he wanted.

"You know, Dad, I've been thinking a lot about your advice on my career path with the firm."

"About time," he said as he ripped open some plastic packaging with his teeth.

"Yes, well, it's such a big firm, and they have a lot of different career paths. It's not quite as clear-cut as the options at Jones-Henderson."

"All the more reason to have a plan."

"Right. So it's an international firm—"

"Well, there's an easy one," said his father.

"What do you mean?"

"The international piece. Even the other US offices. You can cross them off your list right away."

"I can what?"

"Your mother may be sick of worrying about her cancer. She may even believe that she's in remission, but we both know the risks. The cancer could come back at any time, and you won't want to be half a world away when that happens. You can safely narrow down the career options to the ones in the Chicago office. That should simplify things."

"That's true," he said thoughtfully. "It would simplify everything."

Fitz had worked on most of the big projects in the Chicago area, in one capacity or another, during his introductory rotations. His father was right in the sense that his career path would be much simpler if he were willing to limit himself to opportunities available in the Chicago office. That was a reasonable choice, one made by many within the firm. Most people preferred to have a home base. Fitz was the exception—the one with the restless heart and the desire to live in other countries, not just visit them. But he hadn't thought much about how he would feel if he were, as his dad had said, "half a world away" and his mom got sick again. On the one hand, she'd be the first to tell him to go. He was sure of that. On the other hand, he'd be sick with worry and if she got sick again, he would probably take a leave so that he could come back home. That might derail his fledgling career more quickly than anything else.

"Well, good," said his dad, brushing off his hands on his pants. "I'm glad you're getting your head on straight. Now get over to the library and finish this foolish project so you can get back to real life."

"Right."

"Did your mom tell you about dinner?"

"Yes. I'll be here."

"Damn straight you will. See you later."

Fitz had imagined the conversation with his father a million times and in his head it never went well. However, not once had it occurred to him that his father would make a valid point. And not only a valid point, but one so good that it prompted him to rethink his entire plan. As much as it galled him to admit it, even to himself, his father was right. If Mom got sick again, he would want to be close by, not on the other side of the globe. The realization paralyzed him, literally shut down his brain, so instead of trying to think it through, he escaped to the library. Maybe that would bring some clarity.

Dora retreated to her studio on Saturday afternoon in a futile attempt to paint. Oh, it was easy enough to stare at her sketches of David, reliving those kisses over and over again. And it was a pleasure to transfer her favorite sketch—the one of David sitting in the chair, his forearms resting on his knees, hands loosely clasped, his expression so intense that she flushed every time she looked at it—to a larger canvas. As she recreated the moment, she was supposed to be thinking about colors and lines and whether or not she could truly capture him in acrylics. She had spent so long painting landscapes that she had forgotten the challenge of portraits. Her last attempt had been when the girls were teenagers. But instead of thinking about anything artistic, she found herself daydreaming about seduction.

She gave up after a few fruitless hours and hid from the family in her bedroom. Unable to sit still, she paced the room, feeling a bit like a bird who can't find a good perch, all fluttery and nervous. Would the family know by looking at her that something had happened? Dora felt like it was written all over her flushed face. Repeated splashes of water did nothing to help. As a woman of a certain age, her hormones had become unpredictable, and the kiss had kicked everything into overdrive.

Luke came into the bathroom as she was splashing her face for what must be the tenth time.

"You okay?"

Staring at the drain, she suddenly felt like she was going to throw up. She braced herself on the counter and waited for the nausea to pass.

"Honey, you're scaring me," said Luke gently, running a hand down her back. "What's wrong?"

She reached for the towel, her hands shaking, and dried off before turning to face Luke.

"I kissed somebody yesterday," she said. Even her voice was shaking.

Luke had been married to her long enough that he didn't hesitate. He pulled her into a hug and she buried her face in his shoulder.

"The gallery owner?"

She nodded.

"Oh, baby, it's okay." Stroking her back, he waited for the shaking to subside before he loosened his hold.

"It's not okay," she said, her voice more steady now and her gaze serious. "We're still married, and I kissed someone else."

"At least you didn't meet him on the internet."

He was trying to joke, but she wasn't ready to find the humor in it.

"This is not a joking matter, Luke."

"If it makes you feel any better, I kissed Zeke. More than once."

"Of course you did." She swatted him on the chest. "That's the whole point: reuniting with lost love. This is totally different."

"How so?"

She pulled away completely so she could start pacing again. Pacing seemed to help.

"I don't know." His logic was not helping. "It just is."

"You can kiss other people." His voice was soothing, but it had the opposite effect. He was starting to piss her off.

"What if I don't want to?"

"Then why did you kiss him?" Now he looked like he was trying not to laugh. Apparently he didn't want to live a long and happy life. He preferred to be murdered by his wife.

"I don't *want* to want to." She ground the words out through grated teeth.

"Ohhhh...." Finally, the lightbulb went on.

"I don't want things to change," she ranted as she paced. "I want my family. I want my girls, here, all of us together under one roof. I don't want someone new. I want you here, not in Nashville."

"So we can all be a family again," he said.

"Exactly."

"And we can have dinner together every night and breakfast in the morning." He was finally getting the picture.

"And sometimes we can go sailing." She found it so easy to build on the picture he was painting.

"And play music," he said.

"Exactly," she agreed. "Change is horrible. I don't want it—any of it."

He hugged her again, physically stopping her from pacing.

"Oh, honey, I wish we could do that for you, but then what about the girls? Callie and Adam and Danny are working on making their own little family. Don't you want them to get married and build a life together?"

"No," she muttered against his chest.

"And what about Tessa? She and RJ seem to be doing well together; maybe they'll decide to build a life together, too. We'll never know if we don't give them the time and space to do that."

"I don't care." She kept her face buried in his warmth and could feel him laughing, even if he wisely chose not to laugh out loud. She appreciated his restraint on that front, because this storm of feelings was very real. Irrational, yes, and possibly even immature, but she couldn't make them disappear.

"Everybody has a new life except me."

"What about your sexy gallery owner?"

"He's a distraction, not a direction."

"A distraction who also kisses well, apparently."

A flush started creeping up her neck.

"Maybe."

Luke peeled her off his chest and held her at arm's length. "I'm going to tell the girls tonight about the Nashville plan. Well, Callie already knows, but it's time to tell Mel and Tessa. Are you okay with that?"

She couldn't help the childish pout. "You said you wouldn't leave until I was ready."

"And I won't, but you're almost ready, and the girls deserve to know my plans."

"I'm not ready," she insisted.

He tapped her on the nose with his finger. "One more date with this David and you will be."

Dora let Luke hold her for a while longer, treasuring these moments because all too soon he would be off on a new adventure without her. It was all happening so quickly. Luke and Zeke. Callie and Adam. Tessa and RJ. Even Mel and Fitz. Everybody had their new dance partner except Dora.

By this point, the emotional storm had nearly passed, and Dora started to get annoyed with herself. It wasn't in her nature to whine. Or pout. Or begrudge other people their happiness just because she wasn't quite sorted out yet. Maybe David would be her new dance partner, or maybe not. Either way, her family deserved love and happiness wherever they could find it, and she was good with that.

CHAPTER TWENTY-SEVEN

FITZ HAD BEEN MARGINALLY SUCCESSFUL THESE PAST COUPLE OF weeks in avoiding family meals. His father, an early riser, ate long before Fitz found his way to the kitchen in the morning. More often than not his mother had made something nice for breakfast and waited to share the meal with him. Lunch was takeout, eaten on the scaffolding, with no family members in sight. Avoiding dinner, however, took some creativity.

Some nights Fitz grabbed dinner with Rob, after Fitz had finished painting and Rob had finished planting whatever needed planting. Other nights he deliberately worked late so he would miss dinner at home. His mom had caught on to that trick, though, and had started delaying dinner, all while the sun worked against him by setting earlier each day. Instead of letting nature dictate his schedule, he had borrowed some work lights and started telling his mom to go ahead and eat without him.

Frankly, it was easier to avoid dinner than survive dinner. His father, after a full day of retirement projects that seemed to bring him more irritation than fulfillment, had little tolerance for Fitz, and Fitz, after a full workday of his own, had little tolerance for his father.

Tonight he had run out of both luck and excuses. Mandatory family dinner, including his sister and her energetic children, could not be avoided. Her parenting style had changed over the course of her separation and divorce. Playing both good cop and bad cop was exhausting, so she had chosen to be "whatever" cop, who only roused herself if there was risk of blood or fire. His mom didn't seem to mind shrieking grandchildren, and his dad tolerated anything that made his mom happy, occasionally raising his voice to bring the chaos down a notch.

On this particular night, the grandchildren acted as a human shield between Fitz and his father, sucking up all the oxygen at the dinner table. Unfortunately, the kids finished eating long before the adults and were released to play in the basement (something involving running and screaming) until bath time. His sister made it through a handful of questions about the divorce, the kids' behavior, and whether or not she planned to ease off on working now that she had primary custody of the kids before she cracked.

"Enough about me," she said, her voice tight. "Fitz, I haven't seen you in so long. How's work? What's your plan there?" His parents both turned to look at him expectantly, giving Pippa a chance to smirk at his panicked expression and take a huge bite —finally—of her meal.

"It's great," he said, hoping his dad wouldn't feel the need to offer commentary. "I'm between big assignments now, working on this mural project, and it's moving along really well. You should come down to the library tomorrow and we can show the kids."

"Great idea," said Pippa. "You know what's an even better idea? You can take them down there and I'll stay here, put my feet up, and take a nap. What do you think about that?"

He weighed the pros and cons, concluding that sisterly goodwill would be worth a few hours with shrieking children, especially if he later left the country.

"You would owe me big time," he said.

"Yes, I would."

He couldn't help laughing. She really did need a break. It was too bad his ex-brother-in-law had turned out to be a cheating asshole.

The story of the hidden cemetery gave Pippa enough time to finish her meal. His mother took over the storytelling when he got to the bit about the runaway girls. She had gotten the full scoop from Dora and knew some details that he hadn't heard before. As the conversation wound down, Fitz wondered if he should seize the moment and tell everyone now.

As if he could sense Fitz's train of thought, his dad chimed in with, "Well, all I can say is I'm glad the project is nearly finished. It's a distraction from your work, and you really need to focus."

"Actually, Dad, I've applied to join the teams on a couple of big projects. Just waiting to hear back."

"You should be on the phone every day, following up and trying to connect with people already on these projects. You don't win a prime assignment by filling out a form and then sitting on your ass."

"Anthony!" Fitz's mom was pretty laid back about most things, but she did not tolerate swearing at the dinner table.

"Sorry, Margot, but it needed to be said."

Pippa shot Fitz a look that said *What the hell???* and he responded with a discreet eye roll. At that moment, the kids raced up the stairs demanding dessert and the dining room dissolved into chaos. A tiny piece of his big plan had been unveiled, but he'd have to wait to mention the international twist—if he mentioned it at all. He still hadn't decided if he should stay or go. Maybe this reprieve was a sign that he needed to spend more time thinking it through.

His mom got up to lead a parade of little people into the kitchen. Before Fitz could even take a breath, his dad made a not-very-subtle remark aimed at both his children about helping with cleanup. As a bonus, he included a dig about how their mother was far more tired than Pippa, and they should all be taking care of her. He picked up his dirty dishes and immediately headed into the kitchen, while Fitz and Pippa followed more slowly.

"What's the deal with Dad?" whispered Pippa. "Is Mom okay?"

"She's fine," said Fitz, matching her quiet tone. "Dad is the problem. He's freaked out and overprotective."

"Are you sure?"

"She seems fine to me."

"Hmmm...."

Pippa would now be switching into doctor mode, likely on high alert. Maybe that was a good thing. Together they entered the kitchen to find the kids sitting around the table eating ice cream with candy on top.

"Mom, seriously?" asked Pippa.

"I'm the grandma, and I make the rules. It's double dessert night."

This earned enthusiastic cheers of "Hooray for Grandma" from the kiddos. Pippa shook her head.

"Just so we're clear, double dessert night only happens at Grandma's house."

This earned her a round of boos. Pippa gave her mother a pointed look.

"Thanks, Mom."

"Anytime, dear," she answered, completely unrepentant. "Oh, Fitz, did I tell you? I was talking with June this afternoon and there's a place for sale in the same townhouse development as Marcy. You know, the one right by the train station. I was thinking that you and I should go take a look."

"Why?" Fitz was truly mystified. He had never expressed interest in moving.

"It would be perfect for you!"

"But I'm happy in my apartment downtown."

"For now, sure," she said, "but at some point you need to think long term."

His father chose that moment to chime in. "You need to make an investment in your future."

"Right," echoed his mother. "What your father said. Anyway, these townhouses are the perfect size for a single person, but they'll also work for a couple, and even a young family for a few years. Two bedroom, two bath. Walk to the train. Gorgeous finishes."

"Mom, I really don't think—"

"Fitz, listen to your mother."

Fitz gave his dad a dark look and tried to hold on to his temper.

"I'm not sure I'm ready—"

"At the rate you're going," interrupted his father yet again, "you'll never be ready. Your mother has gone to a lot of trouble to learn about this potential real estate investment. The least you can do is give her the courtesy of a visit. Margot, stop doing those dishes. Fitz, you do the dishes. Pippa, you worry about the kids. Your mom needs a chance to put her feet up after slaving away all day in the kitchen."

"Anthony, honestly, I'm fine," said Fitz's mother. "You don't need to—"

"If you won't take care of yourself, I will. Now let's go. Straight to the family room. We'll watch the news while the kids worry about the kitchen."

Expression cranky, she complied, shaking her head as she followed him out of the kitchen.

"Seriously, Anthony..." Her voice faded as she left the room.

Pippa sat at the table with the kids, watching in horrified fascination as they attempted to lick all the ice cream out of the bowls and instead managed to get most of it on their faces. Fitz supposed they were headed to the bath anyway. Pippa didn't seem to care as much about the licking as she would have a year ago.

"Is he like that all the time?" she asked.

"Pretty much."

"God, it must be exhausting to stay here."

Fitz pursed his lips before breaking into a smile. "I spend a lot of time out of the house."

She laughed. "I bet you do. How much longer?"

"About a week if the weather cooperates."

"I'm more concerned about him at this point than I am about Mom. Will you let me know if he gets any worse?"

"Is that possible?" he asked. At her laugh, he continued, "Actually, I'm half-serious. What would count as 'worse' in your medical opinion?"

That got her to stop and think. "Any physical changes in his balance or the way he walks. If his behavior crosses the line from over-protective to controlling. Also any personality changes."

He got up to start on the dishes, saying, "I'll keep an eye on them, but once I leave, we might need to check in with Mom more often. She'll put up with a lot from Dad before she asks for help."

"I know," said Pippa. "That's what worries me." She pushed back her chair and stood in one fluid motion. "And now, my little monsters, give your bowls to Uncle Fitz and let's get you in the bathtub."

In the sudden quiet that followed their departure, Fitz

thought about what his life would be like if he stuck close to home. It would be easier to keep an eye on Mom and Dad, and he would be able to help out his sister when she needed it. If Mom got sick, he would be right here to help. It wasn't a path to achieving his big dreams, but it wasn't a horrible vision for the future, either, just...small.

CHAPTER TWENTY-EIGHT

THAT NIGHT, AS DINNER WAS DRAWING TO A CLOSE, MEL LOOKED around the table and realized this might be the last time they would be together as a family, the five of them. Adam and Danny were having a guys' night, but they would be a regular feature at future family gatherings. RJ had driven down to visit his grandmother, but if things continued hot and heavy with Tessa, he would likely be roped in, too. Tonight, though, without significant others, they could be their own little family. Her mother looked so happy, telling the famous story of the three of them learning to crawl. Before any baby gates had been installed. Mel had managed to explore her way out of the bedroom and down the stairs in a spectacular tumble.

"You were always my little adventurer."

This was it: the perfect opening to tell the family. But before Mel could put the words together, Luke said, "Speaking of adventures, I have some news."

Seriously? Mel's frustration went unnoticed in the flurry of interest from the rest of the table.

"Give me a chance, here," said Luke. "You all know that I've been spending a lot of time down in Nashville."

"That's not exactly news, Dad," said Callie.

"Well, I'm going to be spending a lot more time down there. In fact, I'm going to make the move permanent."

Neither Callie nor Dora seemed surprised. Mel, however, was flabbergasted. Perhaps she had been naive to think that her parents would continue to live together after their separation. Their friendship felt stronger than ever, and Mel had assumed the coming divorce was one step in a long process of figuring out what would come next in their lives. Her mother hadn't hinted at any future plans, but Luke apparently had his new life all figured out. Mom was going to need so much support to get through this, far more than the occasional stay when Luke went out of town for the week. She would literally be starting over without him.

"Can we ask what's prompting this shift?" asked Tessa. "Last time we talked, you wanted to spend more time down there. Making it permanent feels sudden."

Exactly, thought Mel, but she didn't say it out loud.

Was that a blush creeping up her dad's neck? Dora and Callie actually looked amused, which meant they already knew what this was about. Mel's frustration blossomed into anger. How was she supposed to make important decisions about her future when her own family kept secrets from her?

"Yes, Dad, tell us more," prompted Callie, her expression all bright-eyed innocence.

He gave her a grumpy look, but continued. "You all remember my friend Zeke who came up Memorial Day weekend, the one who's been helping Callie with her solo career?" They all nodded. Their father's hidden connections in the music business had come as a shock to all of them except Dora, as had the news that his songwriting had been much more than a hobby. "When I said that Zeke was an old friend, I wasn't being completely honest with you. He and I actually had a relationship a long time ago, one that ended before I met your mother."

"And now?" Tessa asked the obvious question.

Luke responded diplomatically. "We're exploring what a relationship might look like now that we're older and, hopefully, a lot wiser. What we had before was not exactly healthy." At Tessa's raised eyebrow, he clarified, "Zeke was wrestling with drugs, and I really wanted to build a family, something we couldn't do together—not then, anyway."

Mel finally found her tongue. "So are you guys going to move in together?"

Luke looked around the table before answering. "That's what we're thinking, now that Callie is all moved in to her new apartment. Zeke is living alone in an awfully big place."

"You practically live there already," teased Callie.

Luke was definitely blushing. "True."

"So what does this mean for Mom?" asked Mel, because it was clear that Dora wasn't going to speak up for herself. What the hell was her mother supposed to do now?

Luke looked at Dora and they smiled in that happy/sad way that made Mel want to scream.

"I guess I need to decide what comes next," said Dora.

Mel would have asked questions, but Tessa gave her the evil eye before saying, "Take all the time you need."

"And while I'm doing that," said Dora, her eyes squarely on Mel, "why don't we talk about what's going on with you?"

Mel leaned back in her chair and crossed her arms, not in the mood for an interrogation, particularly after the double hit: first Tessa's news and then her father's. Nobody worried about leaving Dora on her own because they all assumed that Mel would be there to hold her hand or pick up the pieces or whatever else needed doing once they all left. If she were a cartoon character, steam would be coming out of her ears right about now. All that anger should probably have been directed at the rest of the family, but Dora was the one jabbing a poker into the fire.

"Well, Mom," said Mel, anger coloring her voice, "why don't you tell me? You seem to know me better than I know myself."

Dora set down her napkin and leaned forward. "I don't think it's complicated, sweetheart." Her matter-of-fact tone was at odds with the loving, this-is-an-intervention look in her eyes. "Your sisters have found their direction in life but you're still floundering. I know it's uncomfortable, but I also know you'll find what you're looking for. The first step is to admit that you miss living here. You've been spending so much time up here but you haven't been willing to say out loud what's in your heart: You want to be here. So be here. Take the plunge."

Mel stared at her mother in disbelief while her sisters shifted uncomfortably in their chairs. Neither one of them spoke up in her defense, the traitors.

"The realtor called today," Dora continued, "and there's someone else interested in your studio space. This isn't the time to waffle. You need to make a move. Take a step toward your future. It kills me to see life pass you by while you wait for lightning to strike. Sometimes you need to make things happen and not let your fears hold you back."

Mel was practically vibrating with anger and frustration by this point. Yes, one could say that this was all her own fault for not sharing her plans with the family, but damn it, it was also their fault for never asking—not once. They assumed they knew what was best for her. It had never occurred to them that her work *was* the plan, that photojournalism could be an actual career.

This would be an appropriate, if painful, time to tell her family about her plans, but she honestly didn't think she could keep it together for long enough to tell the story. They would have to wait. She blinked back tears, refusing to cry. Instead, she cleared her throat and set her napkin beside her plate.

"Well, it sounds like you have me all figured out. I'm not sure I have anything to add to your assessment. I'm sorry I'm such a disappointment to you." Mel pushed back her chair and stood. "If you'll excuse me."

She escaped to the hallway, where she leaned against the wall, her body shaking, and tried to breathe. She needed air. Fresh air. Pushing herself upright, she walked to the front of the house and stepped out onto the screened porch. The chilly air smacked her in the face and she breathed deeply, letting the storm door close behind her.

"What?" Dora knew her voice sounded defensive, but she didn't care. She was not the one in the wrong here. Glancing around the table, she realized that Luke wasn't the only one giving her "the look."

"It needed to be said," she insisted.

Tessa dove in first, of course, defaulting to therapist mode. "I know how much you care about Mel."

Callie picked up the thread. "And how much you want her to find work that she loves."

"She's fully grown," chimed in Luke, "and she needs to make her own choices."

His words stiffened Dora's resolve. "But that's the point, Luke. She's not making choices! She's letting life happen to her."

Everybody was quiet for a moment.

"Are you sure about that?" asked Callie.

"What do you mean?" Dora demanded.

"When was the last time any of us talked with Mel about work?"

Dora threw up her hands. "We talk about it all the time."

"Do you?" asked Tessa "I mean, does she say anything?"

Dora started to insist that yes, of course, Mel talked, too, but stopped. The other day, on their real estate tour, Mel really hadn't really said anything other than smiling and nodding and promising to think about her mother's suggestions. Dora was horrified to realize that her tendency to talk until interrupted might have put a barrier between her and Mel—one that she had made a lot worse with her little speech.

"I just want her to be happy," she whispered.

Luke took her hand and squeezed. "We know, honey."

"I...I should probably apologize."

"Maybe let her cool off first," suggested Callie.

Tessa nodded emphatically, and then, thank goodness, she asked Callie a question about Nashville. The conversation shifted to talk of the music business and Luke's coming move and what that might mean for Callie. Luke didn't let go of her hand, and she held onto it like the lifeline it was. How was she going to muddle through life without him to anchor her? He was her best friend. She wasn't even sure she was a whole person anymore without him by her side.

Guilt sat heavily on her heart. Dora, in her panic about life without Luke, had tried to rush Mel into finalizing her future path. Mel needed time and space to come to her own understanding of what she really wanted. Just because Dora could see it all so clearly didn't mean that she could force Mel to see it, too. The family was right. The more Dora pushed, the more Mel would resist. Dora needed to back off and be patient.

CHAPTER TWENTY-NINE

"How was paddle boarding this morning?" asked Luke.

"Chilly," answered Tessa, "but otherwise perfect. The lake was like glass, and you should have seen the mist coming off the water."

"I did see it, from the comfort of the house with a cup of coffee in my hand."

"Wimp," teased Callie.

"And not ashamed to admit it."

"Mom, I can't believe you didn't come. When was the last time you were out on the water?" asked Callie.

"Yesterday." Dora hadn't been paying close attention and answered without thinking. Too late, she realized there would be follow-up questions. Luke seemed to be enjoying her predicament.

"Sailing?" asked Tessa.

Dora nodded.

"By yourself?"

"I'm certainly capable of taking a boat out on my own."

"Yes, I know," said Tessa, "but you rarely do."

Dora traced the wood grain on the tabletop with her finger,

hoping the conversation would shift again. Unfortunately, she couldn't think of a way to change the subject, and Tessa was relentless when she scented a mystery.

"You weren't exactly alone," said Luke.

Traitor.

"Who did you take out?" asked Tessa.

Dora looked up, not sure if she was feeling more defiant or defensive. "The art gallery owner, David. He had never been sailing, not properly anyway. Big yachts don't count. I wanted to show him the real thing."

Her expression dared them all to question her further.

"So you're going to sign with him, then?" asked Callie.

Dora lifted one shoulder in a half shrug. "I haven't decided yet."

"Mother, are you mixing business with pleasure?" Tessa sounded either scandalized or delighted. Dora wasn't quite sure which one.

"Absolutely not," said Dora, her voice matter-of-fact, but she couldn't stop a tiny smile. "We are going to keep those two things very separate."

Tessa clapped a hand over her mouth and Callie's eyebrows shot up to her hairline. Luke, aka "the traitor," leaned back in his chair, crossed his arms, and watched the show.

"Seriously, Mom? After all the lectures when Brian and I started the band?" Callie couldn't seem to process the idea.

"I never liked Brian," said Dora.

Luke laughed out loud. "Really, honey? We had no idea."

She glared at him. "Shut up."

Dora could feel the heat traveling up her neck toward her cheeks. It must be a hot flash, because she refused to be embarrassed. And she absolutely would not provide any further details for her family's entertainment.

"So," Luke said in a teasing voice, "is he a good kisser?"

She looked at him in horror and he laughed again. "I'll take that as a yes."

"Luke. The children."

At that, Tessa and Callie dissolved into laughter as well.

"I don't know about you, Cal, but I'm scarred for life."

Callie nodded. "Me, too. Years of therapy ahead."

"You all are horrible," said Dora. "I'm going to go talk to Mel."

Dora pushed open the storm door and stepped onto the chilly porch. Mel was curled up in one of the wicker chairs overlooking the lake, but the dim light hid her expression. Hoping she had given Mel enough time, Dora sank into the opposite chair.

"I'm sorry, sweetheart. I'll stop trying to run your life for you."

"It's okay," said Mel.

It wasn't okay, but it was generous of Mel to let her off the hook. They sat in silence for a few moments, but Dora had never been very good at keeping quiet.

"They were giving me a hard time and I was outnumbered, so I came out here to see you."

"A hard time about what?"

Dora hesitated, remembering Mel's reaction to David's visit to the studio, but it wasn't like she could keep it from Mel forever. "I had a date yesterday with David, the gallery owner. You met him the other day."

Mel looked over at her mother. "An actual date?"

"Well, there was no wine and candlelight, but I took him sailing, and, well, there was kissing at the end."

"That's kind of a big deal."

"I know, right? I haven't kissed anybody but your father for almost thirty years."

Mel was quiet, then said, "I've been thinking about that a lot."

"What?"

"You and Dad. Your relationship must be nothing like I thought it was. If he's gay, how did you...? Never mind. Totally not my business."

Dora laughed softly in the darkness and the cold air turned her breath into frozen mist. If they were going to stay out here much longer, she would need to get a blanket from inside. Not yet, though. Things were too fragile with Mel.

"It's fine," said Dora. "I figured you girls would have questions." She thought about what to say next, how much to share. "Your father and I were friends first and foremost, and we love each other very much. Maybe our relationship didn't begin in a storm of lust and hormones, but that doesn't make it any less real."

"I know, but at some point you must have been more than friends. You have us."

Dora considered her words carefully. She didn't want to lie, but there were some secrets she wasn't ready to share.

"There's a lot of comfort to be found in a physical relationship, even in the absence of passion. What's the phrase they use these days? Friends with benefits? Your dad and I might not have had what most people think of as a normal marriage, but we did just fine."

"Tell me again the story of how you and Dad met." Mel's voice was soft and vulnerable in the darkness. "I've always loved that story, but now I suspect it didn't happen quite the way I imagined."

Curling her legs into her body for warmth and wrapping her arms around her knees, Dora began telling the familiar story.

. . .

The love story of Dora and Luke always began the same way, like a fairy tale. "It was summer break after my first year of art school in Chicago. The city was starting to feel like home. I was working part time at the yacht club and taking a class. Most of my friends from school had gone home for the summer, and I was feeling lonely."

Mel filled in one of the gaps in the story. This past summer, their mother had talked about her past for the first time, admitting that she had moved from New York to Chicago after breaking off an affair with a married man.

"You only worked part time?"

"I had some money saved."

Mel wanted to ask where the money came from, but decided to hold her questions until the end. She needed to hear the whole story straight through.

"One night—this was in late July, when the city was sticky and the sun didn't set until late—I went out with some friends. They wanted to hear a new band play. I didn't feel that great, but I was bored, so I went anyway."

Mel studied her mother's face in the low light spilling out of the living room, but her expression was unreadable.

"I wasn't really in the mood to drink," continued Dora, "and my friends were enjoying themselves a bit too much, if you know what I mean. There was a lot of smoke—you could smoke indoors back then—so I moved to a table by myself near an open window, nursing a Shirley Temple and checking out the good-looking guy playing the banjo."

Mel smiled despite her growing list of questions. It was easy to picture the scene. Her mother grumpy and sidelined with nobody to talk to. Her father up on stage. This was the part where her father would chime in about scoping out the crowd, looking for good-looking girls, and seeing Dora for the first time, her blond curls corkscrewing in the humidity and making a halo around her sweet face. She had been the only one in the room paying any attention to the music, according to Luke.

"The band went on a break between sets, and imagine my surprise when that good-looking banjo player came over to say hi." If Luke were here, he would say that he had intended to ask the pretty lady for a dance to the Garth Brooks song playing through the sound system, but she looked a little green. "Instead of flirting, I nearly threw up on his shoes. And that's how our story began."

"So Dad wasn't actually hitting on you?" It felt strange for Mel to rewrite the story she had known all her life.

Dora shook her head. "He came over to make sure I was okay after a different guy tried hitting on me."

"And were you okay?"

"The guy wasn't a problem. I was much more worried about throwing up. I hadn't realized I was going to be sick until the wave of nausea hit me. The next minute, your dad was holding my hair back while I puked my guts out in the bathroom. After I cleaned up, he found me a quiet place to rest while he called me a cab."

"So when did you start dating, or hanging out, or whatever we should call it now?"

"I went to see the band again the following Saturday, mostly because I wanted to say thank you. I was feeling better by then. He was busy with the band, and I was falling asleep, so we decided to meet for breakfast the next morning instead of hanging out that night. The first time we really talked was at breakfast."

"So you and Dad met at the end of July, and you got married and moved up here in August?" Mel wasn't sure what to make of the story if it wasn't fueled by love at first sight.

"It all happened really quickly."

"No kidding. You had three babies to take care of by the following March. That's a lot of change in a very short time."

Dora laughed. "Do you know they only told us we were having triplets two months before you were born? They were worried because I was getting so big and they ordered an ultrasound. It was a bigger deal back then, getting an ultrasound. These days you can get one at the mall."

"I know, Mom." Mel knew the pregnancy story well, but it seemed that Dora was going to tell it again anyway.

"The doctors told me to hang on as long as I could, because triplets like to come early, and I did. I made it almost to term. You girls were each about six pounds, which is amazing for triplets."

"And the snowstorm...?"

Mel decided she might as well encourage her mother's storytelling at this point. It was far better than fighting, or listening to her plans for Mel's future, or breaking her heart.

"That's right. We had a late-season blizzard blow in as I was going into labor. What a night! Your father barely got me to the hospital before you all came popping out, one after the other."

Dora continued on with the story, but Mel had stopped listening, arrested by a sudden thought. She mentally backtracked, walking carefully through the timeline. Dora and Luke had met in late July. She and her sisters were born the following March. Her mother had always taken pride in the fact that she had carried them almost to full term.

The math didn't work.

Mel was old enough now that she had friends with children, friends who tended to over-share when it came to pregnancy, delivery, and childbirth. Full term was forty weeks. She'd been through the countdown more than once. "Almost to term" would mean somewhere between thirty-six and forty weeks, because babies born before thirty-six weeks need special attention. But in order to have a baby in mid-March, the pregnancy needed to start roughly mid-June. Her friend Sunny's second baby had been born on St. Patrick's Day, and

Sunny was confident he had been conceived on the previous Father's Day. It had been a memorable night.

Caught up in the math, the full import of Mel's calculations took a minute to sink in.

Her mother hadn't been feeling well. She had thrown up the first time she and Luke met. Things had moved really fast from that point forward. They were married and moving in together by the end of August. Mel and her sisters were born the following March.

The dominoes fell one by one, crashing around in her brain until she felt dizzy.

Her mother had been pregnant when she met Luke.

Her father wasn't her father.

The world as she knew it ceased to exist.

Mel had gone quiet. Dora wasn't sure how to interpret the silence, but she fought the compulsion to fill it with more stories. It must be difficult for the girls to think about the past in light of Luke's recent revelations. She had thought Tessa would take it the hardest, but Mel seemed to be struggling the most, maybe because everything else in her life was up in the air.

If anything, this only reinforced Dora's determination to take care of Mel, and the only way she knew to take care of her was to set her up with work that she loved and a home that she could call her own. The girl needed roots and a purpose. With those two elements in place, Dora believed Mel would finally thrive, and then Dora could take a few baby steps into her own new life.

The silence stretched between them, the chill sinking into Dora's skin. Mel didn't seem to be affected by the cold temperatures, but Dora had reached her limit. This wasn't the night to push for a discussion Mel wasn't ready to have, so Dora uncurled from the wicker chair and rose to her feet.

"I'm going to help with cleanup, sweetheart. You come in whenever you're ready."

She gave Mel a kiss on the top of her head and then slipped back into the warm embrace of the home she'd built with Luke. One way or another, she'd help her baby girl find her feet.

CHAPTER THIRTY

SOMETHING WAS OFF. FITZ EYED MEL SURREPTITIOUSLY AS THEY worked through the day on Sunday, trying to figure out what was bothering her. Instead of their usual easy companionship, tense silence filled the space between them, punctuated only by his unsuccessful attempts at conversation. The library was closed, making the already peaceful Sunday even more quiet. It was just Fitz and Mel, and Mel didn't seem like she wanted to be here.

As they finished for the day, any pride in their progress had been overshadowed by worry about Mel. He didn't think her cranky mood was directed at him, but it was hard to be sure. Before she left, he decided to reach out one last time.

"Do you want to grab dinner?" he asked. "I'd invite you back to my place to chill and order in, but sadly my place is in Chicago, which is a bit of a hike. I will not invite you to my parents' place. That wouldn't be relaxing at all."

She cracked a smile, the first he'd seen all day. "What I wouldn't give to order in Chinese and kick back on the couch," she said, "but the closest Chinese restaurant is forty-five minutes away, and my mom would definitely not let us eat out of the containers in the living room."

Clouds had been gathering all day, and at that moment the first drops began to fall.

"Oh, crap," said Mel. "Is this going to streak our work from today?"

"I don't think so. We finished up at least half an hour ago. In the time it took us to wash out all the brushes, the paint should have dried. The scaffolding will provide some extra protection if it's not quite dry yet."

"Well, that's a relief." Mel watched the rain thicken as they stood together beneath the scaffolding. "I'd love to grab dinner —I can't handle being home right now—but first I could really use the bathroom. Any chance Mary Evelyn gave you a key to the library?"

"She didn't need to," answered Fitz.

"Bummer."

"No, I mean there's no need for a key. She still hasn't gotten the lock fixed on the back door."

Mel turned to Fitz, overplaying her shock. "Why, Mr. Fitzsimmons, are you suggesting that we break into the library?"

Now this was more like their usual back-and-forth.

"Is it breaking and entering if the door is unlocked?"

"I have no idea," said Mel.

"Me neither. How badly do you need the washroom?"

"Badly."

"That settles it, then. Time for some breaking and entering."

They carried the paint to the storage shed, then casually strolled over to the back door of the library. Fitz gave the handle a shake and a twist, and just like that they were inside. It was dim, with not a lot of outside light making its way in, but they didn't turn any lights on. No need to advertise their presence. Mel made a beeline for the ladies' room, where she did have to turn on a light. It was an interior room with no light from outside windows. Fitz used the opportunity to hit the men's room. After washing up, they met back in the hallway.

"So…" said Fitz, thinking that they should pick a restaurant with a bar. It was early for dinner, but they truly didn't have anyplace else to hang out.

"Did you know that the library has a couple of couches and a TV?" Mel sounded like a tour guide. He had no idea where she was going with this.

"Follow me," she said, and led him to the back corner of the library. The bookshelves ended at a kind of living room with two couches, two club chairs, and a big TV.

"It has cable," she continued, "and headphones."

He smiled slowly. "So we could chill."

"This is what I'm thinking."

"Illegal chilling."

"Possibly."

"All the excitement of breaking and entering, without the running and tripping and falling in the dark," he said.

"Exactly."

"I like the way your mind works."

She turned on the TV and found the remote. With the volume on low, they decided they could skip the headphones. This "living room" was in the far corner of the lower level. That part of the building was set into the hillside so it had no outside windows, which meant no flickering light from the TV would be visible outside—nothing to give them away. Fitz flopped down on one of the couches and kicked off his shoes. She chose the other and began toeing off her shoes as well.

"I think you should come over here and lie down next to me," suggested Fitz.

She checked out his position on the couch, then shook her head. "I would fall off onto the floor."

"There's plenty of room," he insisted.

"Is this a ploy to control the remote?"

"Possibly."

"Let me assess."

She walked over and, after a moment of consideration, removed the back cushions, stacking them in the club chair. He scooted back so she could lie down and she spooned into him, her head cushioned on his bicep. They wrestled for control of the remote, but she dropped it on the floor where only she could reach it, so he conceded and pulled her more tightly against him. It occurred to him that there was no downside to having his hands free. Scrolling through the channels, she found a rerun of *Friends* and then put the remote back down on the floor.

After a few minutes of peaceful TV watching, he said, "You were awfully quiet today."

She nodded.

"Anything wrong?"

"Not ready to talk about it."

Saying it out loud would make it real and Mel didn't want to do that. Not yet. The knowledge was acid in her heart, but she could bear it for a little while longer. She could give her sisters one more day of not knowing, maybe even two.

He kissed the back of her neck, sending a shiver down her spine.

"Whenever you're ready, let me know."

She peeked at him over her shoulder and caught an expression on his face that made her wonder.

"What's up with you?"

He shrugged. "Family drama."

"You, too, huh?" She wiggled around so that she faced him,

ignoring the onscreen drama that was Ross and Rachel on the TV. "How is it?"

"It's bad."

"You want to talk about it?"

"You know how my mom had cancer?"

She nodded.

"My dad has been treating her like a delicate flower, which seemed ridiculous. She's so much stronger now. Back to her old self."

He paused and she waited, but he closed his eyes and didn't seem ready to continue. Assuming the worst, she said, "The cancer is back?"

He shook his head, opening his eyes again.

"My dad has been guilt-tripping me ever since the treatments ended, saying that I need to visit more, spend more time with them, that we could lose Mom anytime, you just never know. It's been driving me crazy, and I think it's been driving Mom crazy, too, but she kind of has to put up with it." He took a deep breath. "Anyway, the other night, I Googled her kind of cancer, so I could have some data to fight back against the guilt. I haven't done that since she was first diagnosed, and I had forgotten a lot of it."

Fitz swallowed, and Mel could see that he was fighting to keep his shit together.

"It turns out my dad is not crazy. Her type of cancer almost always comes back, and each time it's a little worse and a little harder to beat. She won't drop dead tomorrow, but the chances of her being around to go to my wedding or meet my future children, well, they're low. This is why she keeps trying to set me up on dates, and this is what's driving my dad's guilt trips. Real risks, not only fear."

She pulled him close and let her forehead rest against his.

"I'm so sorry. That sucks."

His arms tightened around her. "I'm thinking I should

rescind my request for international projects and request only local assignments instead—exactly what my dad has been saying."

"You can do that," said Mel carefully, "but keep in mind that if you do, the chance might not come again. Once you're more established in your career, and maybe have a wife and kids, it will be really tricky to shift to international work. You might miss out on the opportunity altogether."

"I know. But if I go, I would miss out on what could be the last few years with my mom."

"Do you think she'd want that? For you to stay close even if it made you unhappy?"

"I don't know," he said with a sigh, "but I know she'd tell me to follow my dreams even if it made *her* unhappy, and that's not what I want either."

They were quiet for a while, listening to the *Friends* episode in the background. Fitz stroked her back without pushing for intimacy. He was such a calm, centered person. The world might be crumbling around her, but he wouldn't add to the drama. Safe in the circle of his arms, the knot of tension deep inside Mel began to ease, and she realized she wanted to tell him about her own family drama.

"Yesterday was rough," she began. "In the morning, my sister Tessa said she might move to California, and she assumed I would be here to support Mom. I should have said something then, but I was so angry. I figured I should cool off. So then I was going to tell everyone at dinner, but my dad dropped the bombshell that he's moving permanently to Nashville, which means I'm literally the only one left to be with Mom. And then Mom topped it all off by doing some kind of intervention about me settling down here, and now I'm stuck. I really want to go, but can't bring myself to leave Mom alone. I know I should talk with them before I make a final decision, but the whole thing is making me sick."

"Is that what made you so quiet today?"

She smiled, not because it was funny but because if she didn't, she'd cry, and she wasn't sure she'd be able to stop.

"No, that was the warm-up. When my mom came to apologize for being all in my business, I made the mistake of asking her to tell me the story of how she met my dad."

"And that's bad?"

"Horrible. It turns out they didn't meet until late July."

"Which is important because...?"

Saying it out loud was much more difficult than Mel had imagined. She swallowed hard, not sure she could spit out the rest.

"Long story short, my dad can't possibly be my dad."

"Oh, no."

Understatement of the year.

"It's big, right? I can't even... How do I ask my mom if I'm right? How do I tell my sisters? Does my dad even know?"

"That's huge."

"I don't think I slept at all last night. This morning I hinted that I might be getting my period so that my mom would at least give me some space. If she suspected something was really wrong, she'd be all over me."

"Is there anything I can do?"

"This is helping. Let's stay here for a while." Actually, now that he asked, she realized that there was a way to make this afternoon even better. Looking at him from under her lashes, she said, "And maybe a distraction would be good."

He studied her expression for a minute before lifting a hand to tuck her hair behind her ears. "I'm happy to distract you, but I'm also happy to just watch TV. Are you sure you want to go there right now?"

She snuggled in closer and slid one leg in between his.

"Distract me."

CHAPTER THIRTY-ONE

His smile eased the last of the tension in her body, and she couldn't help smiling back. From that point forward, he took his mission very seriously. Step one in the distraction plan was kissing. He refused to be rushed, no matter how tightly she pressed against him. Every time her hand strayed below his shoulder, he moved it right back up again. Stroking her hair back from her face, he got to know her in small tastes before delving deeper. His hand traced the tendon running down the side of her neck, sending shivers all the way to the soles of her feet, but never roamed below her collarbone. Instead, he cupped the nape of her neck, turning her head so that his mouth could explore the line of her chin. She wove her fingers into his hair, leaning into him. His lazy approach had its merits, but if he didn't take it to the next level soon, she would take matters into her own hands.

To her frustration, instead of speeding things up, he slowed them down even more.

"Turn over," he whispered. "Let's watch TV."

Drunk on all the kisses, she blinked at him until he started coaxing her in the right direction. Once she was spooned up against him, she took a breath, about to tell him he was terrible at both distraction and seduction, but before she could say anything, he slid one hand beneath the hem of her T-shirt, stroking her stomach, and at the same moment he began kissing the back of her neck. The dual waves of sensation short-circuited her brain, and all that came out of her mouth was a happy little hum. She snuggled back against him, pleased to feel his arousal, but when she tried to reach back to touch him, Fitz once again moved her hand.

"Relax," he murmured in her ear. "I've got this."

The pure indulgence of the moment made her feel slightly guilty. Operation Seduce Fitz had turned inside out, becoming Operation Surrender to Fitz, and she couldn't say that she had any regrets about it. He raised himself on one elbow to better explore the nape of her neck, all while his free hand massaged the tight muscles at the intersection of her neck and shoulder. Eager for more contact, she peeled off her shirt before he could object, then resumed her earlier position. Her body sang with need.

"Please," she murmured, "continue."

He chuckled and did as she asked, expanding his field of exploration to include her upper back. As his lips traveled a path down her spine, he unhooked her bra to clear the way for his mouth. Face down and half hanging off the couch, there was nothing Mel could do but bask in the heat of his touch. His free hand traced a path from her stomach upward, stopping at the line of her loosened bra and brushing against the under-side of her breasts.

"Don't stop now," she said.

When he didn't cooperate, she clasped his wrist and moved his hand up until it cupped her breast. Sighing with pleasure, she pressed back against him, hoping to make him as crazy as he was making her. From the hitch in his breathing, she was doing something right. She kept up a gentle rhythm, pressing back against him as he explored first one breast and then the other. His mouth had traveled up her back to the place where her neck met her shoulder, kissing and biting and licking until she was frantic for more, but still he kept the pace slow.

"Fitz." Her voice was low and rough and needy.

"Patience," he said, both his voice and his hand soothing.

She didn't want to be soothed, but when she tried to wriggle out of her pants, he wouldn't let her, instead raising her arm above her head and securing it with his other hand. She whimpered in protest, but before she could get too upset with him, he slid his hand inside her waistband. All it took was the firm pressure of his fingers between her legs and she was bucking against him while he tried to hold her on the couch.

A breath, then two, and she realized what had happened. She could feel the throb of his erection against her tailbone, the heat of his fingers between her legs, and an empty ache inside where he needed to be.

Pulling away, she let herself slide onto the floor and then stood, hands on her hips, staring down at his sexy sprawl on the couch. Without saying a word, she stripped off her pants and underwear at the same time. The smug smile on his face was quickly replaced by a hunger that she fully intended to satisfy. Reaching for the hem of his T-shirt, she had his full cooperation as she pulled it up and over his head and threw it aside. His pants quickly followed suit, but he grabbed them from her, found his wallet in the back pocket, and pulled out a condom.

"I like a man who's prepared," she said, taking the condom from him and rolling it on slowly. Then she climbed on top of him and sank down, slowly filling herself with the heat and strength of him. When he was fully seated inside her, she stilled, leaning down to kiss him before the fire took over. He buried his hands in her hair, holding her in the kiss, and began to move beneath her. As they found their rhythm, his hands found their way to her hips, holding her firmly in place as he slammed up and into her over and over again until the fire exploded between them.

Later, when their hearts and breathing had returned to normal, they disentangled themselves and found a new position to cuddle on the couch. Fitz reached down onto the floor and found a few stray items of clothing to use as a blanket. Mel was plenty warm snuggled up between the back of the couch and the heat of Fitz's body. With his back to her, she traced the lines of his tattoo.

"It's beautiful," she said. "Who created the design?"

"I did."

The illustration was gorgeous, a line drawing showing the escape of a man from a two-dimensional box into a three-dimensional world. Much like the Escher drawing of reptiles emerging from a piece of paper, the tattoo on Fitz's back began near the base of his spine with a man pulling himself out of a flat sketch. Additional images rose along the left side of Fitz's back showing the man climbing to the top of a cliff, building himself a pair of wings, and then flying across the globe toward the horizon. Each image was smaller than the last until the final image in the series, the one barely visible in the shadow of Fitz's collar, featured the map and compass more prominently than the man himself.

"It's a response to your father, isn't it?"

He rolled onto his back, hiding the tattoo, but she could see the answer to her question in his face.

"He's never seen it."

"Doesn't matter," answered Mel. "You know it's there."

Mel let her head sink down onto his chest as the next episode of *Friends* began on the TV. This fling with Fitz was turning out to be more complicated than she had expected. She had hoped for a light flirtation, some uncomplicated sex, and a friendly wave goodbye at the end of it. But after working so closely together these past weeks, and discovering the heat between them, she found that she didn't want it to end. Their timing sucked, given that both of them were supposed to leave the country. Of course, both of them were having second thoughts, and he would make a lovely consolation prize, but she wasn't sure she wanted to win him at the cost of both his dreams and her own. At least one of them should get their chance. She continued to ponder their situation, the sounds of the TV a soothing soundtrack, until her eyes drifted shut, her breathing slowed, and she sank into much-needed sleep.

Later, Mel woke with a gasp as the bright white fluorescent lights flickered on. Tangled with Fitz, who had also jolted awake, she pulled back only to slide onto the floor with a thump and a yelp of pain. Alarmingly, they were both naked. Their clothes, which had been piled loosely on top of them as a makeshift blanket, were now scattered on the floor. They must have fallen asleep on the couch after...well, after the very effective distraction that Fitz offered.

Mel had just found her shirt when Mary Evelyn rounded the end of the last bookshelf, a baseball bat in her hands raised to strike. When she caught sight of Mel clutching her shirt to her chest, her lower body hidden by the couch, and Fitz naked on the couch under a few stray items of clothing, she lowered the bat.

"You two nearly gave me a heart attack," she snapped.

"Sorry," they said at the same time.

Mary Evelyn surveyed the scene, lingering a bit too long on Fitz's half-naked form. Yet another episode of *Friends* was playing on the TV. Mel caught sight of her underwear nearby and reached for them in slow motion. She didn't want to make any sudden moves. Mary Evelyn was still holding the bat.

Narrowing her eyes at the two of them, Mary Evelyn said, "I expect you to clean up this area and head home immediately."

"Yes, ma'am," they said in unison.

"I will be up front taking care of some paperwork."

With that, she turned on her heel and disappeared behind the stacks. Mel and Fitz both began scrambling to find their clothes. The ridiculousness of the situation made Mel want to giggle, but the last thing she wanted to do was further piss off Mary Evelyn. But then she caught Fitz's eye and they both lost it, shaking with silent laughter as they yanked on the rest of their clothes.

They dressed in record time and hustled to the front of the library, where Mary Evelyn waited behind the circulation desk. She was not amused.

"We'll pretend this never happened, and let me be clear: it will never happen again."

"Yes, ma'am."

They kept it together until they made it out the front entrance, then lost it again, this time laughing out loud. When they reached the parked cars, they took deep gulps of air until the hysteria wore off.

Fitz leaned against his car and said, "Still want to grab dinner?"

"Oh, definitely."

They decided to keep it simple and headed down to the Beach for a burger. As Mel drove her car the few short blocks down the hill, she did a little happy dance in the driver's seat. Flinging with Fitz was going to be every bit as much fun as she had hoped it would be. And, as a bonus, she had finally gotten a good look at Fitz's tattoo. After a rocky start, today had turned out to be a great day.

CHAPTER THIRTY-TWO

Monday morning, Dora and Luke were finishing up their breakfast when Tessa came into the kitchen from the mudroom. She might be sleeping over at RJ's every night, but there was better breakfast to be found back at home.

"What's up with Mel?" she asked.

"She just left," answered Dora.

"I know. I was walking into the backyard when she was driving out. She waved at me. Didn't even stop to say hi."

Dora had hardly seen Mel since Saturday night and she was concerned that, despite her apology and their subsequent conversation on the porch, something was still wrong. Mel had mumbled something about PMS on Sunday morning, but it felt like a cover story.

"We're not exactly sure what's going on there," said Dora.

"She looks awful."

"I know," said Dora, "but she won't tell us what's going on."

Tessa poured herself a cup of coffee and joined her parents at the table.

"When did it start?" she asked.

Dora made a face. "She hasn't really been herself since Saturday night."

"I thought you two had a good talk after dinner."

"We did! We had a really nice conversation, although, now that I think about it, I never did ask her about her plans for the future. She wanted to hear the old story of how your father and I met, so I told her. She was quiet afterward, but I didn't think she was angry."

"Huh," said Tessa. "I'll bring her lunch at the library and find out what's going on." She shrugged. "Anyway, I wanted to bring back your sweater from the other day, and to ask a question about the sailing school."

They talked about the sailing school for a few minutes, in particular the timeline for winter closure, and then Tessa had to run. After she left, Dora leaned against the counter, battling a sense of growing unease. The plans that had made so much sense all those years ago were hurting her family—Mel in particular—but there was no going back now.

"What are you thinking?" asked Luke.

The last thing she wanted to do was make him feel guilty for living his life, so she kept her answer vague. "Mom thoughts."

"I have no idea what that means."

Unfortunately, Luke knew her too well and he wouldn't be satisfied until he got to the bottom of her worries.

"I'm wondering what's wrong with Mel, and why she won't talk to me about it. I'm her mother. I want to know that my kids are okay, and that I'm supporting them—not screwing them up. I feel like I've been doing things all wrong with Mel, and now she hates me, and she hates that I'm maybe possibly dating someone, and I don't want to break the family."

"Oh, that's all," said Luke. "Little stuff."

Dora shrugged. There would be no crying this morning. There had been too much of that lately.

"You're a good mom," said Luke, "and Mel is going to be fine. A lot is changing and change is hard. It's supposed to be hard. But you don't need to make it any worse by imagining all sorts of things and blaming yourself for how Mel is feeling. If you want to know what's bothering her, you need to ask. If you want to know her hopes and dreams, ask. She knows you love her. You can't be that far off track."

"I hope you're right," said Dora, chewing on the corner of her lip.

"I'm always right."

She snorted at that. "So not true."

"When have I ever been wrong?" he asked, gathering their dishes from the table and carrying them over to the sink.

"What, I'm supposed to keep a log? It would be a novel. An encyclopedia. A—"

Luke got right in her face and said, "I think you're right."

His words were so unexpected that she needed to hear them again.

"Did you just say..."

"Yes."

"Can I get my phone and record that for posterity?"

"No."

She tried to pout, but a grin broke through. "So what am I right about?"

"You've been Mel's mom for more than twenty-seven years. I think you need to follow your instincts. If you think she needs a nudge, then nudge her. If you think something's wrong, help her. You're a good mom, and whatever you feel is the right choice, that's the way to go."

She pulled him into a hug and squeezed.

"I think that's the sweetest thing you've ever said to me."

28 years ago, August

Dora had decided to paint Luke. He was spending a lot of time at her apartment anyway. Might as well earn his keep by modeling for her. August was shaping up to be painfully hot, and he would agree to just about anything if it meant he could spend more time in her air conditioning. This was fine with Dora, because the more time they spent together, the more she liked him.

Splitting her attention between the canvas and her subject, Dora added a few brush strokes to the line of Luke's arm. One thing she had to give him credit for: he had no shame. He hadn't even blinked when she'd told him to take his clothes off.

Barrett's visit weighed on her mind, but she hesitated to tell Luke, even though he knew all the sordid details of the dysfunctional relationship. It would be so much easier if that part of her life simply faded away. It wouldn't, though, and as her fake boyfriend, he deserved to know.

"Barrett came to see me."

"What?" Luke had been staring out the window, but at her remark he whipped his head around to look at her.

"Pose," she said sternly.

Luke grimaced but looked back out the window. "When did this happen?"

"Yesterday," she answered. "Last night."

"Please tell me you didn't sleep with him."

She shook her head, suppressing a smile. He knew her too well. "I probably would have, if he had gotten me alone, so I arranged to meet him in the hotel bar."

"That was smart."

Grinning, she sat back to study the painting so far and decide what else it needed. "I know."

"How did it go?"

"He believed every bit of it, and he told me I couldn't get married. I told him to fuck off. Well, not in those words, exactly, but that was the gist of it."

"Cold."

"That's what he said," she said with a laugh. "I can't believe I did it. The man still invades my sexy dreams, but in real life, I've managed to cut ties."

"How does it feel?"

"It feels amazing."

Picking up a darker hue from her palette, Dora leaned forward to adjust the shadows on Luke's abs, but stopped herself before the brush touched the canvas. No more. If she fussed with Luke's body anymore, she would ruin it. Time to fill in the background and call it done.

"I have news, too," he said, keeping his eyes on the window like a good model.

"What?"

"I got the job."

This time, when he turned his head to look at her, she didn't yell at him. The news was too good.

"What!?! The one in Wisconsin?"

"That's the one."

"Are you going to take it? You should definitely take it."

"I already told them yes."

She jumped up to hug him but stopped herself just in time.

"Wait. Pose. One more second...."

She needed to capture the wrinkles in the sheets before she let him move. Sticking his tongue out at her, he moved back into position.

"I'm so proud of you," she said as she brushed in the lines of the sheets. "One more minute and I'll give you a huge hug."

He was quiet as she rushed to capture the final critical details, but it was taking more than a minute.

"So I've been thinking," he said. "We should do it."

"Do what?"

"Get married. For real. Not as a cover story for your breakup with Barrett."

She froze mid-stroke and stared at him. "You're serious."

"You're going to need help with the baby," he said. "I know you have money and could hire someone to help, but what fun would that be?" He put up a hand to stop her objection before it could spill out of her mouth. "Hear me out."

Scowling, she put down her brush. There was no way she could concentrate on painting now. "I'm listening. I think you're crazy, but I'm listening."

"You need a barrier between you and Barrett. I need the illusion of a normal life. We could help each other."

"Luke..."

"Let's be real here. I'm moving to a tiny town in Wisconsin. The gay social scene will be nonexistent. And honestly? I don't know how to be a part of it anymore. I'm done with the party scene. I'm ready to get married and raise a family, and if I can't do that with Zeke, then why not do it with you?"

"But what if you meet someone you want to date?" Setting aside her brush and palette, Dora walked over to sit next to Luke on her bed. She didn't care if he was naked.

"In small-town Wisconsin?" His tone couldn't have been more skeptical.

"Yes," she insisted. "It could happen."

"Well, then I'd be married to you, and I wouldn't date them."

"And what if I meet someone?" she challenged, since he didn't seem to care about his own future happiness.

"Same goes."

She stewed over that for a minute before shaking her head. "I'm not sure I'm ready to give up on love. Not forever, anyway."

"How about for eighteen years?"

She cocked her head, not needing to voice the question.

"Well, eighteen and a half. Let's make a deal to raise the baby to adulthood. After that, if we decide we want to go off and fall in love and have adventures on our own, then that's what we'll do."

"You make it sound so reasonable."

"I know," he said, grinning. "I am a very reasonable person."

She was tempted, but she couldn't share his blind optimism. "I need to think about this."

"You do that," he said. Swinging his legs off the bed, he started to pull his pants on. "In the meantime, I'm going to start making some calls and looking for places to rent in Wisconsin. I need to be up there in three weeks."

Dora sat there, blinking. They couldn't possibly do this. Could they?

CHAPTER THIRTY-THREE

Today

MEL AND FITZ WERE ABOUT TO BREAK FOR LUNCH WHEN TESSA'S car pulled into a parking space. When both Tessa and Callie got out, Mel realized she was about to be kidnapped.

"I'm going to need a long lunch," she said to Fitz.

In the middle of rinsing out brushes, he looked up curiously, then caught sight of her sisters approaching.

"Got it. Take your time."

She grimaced. "Want me to bring you back a sandwich?"

"No worries. Rob said he was going to swing by to drop off a few things. He's bringing food."

"See you later—assuming I survive this conversation."

He pulled her into his arms. "Good luck."

Mel didn't know if the kiss was for her benefit or to distract her sisters. She didn't care. In fact, she kind of forgot about them while her toes were curling in her shoes.

"A little distraction, in case you need it," he murmured, their lips only a breath apart.

"Thanks. I think." She gave him one last kiss before pulling away and tromping over toward her sisters.

"So, ladies," said Mel, "what brings you to my place of business today?"

Tessa said the dreaded words: "We need to talk."

"Of course we do. Can we at least eat at the same time?"

"Let's walk over to Lucy's," suggested Callie.

Her sisters stayed mercifully silent on the short walk. It was a Monday, and on the early side for lunch, so they had their pick of tables. Mel headed for a booth on the back wall, which might give them some privacy.

Lucy swung by almost immediately to take their order.

"It's so good to see the three of you together," she said with a smile. "Mel, honey, I hear the real estate shopping went well."

The safest response was a smile and a nod. Her life was such a disaster.

"What can I get you all for lunch today?"

After they rattled off their orders, Lucy said, "You girls better get to work on some grandbabies for Dora. She needs something to keep her busy."

"We'll get right on that," said Callie.

"Well, not you, dear. You're busy. But Tessa, you and that handsome RJ would make adorable babies."

"We'll start tonight." Tessa even managed to say it with a straight face.

"You do that, missy," said Lucy with a delighted laugh. "Practice makes perfect, as they say, and if I got my hands on that RJ, I'd practice all the time."

"And what would your husband say about that plan?" asked Tessa.

"We each have our lists, honey. Hall pass." With that, she swept back toward the kitchen, leaving Mel and her sisters speechless.

Shaking her head, presumably to get rid of the mental image of Lucy with RJ, Tessa said, "So, let's talk."

Mel smiled and tried playing innocent. "About what?"

Her sisters weren't buying it.

"Something's wrong. You've been acting strange and I'd like to know why."

"Actually," said Callie, "before we go down that rabbit hole, let's talk about that kiss Fitz laid on you at the library."

Thank you, Fitz.

"Kiss?"

"Right out there for everyone to see." Leaning forward, Callie asked, "Anything you want to share with us on that front? Did you finally see the tattoo?"

Mel didn't hide her smile. "I may have seen it."

"Does he have tattoos anywhere else?" asked Tessa.

"I don't believe so, although I may have been distracted."

"Hah!" crowed Callie. "I knew it. Although, where in the world did you go? You're both staying with your parents. Did you rent a room somewhere?"

Mel shook her head, wondering if they would guess.

"The summerhouse. Classic." Callie sounded very sure.

"Nope," said Mel. "Way too cold."

"Then where?" Callie was stumped.

"I'll never tell."

So far, so good. Mel wondered how long she could delay the inevitable. The speedy arrival of their food gave her another minute, but then her time was up. Tessa didn't let her eat more than a few bites before she asked, "Are you still pissed at Mom for trying to take over your life?"

Mel chewed slowly, trying to think of what to say, where to even begin.

"That's the least of my worries," she said. "Do you remember the other night when Mom came out on the porch to talk with me?"

Both her sisters nodded.

"I asked her to tell me the story of how she and Dad met. It always made me feel good."

"We've heard it a thousand times," said Callie. "It's a sweet story. I love hearing it."

"But we haven't heard it lately—not since Dad came out," said Mel.

"Good point," said Tessa. She leaned forward on her elbows, food forgotten. "Did the story change at all, now that we know more about Dad?"

"Not exactly," said Mel. "More like I heard it differently."

"How so?"

"The story starts on a hot night in late July. Remember how Mom always says she wasn't feeling well and she almost threw up on Dad's shoes?"

"Right," said Callie. "He held her hair while she puked in the bathroom. If that's not true love, what is?"

"I always imagined it as a passionate love story," said Mel, "but if Dad's gay, that seems unlikely."

"Still," Callie began. "I don't see how—"

"There's another thing," Mel interrupted. "You remember how Sunny's second baby was born on St. Patrick's Day?"

"How could we forget?" said Tessa. "She shared every single detail about the labor and delivery. But what does that have to do with Mom?"

"She also shared the story of how the baby was conceived on the previous Father's Day. *In June.*"

Mel emphasized the last two words and gave her sisters a meaningful look. They didn't seem to follow her logic.

"Our birthday is a few days later," she said, her frustration growing. Did she need to spell it out?

Her sisters nodded.

"And Mom always bragged about carrying triplets to term."

They nodded again, but more slowly this time.

"So if Sunny's baby was full term and he was conceived in June, how could we be full term if Mom and Dad didn't even start dating until the end of July?"

As understanding sank in, Mel watched her own reaction play out on the faces of her sisters, the shock and denial almost as painful the second time around as the first.

"Stop it," said Callie, her voice shaky. "You're freaking out about nothing. So what if the timeline is tight? Maybe Sunny was a little late, and maybe Mom didn't quite make it to term. There's still no reason to create some kind of conspiracy about the whole thing."

Of the three of them, Callie was closest with their father, and the one who would hurt the most if their parents had lied to them all their lives.

"We should give them the benefit of the doubt," said Tessa slowly, "but we have to ask."

"No we don't," said Callie. "Can you imagine how hurt they'll be?"

Tessa picked up a chip and ate it before answering.

"If we've learned anything this summer, it's that Mom and Dad have kept a lot of secrets. Most are their secrets to keep, but this one affects us directly. We can find a loving, respectful way to ask them, but we need to ask."

"You ask, then," said Callie. "I want nothing to do with it."

Feeling sick, Mel knew she had to do something. Say something. This question had the power to blow up their family, and that was the last thing she wanted.

"I'm so sorry," she said. "This is exactly what I didn't want to happen, and why I didn't come to you right away. Talking about it makes it feel real, and I hate that. I can't tell you how much I hope I'm wrong."

"I know you're wrong." Callie's voice wasn't shaky anymore. It was sharp and strong.

Mel squeezed her hand and didn't contradict her.

"I'm the one who opened this box, so I'll ask Mom about it," said Mel.

"Are you sure?" asked Tessa. "Maybe we should ask her together."

Mel shook her head.

"Nope. This one's on me."

CHAPTER THIRTY-FOUR

28 years ago, August

DORA WAS STILL PONDERING LUKE'S CRAZY PROPOSAL WHEN SHE agreed to accompany him on his house-hunting trip up to Wisconsin. He needed a wingman and she needed to get out of the city. Chicago in August rivaled New York City, the humidity making them equally unpleasant. She could use the time to decide if Luke's plan was brilliant or plain crazy.

The second time around, Dora found the transition from city to suburbs to farmland even more fascinating. Her stress level notched downward as the miles passed, and by the time they arrived in Hidden Springs, she felt like she was coming home.

The real estate office was easy to find, down the block from the little diner where they had eaten lunch on their last visit. Within two hours, they had seen the best of the local rental properties, and both Dora and Luke were feeling discouraged. They had hoped for a cute little cottage, or maybe a creaky old Victorian, but instead they had seen two mid-century ranches, both in a sad state of disrepair, and one depressing beige apartment in a new and architecturally painful building. None of the rentals were anywhere near that gorgeous lake.

They promised the real estate agent that they would be right back and ducked into the diner for some lunch. The girl with spiky purple hair remembered them. Her name was Lucy. Dora ordered the grilled cheese again because, weirdly, the cheese really did taste better in Wisconsin. The food helped to renew their optimism, and they returned to the real estate office determined to find something workable.

"Well," said the agent, "to get the kind of place you're looking for, we could widen the search area to include the surrounding towns. There aren't that many rentals in Hidden Springs. Have you thought about buying? If you could pull together a down payment, we have a number of local listings that would be perfect for a young family."

"Let's widen the search area," said Luke. "How far away would we have to look?"

While they discussed options, Dora wandered over to browse the bulletin board with photos of adorable little houses for sale. She really shouldn't meddle in Luke's decision about his housing. She couldn't imagine living out here in the sticks, lake or not, and he didn't even know if the job was going to work out. It wasn't logical to daydream about a perfect house right on the lake with a dock and storage and more than enough room for the two of them and a baby.

Oh my God, it was perfect.

Not that she had agreed to this plan, and not that she was serious about buying a house in rural Wisconsin, but the listing in front of her on the bulletin board might as well have been written to lure Dora into this life. The old, sturdy house overlooked the lake, with a flagstone path leading down toward the water. It came with its own dock and a small boat storage building right on the shore. An enclosed porch of some kind sat on top of the storage building, so that you could spend time down by the water but sheltered from the sun.

She glanced over at Luke, who was still deep in conversation with the agent.

"What about this one?" Dora's voice, unexpectedly loud in the small office, cut right through the middle of their conversation.

Sensing the possibility of a much larger commission, the agent jumped up and hurried over.

"That's a beautiful property," she said. "It's also vacant, so if you'd like to see it, I could take you right over. No need to make an appointment."

Dora smiled. "That would be wonderful."

"Let me find the keys," said the agent as she headed toward the back room.

Luke took one look at the price tag and pulled Dora away from the bulletin board.

"What are you doing?" he whispered. "There is no way we could possibly afford that."

She whispered back, "We could if we made a big down payment."

He burst out laughing. "Right," he said, struggling to keep his voice low. "Of course. Why didn't I think of that? Oh, right, because it's not even in the realm of possibility."

With a glance at the agent, who had returned with a set of keys, Dora kept a smile on her face and said softly, "I may not have told you everything about my financial situation."

That shut him up.

"Shall we?" asked the agent.

"Let's go," said Dora, taking Luke by the arm and leading him outside. "We'll follow you."

On the short drive to the house, Luke started to freak out.

"What the hell is going on, Dora? You can't possibly have a few hundred thousand dollars in the bank, ready to plunk down on a lake house. Why are we wasting this agent's time?"

Dora didn't answer right away, despite the fact that Luke gave her a death stare every thirty seconds or so. Thank goodness he had to keep his eyes on the road.

"You're right," she said at last. "I don't have a few hundred thousand dollars in the bank. I have a few million dollars in an investment portfolio."

A look of appalled horror replaced the death stare.

"Watch the road, please."

Silence filled the car.

"Luke?"

"You can't just...buy a house."

"Why not?"

"That's—" he sputtered. "That's not how it works."

She couldn't help laughing. "It is if you're sitting on a few million dollars."

"A house is something you earn, not something you buy."

She cocked her head to one side, wondering where that came from. "Your parents wouldn't approve?"

His jaw tightened, but he didn't say anything.

"I thought you didn't speak to your parents."

"They don't speak to me."

Dora could see the tension in the set of Luke's shoulders. If they were really going to raise this baby together, they would have to work through their baggage because she certainly didn't want to dump it on the baby. He would also need to make peace with the fact that she was sitting on a giant pot of money. She needed to find a way to make him understand that it wasn't the money that mattered.

Luke followed the agent when she turned down a long, winding driveway. The glimmer of water through the trees suggested they were getting close, so Dora chose her words carefully.

"I believe that we can make a home for this baby no matter where we live."

"I agree, but—"

"It doesn't matter if we live in an apartment in the city or a row house in the suburbs or even a house on a lake. Wherever we live, we'll make it our home."

They pulled up behind the house and parked beside the agent. It wasn't quite as charming from the back, but Dora had high hopes. Luke put the car in park and leaned his head back on the headrest.

"It's too much, Dora. I can't wrap my head around it."

"Please. Let's take a look."

He sighed. "Fine, but don't you dare fall in love with it."

Today

When Mel returned from lunch with her sisters, Fitz was back at work painting and Rob, along with a couple of helping hands, was busy planting things near the base of the scaffolding. Mel wasn't in the mood to chat, not even to tease Rob about his new relationship with her friend Kat. She dove back into work with a vengeance and didn't really surface until she and Fitz were cleaning their brushes at the end of the day. Rob and his crew were long gone.

"So," said Fitz, "did you tell your sisters?"

She nodded. "I volunteered to be the one to ask my mom about it. No need to freak out my dad if there's a rational explanation for everything."

"At least you'll know."

"That should be better, right? The not-knowing sucks."

He quirked a smile. "Maybe you should tell the family about your plans tonight, too. Get it all out at once."

"Can you imagine?" she said on a laugh. "The ultimate one-two punch. 'Hey, Mom and Dad, let's wrestle with this huge identity crisis, and then when everyone is emotionally exhausted, I'll tell you I'm abandoning you.' I don't think so." She shook the water out of her brushes with more force than strictly necessary.

"The clock hasn't stopped ticking, Mel."

"Yeah, well, maybe I'll have to stop it," she said grimly.

"Meaning?"

Laying out the brushes to dry, she put her hands on her hips. "It's becoming clear to me that this is not the time to go halfway around the world. I mean, how many ways can the universe clobber me over the head before I finally listen? Dad and Callie are going to be in Nashville. Tessa and RJ are off to California. Mom is going to need some kind of support, and she's not going to get it from this random guy she just met who's going to go back home to Peru or Ecuador or wherever. She needs someone *here*, and as usual I'm the only one available. I'm not going to leave her all alone." Mel shoved the lid back on a can of paint. "Besides, we're going to have some serious baggage to work through. Can't do that from the southern hemisphere."

It didn't matter that she could feel her soul tearing in half. Some things were important enough to sweep aside the most carefully laid plans. Her family counted among those things. If she had to delay her plans for a few years in order to rebuild her family, then that's what she would do. And if she had to lease a photo studio and photograph an endless string of weddings, then that's what she would do. As she ruminated on the implications of staying, she realized that Fitz hadn't responded. He'd been patiently tapping the lids back onto the paint cans.

"You're awfully quiet over there."

"I guess I'm surprised," he said, rising to face her.

"Why? You're wrestling with the same bullshit."

"I know. I was just trying to figure out when it ends."

She crossed her arms, unable to help feeling defensive. "It's not a good time. In a couple of years I can try again."

"And then what?" he asked. "One of your sisters will be getting married, or having a baby, and once again it won't be a good time? You realize it's never going to be a good time, right?"

"It will."

"Why are you here, Mel?"

"What the hell?" she cried, throwing her arms out wide. "I'm here to help you get this stupid mural done, thank you very much."

"No," he said, his voice intense, "you're here because you don't know how to say no to your family."

"Sounds like the pot calling the kettle black to me," she snapped.

"Maybe so, but that doesn't make it any less true."

"So you've told your family?"

If he was going to point out her failings, she might as well return the favor.

"No. I told you already, I'm waiting until there's something to tell."

"I bet you don't take it," she said.

"What?"

"Even if you get an international assignment, I bet you don't take it. I bet you crumple just like me and switch to the local track."

"You can't know what I'd do."

"Oh, please. It's not hard to guess. Do you think this is your mom's dream for you, to be her puppy?"

"It's not like that."

"Whatever," she said. "I'm out."

He could finish cleaning up by himself.

Regret was not a comfortable feeling. Fitz watched Mel drive away and faced the fact that he might have destroyed their growing friendship. He had goaded Mel into a fight when every single one of his questions should have been directed back at himself. He was the one who didn't know how to say no to his family. He was the one fighting the right course of action because he didn't want to admit his father was right. Not exactly a paragon of maturity here.

With a groan, he picked up two of the paint cans and carried them over to the storage shed. If he was very lucky, Mel would show up tomorrow morning and he could apologize. If he was not so lucky, he would seek her out. One way or another, he would deliver the apology.

CHAPTER THIRTY-FIVE

DORA LIT SOME CANDLES IN HER STUDIO TO OFFSET THE GLOOMY day. There would be no more summerlike days. October had well and truly arrived. Mel and Fitz were racing to finish the mural before daytime temperatures dropped below fifty. Luke was off chasing an antique banjo in northern Wisconsin that he had found on Craigslist. Tessa would be with clients all day, and Callie had a special outing planned with Adam. Dora had the house to herself—no interruptions—and she had invited David to join her.

Never before had this house hosted a romantic interlude. Lots of family fun, lots of giggling girls, but never romance. She and Luke had been friends, first and always, and any physical comfort they found with each other had been about connection and comfort, not passion.

As the clock ticked toward David's arrival, Dora's stomach churned with nerves. She had mixed feelings about the coming changes to her life—and about David—but she was determined to push through. Once upon a time, she had been brave, confident in her body and her sexuality. That was a long time ago, and she had changed. Her body had changed. Nothing like pregnancy followed by years without regular exercise to reshape a person. Dwelling on the changes, though, would only make her more nervous, so instead she tried to reconnect with her younger, sexier self and ignore the voice of wisdom and maturity that nagged in the back of her mind.

Spotting a car coming down the drive, Dora hustled down two flights of stairs to meet David at the door.

"Welcome back," she said, battling sudden shyness and gesturing for him to come inside.

It was so odd, to be without the illusory bubble of protection that marriage provided, as if a wedding band on her finger was a magical talisman, warding off flirtation, or at least rendering it inert. She felt exposed and vulnerable. A vague memory surfaced. She used to feel this way all the time, in the time before Luke.

David came into the kitchen and Dora moved to take his jacket. She was fussing but couldn't seem to stop herself. She used the excuse of sliding the jacket off his shoulders to touch him briefly. The jacket held his heat and his scent, soap with a hint of cologne. While Luke's scent had become invisible to her over the years, David's caught and held her attention.

She hung up the jacket and took a deep breath of air that didn't smell like David. Leaning against the counter, she took a moment to appreciate the view. He had stuck with business casual today: slacks, a white button-down shirt, and a sport coat. She wondered if he was more relaxed at home with family.

This afternoon could play out in many different ways, some boring, some interesting, and some just plain terrifying. He might leave after she agreed to work with him, all of his flirting simply part of the sales process. He might stay, but choose to keep things professional, and she wouldn't blame him for choosing that path. Or they might pick up where they left off after sailing, and who knew where that might lead? A shiver walked down her spine. This afternoon might see one or both of them naked, and damn it, she was going to be ready.

"I'd like to work with you," she blurted out.

Great job, there, Dora. Very businesslike.

He smiled slowly, the kind of smile that warmed up her insides.

"I'm glad to hear that."

"Do you want me to sign something?"

"There's no rush."

"Okay."

He moved closer to where she leaned against the counter and placed his hands on her hips.

"May I greet you properly?" he asked.

She nodded as her brain started to pop and fizz.

He leaned in and their lips touched, gently at first. Her fingers smoothed up the front of his shirt inside his sport coat, then moved up into his hair as he deepened the kiss. When he pulled her against his hard body, her whole body started to burn. She hadn't felt a physical response this intense since before the girls were born, and she wanted more.

But he pulled away and rested his forehead on hers. They were both breathing heavily. She tried to pull him close again, clearheadedness holding no appeal, but he stopped her.

"A moment, *querida.*"

"Okay," she breathed.

He smoothed the hair back from her forehead and tucked a lock behind her ear.

"I promised myself that I would not move so quickly."

"And I promised myself that I would," she said, feeling bold. "We have the house to ourselves all afternoon. I don't want to waste a second."

"I fear that would be a mistake."

She pulled away to get a better look at his face, and saw only frustration and heat and regret.

"How can you call this a mistake?"

"You are still mourning the end of your marriage."

His words took her by surprise and she found she was mildly insulted. "I am a grown woman, perfectly capable of deciding if and when I'm ready to connect with someone new. I'm ready. End of discussion."

"I would not lose you because we moved too fast."

Her eyes narrowed. "You risk losing me by moving too slowly." Feeling her temper rise, she pulled completely out of his arms and put some space between them.

"But your husband—"

She stopped on the far side of the kitchen island and planted her hands on the counter.

"My soon-to-be ex-husband is a wonderful man and a good friend, but we didn't marry for love, and our hearts are not broken by the end of the marriage. Change will be difficult, but there is nothing to mourn, only a family to celebrate."

"I will not be a temporary balm to ease your pain."

Now he sounded insulted, and she found that a bit rich.

"We hardly know each other. It seems a bit early to be talking about anything permanent."

Hah. Counter that, Mr. Sexy-pants.

"This is exactly why we should move slowly."

Dora was having none of it.

"I've waited almost thirty years to find chemistry like this. I see no reason to wait any longer."

Beneath the anger, she was horrified to feel the prick of tears at the back of her eyes. Damned if she would cry about missing out on hot sex after so many years of "Luke-warm" comfort. Ugh. It was a terrible joke, even in the privacy of her own mind, but Luke would love it, and that thought made her half laugh, half hiccup. At this point, David probably thought she was crazy.

"When I touch you I find it very difficult to stop."

She couldn't help smiling at his words, even though she was still angry at him. He was trying really hard to do the right thing, and she couldn't fault him for that, no matter how impatient she might be.

"I have the same problem," she replied.

"I am not a man who seeks casual comfort in the arms of a stranger."

Her shyness had disappeared with the kiss, and any remaining nerves had burned away in the heat of temper, leaving her strangely calm, even confident. David was trying to do the right thing, struggling—as she was—to navigate the possibilities between them. She had expected him to take the lead, but perhaps she needed to be the one.

"I have a proposal." She moved slowly around the counter toward him.

"I'm listening," he said, his voice cautious.

"We may not know each other well, but we're hardly strangers."

"True."

"I propose that we get to know each other while also touching one another."

She had reached him at this point and wound her arms around his neck. Her brain didn't function all that well when she was this close to him, but this didn't need to be complicated.

"My name is Dora, but it's actually short for Eudora. I'm named after my grandmother."

After what seemed like forever, he slid his hands around her waist. "I have two children. Sebastian is twenty-five and runs the family gallery in Quito. Carolina is a senior at the University of California at Santa Barbara."

She leaned closer and began to kiss her way up his neck toward his ear.

"My favorite color is blue," she murmured, "because it comes in so many different hues."

He tilted his head to give her better access.

"I read mystery novels," he said, his voice gruff, "but not thrillers."

When her lips reached his ear, she whispered, "Do you like my approach?"

He turned his head to tug on her earlobe with his teeth before replying.

"I can see the merits of your idea."

"Follow me," she said, slipping from his arms and taking him by the hand. "I'd like to show you some of my works in progress."

CHAPTER THIRTY-SIX

28 years ago, August

Dear Lauren,

Well, it's official. I'm getting married! Luke found a job as a music teacher in Wisconsin. It's a small town on a lake, which means there will be sailing. It probably seems quaint and quiet to you, this new direction my dreams have taken, but it suits me in a way that New York City never did. I'll send you our new address once we're settled. Please give my love to the children, and share the news with Barrett. I know he would prefer to have everything back the way it was, but this will be better for all of us in the end.

With love,
Dora

SEEING THE WORDS ON PAPER MADE THE PLAN SUDDENLY SEEM very real. So much had changed in only a few weeks. She had quit her job. She had deferred her second year of school. She was getting married. Luke's logic won her over. He seemed so certain that he wouldn't have regrets, and she didn't want to do this alone.

The parts and pieces of their lives fit together like a jigsaw puzzle. She liked the idea of living on a lake. He found the prospect of fatherhood appealing. She didn't want to get sucked into a toxic relationship again. He didn't plan on falling in love anytime soon. They could be friends who got married and had a baby, and nobody needed to know their marriage wasn't real. For all intents and purposes, it would be. They might even have sex sometimes, just for fun. She was open to it, and he could be flexible. And so the plot was hatched and the decision made. They would build a life together.

Dora had already shared most of her story with Luke—her less-than-ideal childhood, her complicated relationship with Barrett, and the role she had played in his family. It seemed only fair that, if she and Luke were going to join forces, he should know about the skeletons in her closet. What if one of those skeletons came knocking one day? He knew she had money; she revealed that it hadn't been an inheritance but a parting gift from Lauren.

They were quite the pair, damaged but determined, and she thought they had a fair to middling chance of making it work as long as neither of them met someone else. They talked about that possibility, promised to be honest if anything came up, and to set each other free when the time came. At some point, their child would be grown and flown, and they might want to look for love again. Maybe. It was all hypothetical and a long time away. For now, Dora was grateful to have a partner as she grew a tiny human inside of herself.

A part of her would always wonder, what if she had chosen to stay? Her heart remembered the joy of being part of a family for the first time. (The people who raised her could be called by many names, but family wasn't one of them.) Her body remembered the overwhelming chemistry with Barrett. He and Lauren had given her everything she had dared to hope for, and in doing so, they had taught her to hope for more. Luke was wonderful, and together, they would build a happy life. What they lacked in passion they would make up for in friendship and commitment, much as Lauren and Barrett had. As odd as their marriage might be, they valued and protected it. Barrett would understand that she needed to do the same. He would finally stop pursuing her, and he wouldn't question their rush to start a family. After all, he knew how much she loved babies.

The baby she carried now was Barrett's, and if she were truly a good person, she would tell him. However, it seemed she wasn't a very good person. Given her track record of questionable decisions, this didn't exactly come as a surprise. While she didn't like the feeling that she was living a soap opera-style plot line, she could see no upside to sharing this news with him. Her baby would be born within a stable marriage and would want for nothing. Nothing bad would come of keeping this secret.

Sharing the secret, however, carried more risk. Barrett might demand access to the child. He could use that as leverage to force her return to New York, and to the half life she had left behind. With a child connecting them, she would never escape his influence, forever trapped in the toxic chemistry of their relationship.

It was this fear, more than any other consideration, that drove her decision. Luke didn't seem to mind keeping the secret. Barrett had no reason to suspect, as the doctor had speculated, that antibiotics had interfered with her birth control pills. Deceptions like this went on all the time with no one the wiser.

It was decided, then. Dora would keep the secret, and the baby, and build a life with Luke.

Today

Dora started to lose her nerve as she led the way up the creaky stairs to her attic studio. The candles did a nice job of setting the scene, but she hadn't thought through the practical aspects of seduction. Where exactly were they supposed to sit? Neither the stool nor the armchair were particularly good candidates. It would have to be the chaise longue, currently buried under a pile of blank canvases, sketches, and a box of supplies.

She had dragged him up here under the pretense of showing off her work, so she started there. Ignoring the candles, which suggested an ulterior motive, she made it a point to show him a few finished canvases stacked against the far wall. His fascination with her work was both flattering and convenient, as it bought her some time to clear off the chaise.

If only there were somewhere else she could take him, but memories clogged the rest of the house. Realistically, where could they go? The living room, where she would be surrounded by memories of Christmas mornings and family movie nights? The bedroom that she still shared with Luke? One of the girls' rooms? Definitely not. The porch might work, if it were warmer, but it didn't offer much privacy. Really, the only option would be the kitchen or the dining room, and she just couldn't see it working. The kitchen would require an adventurous approach to seduction, one requiring more athleticism than she currently possessed, and the dining room wasn't all that comfortable either. She wasn't twenty-two anymore. She needed low lighting, cushioned surfaces, and preferably no family photos observing the proceedings.

When the chaise was clear, she sat down and tried to arrange herself in a seductive pose, but gave up after about ten seconds. She leaned against the angled side of the chaise and waited for David to finish pondering her finished canvases. He finally set aside the last one and walked over to sit beside her.

"Your work is beautiful, as always," he said, "but I find I cannot give it the attention it deserves."

She wasn't the only one who was nervous, and the realization did more to alleviate her anxiety than anything he could have said or done. Confidence restored, she sank back onto the chaise and draped her legs across his lap.

"Let's play a game."

"What are the rules of this game?" he asked, his eyes intrigued but also wary.

"We'll trade buttons for questions," said Dora. "If I want to ask you a question, I must undo a button on my shirt, and vice versa."

"You know that buttons are not necessary," he said. "I would gladly answer your questions."

"Now what would be the fun in that?" she asked with what she hoped was a seductive smile. It appeared to be working. His expression had shifted from intrigued to intent.

"I'll go first," she said. His eyes followed her fingers as she released the first button on her blouse. "When did you know you would join the family business?"

As he answered, he reached over to caress the tiny triangle of newly revealed skin, sending shivers skittering down her body.

"When I realized that I was not destined to be an artist myself," he answered. His fingers continued their exploration, which made formulating an answer difficult.

"May I see your early work?"

"Definitely not," he said, "and that was another question." He helpfully undid another button. "When did you decide that you would be an artist?"

Returning the favor, she undid his top button, letting her fingers linger on the hollow of his throat. "When I was a teenager. I had always loved art, but I came to realize that I had talent, and that's when the dream of going to art school was born."

She released another button on his shirt, tracing the patch

of skin now visible. He hadn't asked another question, but didn't seem to mind.

"Tell me again the names of your children," she asked.

Sliding another button free, he answered, "Sebastian and Carolina."

Dora was finding it difficult to breathe.

"If you did not marry for love, why did you marry?" he asked.

She fumbled with his next button as she answered. "I was pregnant, and the father was not willing to marry me. Luke and I were friends, and we realized that we could build a good life together."

"He did not wish to marry for love?"

The next button sprang free, and she slipped a hand inside his shirt. The rough texture of the hair on his chest made her palm burn, a fire that was reflected in his eyes as he leaned closer, resting his forearm above her head on the edge of the chaise. She was losing track of questions and buttons, not that it mattered, and she moved on to the next button.

"Did you marry for love?"

"I did," he answered. "We had a strong marriage."

The next button revealed her bra strap, where the cups met in the middle. Brushing his fingers along her skin, he slowly traced her collarbones and across the hollow of her throat, then down and up the deep vee of her bra, only to repeat the caress again. She could feel it all the way to the soles of her feet.

"You did not answer my question," he said. Not surprising, as she couldn't think clearly. "Did your husband not wish to marry for love?"

David needed to understand this aspect of her relationship with Luke, and she didn't think Luke would mind her sharing a part of his story. "His love was lost to him, and he didn't want to fall in love with anyone else. He would not have been able to have a family with his love, as families with two fathers were frowned up on at the time."

Understanding dawned in David's eyes, and with the release of the next button, he slid her shirt off one shoulder.

"This is very enlightening."

He watched her as he slid his fingers toward the next button, waiting to see if she would ask a question, but she answered by undoing another of his buttons. He followed suit, and a moment later both of their shirts had fallen open.

She had been feeling quite bold until a breath of cool air hit her stomach. If only she had started those exercise classes at the YMCA along with the rest of the book club. As if he could read her mind, he ran his fingers along the waistband of her pants.

"You are very beautiful," he said. Something about his voice caught her attention. He wasn't really seeing her, and he definitely wasn't thinking about her abs or lack thereof. Like her, he was noticing the differences between this new person and the one who had come before.

"Beautiful but different," she said. There was no need to shy away from the truth.

"Yes." He looked up to meet her eyes and she saw the echo of grief.

"Have you been with anyone else since you lost your wife?"

"No."

She wasn't sure if that would make this easier or harder. "You're also my first," she said. "Although I haven't lost Luke, we have always been faithful to each other. He's the only man I've known for a long time."

His fingertips grazed her cheek, her neck, the hollow between her breasts, and returned to the edge of her waistband, making her suck in a breath.

"It is a privilege," he said.

"Likewise." She traced the same path on his chest that he had traced on hers. "There is no rush. We can take as much time as we like. As much time as you need."

Leaning closer, he said, "Right now, I need this." And his mouth closed over hers.

CHAPTER THIRTY-SEVEN

Dora closed the door behind David and floated back into the kitchen, only to be brought up short by a photo on the refrigerator. It was one of her favorites, the triplets on their first day of kindergarten. Sure, it was yellowing after all these years, but it had never lost its place of honor on the fridge. Dora could remember that morning like it was yesterday, and the memory brought her crashing back down to earth.

What had she done?

Mel would be home soon, and it would be just the two of them for dinner. Oh dear God, the truth of this afternoon's activities would be written all over Dora's face, no scarlet letter required.

Her phone. It was still up in the studio. Dora rushed upstairs and searched frantically until she found it under a sketch on her worktable.

Dora: Can you meet me for dinner? Urgent.

Lucy: Sure thing. Where?

Dora: Anywhere but here. Your house?

Lucy: Come on over. We'll have the place to ourselves.

Dora: On my way.

Scribbling a quick note for Mel, Dora was out the door within five minutes. Escaping for the evening didn't solve the larger problem, but at least it bought Dora some time. When she saw the family again, she needed to have her head on straight.

Lucy's husband might be out for the evening, but when Dora arrived she discovered that Lucy wasn't alone. Through the window in the side door, Dora could see Lucy's mother, Mary Evelyn, sitting with her in the kitchen, and in the center of the table sat a huge platter of cookies. Lucy waved her in, and soon Dora was seated at the kitchen table with a glass of wine.

"Are these fair game?" asked Dora.

"Absolutely," said Lucy. "I had a feeling you might need comfort food."

Dora didn't hesitate, taking two snickerdoodles and planning to save room for more. Nobody made snickerdoodles like Lucy.

"Have you checked on the mural progress lately?" asked Mary Evelyn.

When Lucy shook her head, Mary Evelyn said, "You need to go see it. They're almost done, and even behind the scaffolding it looks amazing. Fitz was saying this afternoon that there are a few fussy details to do in the morning, and then they'll start sealing it. Should be dry by the weekend. If the weather holds, we might be able to do the unveiling this weekend instead of waiting until spring."

"And how is our muralist doing? I haven't had a chance to ask Mel."

"You should definitely ask her," said Mary Evelyn. She didn't quite pull off the suggestive eyebrow waggle.

"Oh really?" Dora had witnessed the one kiss, but she wasn't sure it would merit the eyebrows.

"I'd say Mel and Fitz have grown very close over the last few weeks."

"And what led you to this conclusion?" asked Lucy.

"I caught them in a compromising position."

Lucy and Dora stared at her in shock.

"You're kidding," said Lucy.

Mary Evelyn shook her head.

"Where?" asked Dora, imagining them getting up to mischief on the scaffolding. They would have needed blankets, surely.

"I stopped by the library on Sunday afternoon to catch up on some paperwork. Lo and behold, who do I find snoozing naked in the library's back lounge?"

"They didn't," said Dora, equal parts horrified and delighted.

Lucy snickered. "Good for them."

"Nearly brained them with a baseball bat before I realized who they were and what they were up to."

"Did they wake up?" asked Lucy.

"Of course. I turned on the lights and they woke right up." She chuckled in satisfaction. "Got a good look at Hot Muralist's tattoo before he thought of his modesty. If only I were forty years younger. Hell, even thirty years younger would do it."

Dora pressed her fingers against her lips but couldn't hold back the smile. "It sounds like things are going very well indeed. I'll stay out of their way and cross my fingers that this one sticks. Mel tends not to keep them around for long. Easily bored, I think."

"The muralist is definitely not boring," said Mary Evelyn. "And on that thought, I'll leave you ladies to your wine. I need to get home."

After saying their farewells and ushering Mary Evelyn out the door, Lucy turned her full attention to Dora.

"So what's so urgent that we needed to get together tonight? Did you see your international man of mystery again?"

Dora kept her eyes on her wine, but could feel the blush creeping up her neck.

"Ah," said Lucy, "I see that you have. Details, please."

"He's amazing."

"Mm-hmmm."

"And interesting."

"And..."

"And I feel like I'm twenty-two. I can't wait to see him again and it's driving me crazy."

Lucy laughed out loud, a big belly laugh.

"I knew it," she crowed. "I'm so glad I introduced you. Business, my ass. That man has had the hots for you since the first time he saw your picture. He was already into your art. All he needed was a little bait."

"Wait, my picture? I never gave the gallery my picture."

"No, you didn't, did you? Lucky that I happened to be in the library when that gorgeous hunk of man stopped by to see your work on display. He was asking all sorts of questions about you, and I may have volunteered to show him some photos of you on my phone."

"You didn't."

"I most certainly did."

"You are a terrible friend."

"Or an amazing friend. Depends on your perspective, I guess. Did you by chance get laid today?"

Dora swatted her on the arm. "I can't believe you did that."

"Best friend ever. Are you going to keep him?"

"Like a pet, you mean?"

"Well, if you're into that." Lucy shrugged nonchalantly. "I just meant, are you going to let this develop, see where it goes?"

"What choice do I have?" Wasn't that how relationships worked? One date at a time?

"Well, you could use him for hot sex and then cut him loose."

Nearly choking on her wine, Dora said, "You're awful."

"I know."

"The answer is yes. I'm going to let this develop naturally and see where it goes."

"And have hot sex."

"Well, of course." Eventually. When they were ready. Which would hopefully be very soon.

"Great. So why the panic attack?"

"Oh, that," said Dora. She nibbled on a cookie to buy herself some time.

"Yes, that."

Now that she was here, embarrassment had set in. Maybe she was overreacting.

"Do you think we might be moving too quickly?"

"No," said Lucy emphatically.

Maybe another cookie would help.

"Dora, you're not taking things too fast. You're a grown woman, and you are allowed to have sex with whomever you please."

"Technically," said Dora with a mouthful of cookie, "I'm still married."

"Don't give me that. You're separated, and your husband has basically moved in with his true love. You have a free pass to do whatever wild and crazy thing you like."

"Don't you think I should tell the girls first?"

"Why? So they can disapprove and then you can stop because you don't want your poor babies to be uncomfortable?"

"Well...yes."

Lucy's snort was not a nice sound. "Take your pleasure, honey. The girls will be fine."

"But—"

"They'll be fine. They're grown women."

"Sometimes I'm not so sure."

Laughing, Lucy pushed back from the table. "Let's scrounge up some dinner. I need food to soak up this wine."

Over the course of dinner and conversation, one thing became very clear to Dora. In order for her to move on with her life, she would need to see Mel settled. Coaxing had led only to resistance, and waiting had clearly failed, so Dora was working on a different plan. Luke's advice was to trust her instincts, and those instincts were telling her to give Mel the nudge she needed. A forceful nudge, if necessary.

Still buzzing with anger and frustration after her unexpected fight with Fitz, Mel tried to calm down on the short drive home. She had promised her sisters that she would ask Mom about their paternity tonight, and there was no way she could do it in this frame of mind. But when she arrived home, she didn't find her mother, or her father for that matter, only a note on the kitchen counter.

> Mel,
>
> I'm off to book club, and your father won't be back from his field trip until late tonight.
>
> See you later.
>
> Love,
>
> Mom

The unexpected reprieve left Mel feeling oddly deflated. She ate a solitary dinner in the kitchen, wondering if this would be a typical night for her going forward. Dora had an active social life, while Mel had very few local friends left. She'd always been closest with her sisters, and her small circle of friends had all moved on to greener pastures—or, in this case, not-greener cities with an actual social scene for people in their twenties. A few had married and had children already, like Sunny, who lived in Madison now. For Mel, moving here to Hidden Springs was a lonely prospect, one she didn't think she could handle for more than a few years.

There was one person she could call. Maybe Kat would have some perspective on this situation. She dealt with screwed-up families all the time for work, and her own situation had been beyond messy. If anybody would have good advice to offer, it would be Kat.

Mel: Need your sage advice. Meet at the Beach?

Kat: Give me half an hour to finish what I'm working on.

Mel: Works for me. See you there.

Mel found Kat at what had become their usual table in the corner. It was the best location for people-watching. Mel scanned the crowd as she walked through, but didn't see any gossip-worthy pairings. She stopped at the bar to order a beer before continuing on to the table.

"It's been awfully quiet at the library without the community service kids. When will you get a new crew?" asked Mel, once she had taken a seat.

"I guess that depends on how the local teenagers behave. It's been quiet lately."

Not surprising after the drama of the runaway kids a couple of weeks ago. Speaking of which, Mel asked, "How are Hannah and her little sister doing?"

"They're going to be fine. Not everything is resolved with their stepdad, but in their case, the system and the process are working. Their mom also seems to be doing much better now that her own mother is living with them."

"I'm glad," said Mel. "There were so many ways that the whole thing could have gone sideways."

"I know," said Kat. "In my line of work, not every story has a happy ending. I'll take the good outcomes whenever I can get them. But enough about work. What's up with you and Hot Muralist?"

Mel choked on her beer. Did everyone in town call him that?

"That's what I thought," said Kat. "And the tattoo is...?"

"I don't kiss and tell," said Mel primly, although she was tempted.

"Well, at least you admit that you've been kissing. Anything else you want to share?"

Mel considered her options and decided she could share at least one little detail. "The couch in the library's lounge is very comfortable."

This time it was Kat who choked on her beer. "You didn't."

"We did."

"Remind me never to sit on that couch again."

Laughing, Mel said, "We left no evidence behind."

"Or so you think. All I need is a black light."

"I'm sure the couch has been thoroughly cleaned. Mary Evelyn caught us."

"No!"

Mel nodded. "Yes. Scared the hell out of me. I haven't been busted like that since I was a teenager."

Kat covered her face with her hands. "Oh my God, I can't even imagine."

"It was a little strange."

"I bet. So how is this going to work? Are you going to keep things going with him after you leave?"

Mel looked down at her beer bottle and swirled the liquid around a few times.

"I'm not sure I'm leaving."

The teasing expression on Kat's face faded, leaving only concern behind. "You'd ditch your plans for him? You've only known him for a few weeks."

Mel gave a half-hearted smile. "Not for him, although he would be a lovely consolation prize if he sticks around. There's some other family drama that's making me think I should put my plans on hold."

"Drama you can share?"

Tracing shapes in the condensation on her beer bottle, Mel said, "It looks like my dad isn't really my dad."

"Oh, no," said Kat. "Did you guys do one of those personal DNA tests?"

"I never even thought of that," said Mel. "I guess one way or another the information would have come to light. No, we didn't do tests. We just realized that the story my parents have always told about their whirlwind courtship doesn't add up. We knew it happened fast. They met, got married, moved up here, and had us, all within a year. When you consider the timing, it looks like my mom was pregnant when she and my dad first met."

Kat considered the options. "Were you preemies?"

Mel shook her head. "The opposite. My mom brags about carrying us to term."

"Oh."

"Exactly."

"Have you asked her about it yet? Maybe your mom misspoke."

If only Mel could believe that. Callie still held out hope that it was all a big mistake, but Mel had seen the acceptance in

Tessa's eyes. Luke had raised them, and he would always be their father, but he hadn't contributed his DNA to their creation and Mel really hoped he knew that.

"That was supposed to be my mission for tonight, but when I got home my mom had already left for her book club."

"I'm so sorry. Everything must feel upside down."

Mel nodded. Upside down. Backward. Inside out. Half the time Mel felt like she couldn't breathe. Nothing made sense anymore.

"Not to be coldhearted or anything, but are you sure that's a strong enough reason to ditch your plans?"

"I can't imagine flying halfway around the world when I'm not even sure which way is up."

Kat took a sip of her beer, nodding.

"Maybe once we figure all this out, and I know the family is going to be okay, then I can try again."

"I hope you do," said Kat. "You've been planning for this a long time."

CHAPTER THIRTY-EIGHT

OVER BREAKFAST, FITZ WONDERED IF MEL WOULD SHOW UP TO paint today. They had never fought before, so he had no idea how long it might take her to cool off, or if she might be one of those people who couldn't get over a fight. Hopefully not. Their friendship had become important to him and he wanted it to continue. Fitz brought his breakfast dishes over to the sink for a rinse, but his mother took them from him.

"Don't worry, dear," she said. "I've got this."

She was puttering around the kitchen, unloading the dishwasher and setting everything to rights after breakfast. Before Fitz could thank her, his father came into the kitchen from the garage. It was awfully early in the day to be carrying that much tension around, but he was clearly in a terrible mood.

"Are you ready?" he asked. "We're going to be late."

"Almost," said his mother. "Give me a sec."

"We don't have a sec, Margot. We need to head out now. Fitz can finish cleaning up." This directive accompanied an irritated look in Fitz's direction, as if Fitz could prevent his mother from puttering around her own kitchen.

She gave her husband a warning look of her own and continued to straighten up. "The doctor's office is only ten minutes away," she said. The words were clipped and her tone not all that friendly. "We have a sec."

He threw up his hands in exasperation. "I'll be in the car."

"Anthony," she said, halting him on his way out of the kitchen. "You need to stop. This—" She gestured vaguely toward him. "—needs to stop."

"What are you talking about?"

If only there were a way for Fitz to sink into the floor, or at least fade into the background. Rather than be an unwilling witness to the coming battle, he started to back slowly toward the living room, but froze when his father's eyes flickered in his direction.

"You're smothering me," said his mother. "I don't know if it's retirement or the stupid cancer or what, but I can't live like this. Maybe retirement isn't the right choice for you. Maybe you need to go back to work."

"What?"

With his father's attention firmly back on his mother, Fitz took the opportunity to slide into one of the kitchen chairs, trying to fade into the background. He didn't think he could make a full escape without drawing attention to himself and, to be honest, he didn't really want to miss this.

"I can't go back to work," shouted his father. "You could relapse any day."

"So it's the cancer then, not retirement," she said, the words clipped and not particularly friendly. "You're treating me this way because you think I'm a lost cause."

"What? No. I think we need to be vigilant."

She nodded in agreement. "Cautious."

"Exactly." His father seemed to be calming down, soothed by her agreement. Fitz started to feel sorry for him. He had no idea how much trouble he was in.

"No risks, no adventure," his mother continued, her voice hardening.

"Wait—"

"No more fun for me," she said. "Just a porch and a rocking chair."

"That's not what I said."

"That's what it sounded like to me."

"Look," said Anthony. "I'm the only one in the family who seems to take the cancer seriously. Pippa is no help. She's too caught up with the kids and her job to make time for you. And Fitz is running around painting murals instead of doing actual work or spending time with you."

"Because these could be my final moments. Don't want to miss a second of the death watch."

"That's not what I said."

Never had his dad sounded so lost.

"It's what you mean," said his mother. "Why the hell should Pippa or Fitz put their lives on hold while they wait for me to die? If I caught either of them doing that, I would kick their asses."

Fitz's eyes widened. His mother never swore. As if she could hear him thinking, she swiveled abruptly to face him. So much for fading into the background.

"Fitz, you're not putting your career on hold, are you? Don't you dare tell me you're putting your life on hold."

In that moment, all of Fitz's jumbled thoughts about the future crystallized into a single realization: he would not let his mother down. If the cancer came back, he would adjust, but until then, his dad would have to deal with his son's life choices.

"I promise I'm not putting my life on hold."

She narrowed her eyes at him. "How can I be sure of that?"

"I applied for an international assignment that could last two years, and I'm sorry but I'm going to have to decline to go out on a date with...what's her name? Marcy."

In all his nervous hand-wringing about how this revelation might play out, this was one scenario he had never envisioned. Weirdly, it was not stressful at all.

His mother laughed, sounding maybe a little unhinged. She gave him a swift hug and a kiss. "You are definitely my favorite son."

"I'm your only son," he said dryly.

"And that makes you the best."

Fitz's father was looking at the two of them as if aliens had taken over their bodies. Sighing, Fitz said, "Dad, I'm sorry if this disappoints you, but it's something I've always wanted to do."

"Oh, sweetie," said his mom, "you could never disappoint us." But when she turned back to face her husband, he couldn't bring himself to agree.

"Oh, yes, he damn well could," said his dad. "I thought we discussed this. You need to focus on career progression, not murals and definitely not some pleasure trip. You need to be here, in Chicago, not halfway around the world, when your mom's cancer comes back."

"What did you just say?" Now Mom was well and truly pissed off. Fitz knew that tone of voice all too well from his teenage years. "Did you say 'when' my cancer comes back?"

"Calm down, Margot. Stress isn't good for you."

Fitz took one look at his mother's face and hoped his father would survive the next five minutes.

"You know what isn't good for me, Anthony? An over-bearing husband who doesn't listen to his wife when she tells him to stop. Just stop. I am not going to live the rest of my life, no matter how short or long it may be, in bubble wrap. In fact, I will be traveling the world, visiting my son on his exciting over-seas project and seeing all the places on my bucket list. You may or may not be invited to join me."

"But, Margot—"

"Don't even start, Anthony." Turning her back on her frantic husband, she said, "Fitz, I'm going to need you to come with me to my doctor appointment this morning. Your father is not invited, but I think it's still important to have a second set of ears there. Can you give me an hour?"

"Ah...no problem, Mom. I'll grab my shoes."

He should probably also text Mel so she didn't think he was blowing her off. That would not be a great way to recover from the fight.

"I'll be waiting in the car," she said.

His father stood there, blinking, in the center of the kitchen, as his wife swept past him.

After the appointment, Fitz dropped his mother back at home and headed over to the library. The doctor had offered reassurance along with normal blood test results. However, instead of making his mother feel better, this had left her in a foul mood, muttering about continuing the "discussion" with her husband all the way home. Fitz was really glad he had somewhere else to be.

Mel had already begun sealing the wall when Fitz arrived. He had talked her through the process on the way to the doctor appointment, and it wasn't actually that complicated. If her progress so far was any indication, they would finish the project today.

A selfish part of her wanted to drag out this last step, if only to extend her time with Fitz. Once the mural was done, they would see each other at the unveiling, but then—assuming he stuck to the plan—he would be off on his international assignment and she would be here, bogged down in the never-ending drama that was her family.

He looked kind of shell-shocked, and since he had texted

her to say that he was taking his mom to her doctor appointment, her mind immediately went to the worst-case scenario.

"Is your mom okay?" she asked, concern lacing her voice, as he climbed through the hole in the scaffolding to meet her on the top level.

"She's good," he said. "Great, actually. Her blood work is normal and the doctors say she can resume all her normal activities. She still needs to get a flu shot, but otherwise she's in the clear. Next checkup in six months."

"That's wonderful. You must be so relieved."

"I am."

He was nodding and he had said all good things, but he didn't seem himself, staring at the completed section of wall like it would tell him what to do next.

"Fitz?"

"Hm?"

"What's wrong? You seem really out of it."

He shook his head, then rubbed his face with his hands before turning away from the mural to sit abruptly on the scaffolding and hang his feet over the edge.

"I told my parents this morning."

"Oh my God. How did it go?"

"My mom is thrilled. My dad is pissed. However, since my mother basically said she would never forgive me if I changed my plans because of her, I guess I'm sticking with the original plan."

Mel plopped down beside him and threw her arms around him. "That's amazing!"

"I should be thrilled, right?" he asked. He gave her a squeeze before letting go. "Instead I feel kind of empty. I always knew there was no way to please both of them, but I guess I didn't realize how screwed up my dad is right now. I think he's out of his mind with fear that he's going to lose my mom."

"It can't be easy for him."

"Pretty sure my mom is going to kick his ass, though, now that she understands the problem. Maybe even make him go to therapy."

"Do you think it will work?"

Shrugging, Fitz said, "He'll go if she tells him to go, and that's half the battle." He looked over at her. "What about you? Did you talk to your mom last night?"

She shook her head slowly. "We were supposed to have dinner together, but I came home to a note saying she had book club. I think she might be avoiding me." Frowning at the view, she said, "We have family dinner tonight, and if she keeps avoiding me, we'll have to tackle it then."

"I hope it goes okay."

"You and me both."

It was really too bad Fitz was back on the international track. If he stayed, maybe they could spend weekends together here at the lake, or she could go visit him down in the city. He was exactly the kind of guy she wanted to know better. Feeling the time slipping through her fingers, she grabbed his shirt and pulled him close for a kiss, then let him go as he was getting over his surprise and sliding his arms around her.

He didn't let her slip away, instead saying, "I'm sorry about yesterday."

"Forget about it." She leaned in to kiss him again, but he wouldn't let her.

"I was angry and frustrated and I took that out on you, and I'm sorry. If I ever try to pull that shit again, you should call me on it."

"Now, Fitz, that sounds suspiciously like planning for the future. I thought we agreed not to do that."

Mel wouldn't mind visiting him overseas. It would help to ease the sting of staying home. But they had gone into this fake-dating arrangement with clear expectations, and she wasn't going to back out of the deal.

"Let's just say I'm keeping an open mind."

CHAPTER THIRTY-NINE

MEL CONFERRED WITH HER SISTERS VIA TEXT TO DETERMINE their next steps. Dora might be able to avoid a one-on-one conversation, but she was the one who had organized another family dinner for tonight. She couldn't skip dinner at her own house. Well, she might, if she knew the planned topic of conversation, but she didn't. Mel hoped they were doing the right thing by raising the issue with both her parents. If this turned out to be the first time her father had considered the possibility, she would feel horrible.

Mel: Ok so who will bring it up? I vote Tessa.

Callie: Me too

Tessa: I thought Mel had already planned out what to say???

Mel: You're the professional...

Tessa: Fine. But you all have to talk, too

As dinner drew to a close, Tessa said, "So, we've got a question for you two." At the same moment, Dora chimed her knife against her wine glass and said, "I have a surprise."

A Canadian standoff ensued ("You first." "No, you first.") until Luke looked at Dora and said, "You go first, honey."

Mel's heart sank when her mother looked directly at her.

"Okay, so Mel, sweetheart, I know you've been feeling stuck and have hesitated to make any big decisions. I'm sure the money involved in committing to a lease is intimidating. I can't stand on the sidelines when one of my girls needs help, so I decided it was time to make a move."

"Oh, Mom, you didn't…"

"It's a done deal," she said. "You have a one-year, prepaid lease on that beautiful space we saw. I hope this gives you the freedom to build the kind of photography business you want, and I don't want to hear a word about paying it back. This is on us."

Luke raised an eyebrow, but Dora stared him down. "It's on us. No strings attached."

Mel buried her face in her hands, and the table went silent.

"Honey?"

Mel looked up and saw her mother's face fall, which only made her feel worse. She reached across to squeeze her mother's hand.

"Mom, it's amazing that you would do this for me, and I appreciate it. I really do, but there's a lot I haven't told you—any of you."

This was all happening out of order, and Mel knew that they should figure out the family thing first, but after hearing Fitz's story today, she had realized that she owed her family the full story, whether she ultimately left town or not.

Her sisters looked surprised and wary, Dora looked panicked. Luke was the only one who appeared calm.

"What's going on?" asked Dora. "I thought… But you said…"

"I know, and I'm sorry. I've tried to tell you so many times. This vision you have of a photography business here in town— it's beautiful, and I wish I wanted it as much as you do."

"But I thought you did."

"I'm sorry, Mom. I don't."

"Then what are you going to do? You can't freelance and couch surf forever."

"Honey, I hardly think—"

"It's okay, Dad," said Mel. She knew her mom's heart was in the right place. Sometimes she just went overboard. "Mom, I know it makes you really uncomfortable that I don't have a regular career."

"It doesn't have to be ordinary, sweetheart."

"Here's the thing. I do have a career, even if it doesn't make sense to you."

"So explain it to me." Dora looked like she was going to cry, and it killed Mel to see her like this.

"I don't talk very much about my freelance work because I know it upsets you. It's not the safest job in the world."

"You could do your photography anywhere," said Dora, repeating an old refrain. "There's no need for you to accept dangerous assignments."

"Well, it's those assignments that have allowed me to build a portfolio and a reputation, and to take the next step in my career."

"Which is what? More dangerous assignments?" The expression on Dora's face was shifting from hurt to angry, and Mel knew she needed to tread carefully if she wanted her mother to hear her out.

"You know I love to travel."

"Well, of course, but—"

Mel interrupted her mother. She needed to get this all out.

"I've landed an international photojournalism contract. I'll be traveling in Central and South America for the next couple of years, visiting UN program sites and documenting their work. I'm considering backing out of the contract, given everything that's going on in the family, but I'm worried that if I do that, I won't get another. I'm so sorry."

It was quiet for a moment as the family absorbed her news, and then everyone started talking at once. In the middle of the confusion, Dora held up a hand and they all shut up. Her eyes were full of unshed tears.

"Why are you sorry?"

"Because I know how much you want me to be here," she said. "Well, that, and you hate my career. You're going to be lonely with everybody heading off to do their own thing, and you were so excited about the idea of my photography business here. I hate to take that away from you."

"Oh, sweetheart," said Dora as the tears started to fall. "All I want is for you to be happy. I'm the one who should apologize. I had no idea."

"But you'll be alone," said Mel, doing a terrible job hiding the hitch in her voice.

"There are worse things," said Dora gently. "Besides, it won't be forever, and it won't be all the time. Maybe I can use some alone time to figure out what comes next for me."

"Maybe you'll spend some time with a sexy art gallery owner?" asked Tessa. As a tension-breaker, it worked really well. Everyone laughed except Dora, who threw her napkin at her daughter.

"Hush, you. This is hardly the time."

Luke stepped in, saying, "That's enough, girls. It seems your mother may need privacy while she figures out this next chapter in her life."

Callie snorted. "I'm thinking she needs *a lot* of privacy."

"What were you going to ask earlier?" Dora had recovered

enough to try to change the subject, and she directed her question at Tessa. She had no intention of discussing what may or may not be happening with David with the entire family. Nope. Not happening.

"Oh, well..."

Tessa, Callie, and Mel exchanged glances, looking panicked.

"Girls?" Dora let her voice get sharper this time. She knew when her girls were trying to wiggle their way out of trouble. Not surprisingly, Tessa ended up as the designated spokesperson.

"The other night, you told Mel the story of when you and Dad met."

Dora nodded. This was not news, so she had no idea why the girls were acting so strangely.

"You talked about how hot and muggy it was that night, that it was late July."

The girls had never asked about the exact timeline of the pregnancy, and Dora had always been carefully vague about the dates. She shot a glance at Luke and could tell he was thinking the same thing. Unfortunately, her poker face had never been particularly good.

Callie picked up the storyline from Tessa. "You've always said that the doctor was proud of you for carrying us to term. We didn't have to stay in the NICU."

Nodding, Dora tried to think of something—anything, really—to say.

"When we did the math," said Tessa, "we came up a little short."

Dora covered her mouth and looked helplessly at Luke. This was her nightmare, and she needed him to make it stop. Instead, he said, "We should have told them years ago."

Tessa looked back and forth between Dora and Luke. Now *that* was a good poker face. Callie and Mel were trying to do the same, but they weren't as good at it, and Dora could tell they were upset.

"Would either of you like to help us understand the real story?" asked Tessa.

Swallowing, Dora shot a pleading look at Luke, but he smiled and shook his head. "It's your story to tell."

When she didn't say anything, Callie asked, "It's Barrett, isn't it?"

Dora couldn't get her brain to connect with her mouth for what felt like a year. Then all she could manage was, "How...?"

"There was something in the tone of the letters," said Callie. "Maybe it was the way Lauren talked about us. Did she know?"

Nodding slowly, Dora said, "I didn't tell her until this summer, but she had a hunch, and as she watched you girls grow up in pictures over the years, she became more certain. We talked about it at the hospital before she died."

"Does Barrett know?" asked Tessa.

"I never told him. If he had known—or even suspected—he would have been here in a heartbeat." When she remembered those early days, she felt ready to go to war. "But Lauren said something in the hospital that made me wonder if she had told him. It would certainly explain his recent communication." The old dread and panic started to bubble up in her stomach, and she looked at Luke. "He can't have them. I don't care if he figures it out. The girls are yours and mine—nobody else's."

Standing, Luke walked around the table to pull Dora out of her chair and into a hug.

"Nobody can take the girls away from you," he said. "It's going to be okay."

CHAPTER FORTY

THE HUG FROM LUKE HELPED TO CENTER DORA, WHICH WAS A
relief, because only a moment before she had felt like throwing
up all over the table. The girls probably thought she was crazy,
but she didn't care. They had never met Barrett, didn't understand the resources at his disposal or his frustrating ability to
scramble their mother's brain.

"Mom," said Tessa. "Even if this guy Barrett is our biological
father, we're adults now. He can't take us anywhere."

Luke gave her one last squeeze and then pulled away.

"Your daughter has an excellent point," he said. "Things are
very different now that the girls are grown."

After blowing her nose, Dora took her seat back at the
table, while Luke went into the kitchen to put on the kettle.

"You're right, and in my head I know that, but in my heart I
was always so afraid that he would make a claim to you girls,
and we would have to go back to New York with him."

"How could he claim us?" asked Mel. "Dad is listed on our
birth certificates."

In all the years spent dreading this conversation, Dora had
never actually rehearsed it in her mind. Now she scrambled to

find the right words and to decide how much to share about that complicated and difficult time in her life. Tessa had been right to point out that they were fully grown. Twenty-seven should be more than old enough to handle the truth—no matter how complicated. The question wasn't whether or not the girls could handle it. It was whether or not Dora could handle it.

"You need to understand that Barrett comes from money. Old New York money. If he had wanted to conduct a paternity test and sue me for custody of you girls, there was nothing standing in his way."

"Do you come from money, too?"

This time it was Callie asking the question, and it was a reasonable one. Still, it was so far off the mark that Dora burst out laughing. Callie gave her a funny look, making her realize how much she had to explain.

"No, I do not come from money. The opposite, actually. I grew up on Long Island in a working-class family. I know I don't talk about it much. We were not a happy family."

"I only asked because, when I look back, it seems like we had more money than we should have. It's not something I noticed when we were little, but once I was out on my own it was obvious. Now we know that Dad made money from his songwriting. That wouldn't have made a difference in the beginning, but somehow you were able to buy this house."

"The answer is complicated, but then, everything about my relationship with Barrett and Lauren was complicated." Dora smiled gratefully when Luke slid a cup of tea in front of her. "Any time you're friends with the wife and sleeping with the husband and everybody knows about it and is okay with it, well, that's complicated. But for us there was an additional wrinkle."

She took a deep breath, steeling herself for the hardest part. She wasn't ready—not that she ever would be—but she had to tell them. Luke, her anchor, stood beside her with his hand on her shoulder, but he couldn't eliminate her fear. What if the girls hated her for the choices she made? What if they never looked at her in the same way again? Maybe it was for the best that Dora hadn't seen this conversation coming. Time to prepare would have become time to freak out.

"I wasn't just friends with Barrett and Lauren. I was their surrogate. They paid me very well for providing that service, and Lauren gave me even more when I left, to make sure I would be okay on my own. That's how we bought this house, and started the sailing school, and how we were able to send you girls to college without taking out loans."

Silence.

Tessa recovered first, and she zeroed right in on the bombshell. "Surrogate, as in, you had a baby for them?"

Dora nodded, but before she could clarify, Callie said, "Twins."

Nodding again, Dora said, "Nobody expected it to be twins."

"It doesn't sound like you had a formal arrangement, the way it would happen today," continued Tessa.

"No," said Dora. "Lauren's fertility was impacted by cancer treatments when she was a child, so not only could she not get pregnant herself, she couldn't even donate the eggs. Barrett and I met just as they were looking into adoption. Surrogacy wasn't really on their radar."

"So, when you say surrogate," continued Tessa, "what you really mean is that you and Barrett had sex and made babies the old-fashioned way. No turkey basters involved. No IVF."

"That's correct," said Dora. She was starting to feel like a witness in a trial.

"And Lauren was on board with this plan?" asked Mel.

Sipping her tea, Dora thought about how she could explain the dynamic in a way that would make sense to outsiders. The relationship between herself, Barrett, and Lauren had worked for them, for almost two years, but she'd only ever explained it to Luke.

"Lauren and Barrett had been friends their entire lives," said Dora, "and their marriage was an extension of that friendship. I honestly don't know if they ever had sex. By the time I came on the scene, they slept in separate bedrooms, and Lauren didn't seem to mind Barrett's girlfriends, as long as he was discreet and she always came first in the pecking order."

"You were one of his girlfriends?" Tessa's calm facade was slipping, and Dora could tell she was struggling to understand.

"In the beginning, yes, once I was sure that they had an open marriage."

"How could you be sure?" asked Mel, her face alight with curiosity.

"Lauren told me."

The expression on Mel's face was priceless.

"Right," said Tessa. "That must have been an interesting conversation. When did you all decide to try for a baby? Or was it an accident?"

"No, Barrett was very careful. He actually invited me to their place in the city for dinner one night, and we all discussed it over chicken Kiev and chardonnay."

Callie smothered a laugh. "That sounds very civilized."

"It was," agreed Dora. She could still remember walking into their building for the first time, meeting the doorman, hearing the squeak of her boat shoes on the marble floor. It had been a surreal experience, discussing the making of a baby over the fanciest dinner she'd ever eaten.

Luke gave her shoulder a squeeze and headed back into the kitchen. So far nobody was in hysterics, which was probably why he felt he could leave her on her own. He didn't leave for long, though, returning with the kettle, four more mugs, and a selection of tea on a tray. What was she going to do without him?

"So you were like a handmaid, from that book," said Mel with a frown.

Dora flinched. Maybe she had relaxed too soon. "We may have been unconventional, but we all chose to be a part of it. There was no coercion. I was happy to do it."

"Sorry," said Mel. "I didn't mean it that way. I meant the mechanics were the same—regular sex, living together during the process. Although somehow I doubt Lauren was in the room when it happened."

"God, no," said Dora. "That would have been... No. Definitely not."

The girls snickered at her discomfort. It was silly to be squeamish when she was the one who had done all the unconventional things in the first place.

"Wasn't it complicated, legally speaking?" asked Tessa.

"We didn't involve any lawyers until after the babies were born. From that point, it was basically a standard adoption. Very neat and tidy. Barrett hired expensive lawyers to make sure it was all done right. They planned to tell the kids later that they had used a surrogate, with the implication that it had all been very clinical."

"Did they? Tell the kids, I mean?" asked Mel.

"I don't know," said Dora. "I wasn't a part of their lives after that first year, and Lauren never mentioned it in her letters."

"You lived with them for a year?"

Dora nodded. Of all the girls, Tessa seemed to grasp how difficult it must have been, and how painful to leave. She was right to be shocked. To bond with your own babies, breastfeed them late in the night, care for them for a year, and then leave —it had been excruciating.

Instead of wallowing in the experience all over again, Dora simply said, "It wasn't easy to leave."

"What made you decide to go?" asked Tessa. Of course she would want to know the most painful of details.

"They started to talk, and they called Lauren 'Mama.'"
Dora's tone of voice did not invite further questions.

Everyone was quiet for a moment, and then Callie asked,
"Have they ever tried to get in touch with you?"

Dora shook her head.

"They have my medical history. I don't think they would
have any curiosity about their surrogate beyond the necessary
facts. As far as they're concerned, they grew up with a mom and
a dad."

"But still," said Callie.

"You're curious." Dora could still read her daughter's face,
even though Callie might not like it.

"There's an unknown human out there in the world who
contributed half of our DNA. It's hard not to be curious." Callie
looked over at Luke. "And you knew? All these years?"

He nodded.

"Why did you do it?"

Callie had always been closest to Luke. To learn that he
wasn't her biological father—that he had knowingly kept that
information a secret—must be very difficult for her. Dora
wished she could think of a way to make it all easier.

"For me," said Luke, "having a family of my own seemed
impossibly out of reach. At that time, there was no way a single
man could have adopted a child. And if I'd been living with
Zeke? Even worse. As your mother and I got to know each
other, we realized that we could build a really good life
together, and I wanted that life." He held up a hand to delay the
questions that were coming. "At school, everyone knew I was
married, so I could pursue a career without fear of being 'out-
ed.' At home, I was your father in every way that mattered.
Screw Barrett." This surprised a laugh from Dora and the girls.
"I'm the luckiest guy in the world. No matter how things may
change in the coming years, it's important that you know that.
We're still a family."

"No matter what," said Dora.

"Even if I'm halfway around the world?" asked Mel.

Dora stood up and walked around the corner of the table to give her a huge hug. "*Especially* if you're halfway around the world. In fact, I'll have to come visit you."

"And Barrett?" asked Tessa. "Do you think you'll ever talk to him about it?"

Dora looked around the table at Luke and their girls, and her heart filled with so much love that she thought she might explode.

"Barrett has his family and I have mine," she said. "Someday, if you'd like to meet them, we can make that happen. Maybe one day they'll reach out to us. But for me, for now, this family is all I need."

The following morning, Fitz's phone buzzed with a call from his sister right after he arrived at the library.

"What's going on?" she asked. "I just got a very weird phone call from Mom."

"Short version? I'm planning to work overseas for a few years. Mom is thrilled. Dad, not so much."

"That's awesome! Congrats, little bro. That's very cool news, but I'm not sure how it relates to Mom's phone call."

"What did she say?" he asked as he climbed the scaffolding to the top level.

"She called yesterday to say that she loves me and she's so proud of me and the way I'm juggling work and the kids and if I ever shortchange the kids in order to spend time with her she'll kill me."

"Huh."

"That's what I said. So, maybe there's more I need to know?"

"Nothing new, exactly. You saw how overprotective Dad was being. He's been driving Mom crazy, and yesterday morning it all came to a head. He basically said that we all need to spend time with her now because the cancer is going to come back and she's going to drop dead."

"Nice."

"Mom did not take it well."

"So that's why she asked if I liked the couples counselor we saw before the divorce."

"Yeah. Mom seems solid, but Dad is losing his shit. Counseling would be a great idea."

"If she can get Dad to agree."

"Something tells me he won't have a choice," said Fitz.

As he hung up, Mel pulled into her usual parking space. They planned to check the wall for any last touch-ups, and then call the rental company to come take down the scaffolding. Fitz had already told Mary Evelyn that the official unveiling was a "go" for Saturday so she could tell the newspaper and put some posts on social media.

He watched Mel walk over and disappear underneath the scaffolding below. She looked good. Really good. As if a weight had lifted from her shoulders.

When her head emerged from the hole in the floor of the scaffolding, Fitz said, "You told them."

She nodded, then broke into a huge grin.

"And you're still going on the trip." It wasn't difficult to read the news on her face.

"Yes, I am," she confirmed, then flung her arms around him and planted a big kiss on his mouth.

Several minutes later, he said, "I'm so glad to hear that. You know, you never told me exactly where you were going. You only said South America."

"That's because I'm going to hit ten different countries over the two-year period. You name a country, I'm probably going there."

"Any chance you'll be in Chile?"

He was definitely breaking the rules at this point, thinking about the future, but Mel didn't seem to mind.

"Why yes, I believe I will." She wound her arms around his neck and leaned back in his arms, giving him a flirty look from under her lashes. "And you?" she asked. "Any chance you'll be in Chile?"

"As it happens, I received an email this morning asking me if I'd like to join a project team in Santiago. It looks like I'll be spending a lot of time in Chile."

"Maybe we could meet for coffee."

"I'd like that."

CHAPTER FORTY-ONE

28 years ago, August

DORA BLINKED AWAKE. SOMETHING HAD WOKEN HER, BUT WHAT? Sunshine streamed through the high windows of the loft. The sound of the shower running confused her for a moment, until she remembered that Luke had slept over last night. They had talked late into the night about their plans for their new life together.

Never had she and Barrett simply slept together, without sex, and it hadn't occurred to her that they could. It had certainly never happened while they lived together. Last night, though, she had learned what she was missing—the comfort of curling into a warm body, the feeling that she wasn't alone in the world—and it made her angry with Barrett all over again. He was asking her to sign up for a life without this.

The sound of the buzzer jolted her fully awake and she sat up, wondering who in the world would be coming to see her this early in the morning. None of her friends voluntarily got out of bed before noon—Luke being the exception.

She made her way over to the call box by the door and pressed on the talk button.

"Who is it?"

"It's Barrett. I need to see you."

She thunked her head on the doorframe. "Is there really anything left to say?"

"Let me in, Dora."

She buzzed him in, wondering what she could say that would finally get through to him, because apparently he thought he could talk her out of getting married. The ancient elevator would take a few minutes, if he could figure out how it worked. She had dumped coffee grounds into a fresh filter and pressed the start button on the coffeemaker when he knocked. Her oversized T-shirt and boxer shorts would have to do, because she certainly didn't have time to get glammed up now. Resigning herself to the coming confrontation, she slid the deadbolt open. He'd seen her in less. If he couldn't deal with morning Dora, then he shouldn't be here.

"Come on in," she said. "Have a seat."

She motioned toward her tiny kitchen table, flanked by two chairs, then walked over to the fridge to hunt for some food. Her apartment might be large by student standards, but it was still a studio. Barrett could survey it all with a glance. If he was smart, he would notice that she wasn't inviting him to sit on the bed or even the couch. Hopefully this wouldn't take long.

"Coffee will be ready in a minute," she said. "Want some toast?"

He seemed taken aback by her casual attitude. Did he think she was going to greet him naked at the door even though she was engaged to someone else? If so, he needed to readjust his thinking.

"No, thanks," he said, then took off his coat and put it over the back of his chair before sitting down.

She started some toast for herself and Luke. The coffee

maker had begun to percolate by the time she sat down opposite Barrett.

"What can I do for you so early in the morning?"

The sound of the shower shutting off signaled the presence of another person in the apartment, and he gave her a sharp glance.

"You have a roommate now?"

"Not exactly."

His eyes narrowed. "There's a man here?"

She laughed. This was much more fun than she had expected, and knowing Luke was in the apartment seemed to make her immune to the chemistry between them. It allowed her to relax and enjoy the moment.

"You sound like my mother." Not that her mother would speak to her anymore, but she had been full of moral judgments and had sounded just like that. "My fiancé is here. I'm sure Lauren told you about him."

"How can you focus on school if there's a man in your life?"

She didn't bother to hide her snort of derision as she stood. This conversation was going to require coffee. Now. The pot hadn't finished brewing, but there was enough for the first two cups. She popped a mug under the drip as she slid the carafe out of the machine. Pouring each of them a cup, she repeated her maneuver in reverse, then looked at Barrett over her shoulder.

"I never suggested I was going to become a nun. This may sound strange to you, but I'm perfectly capable of studying art and having relationships with other human beings at the same time."

His lips pressed together. She was getting under his skin. Good. She handed him his coffee (black, as he preferred) but instead of returning to the table, she leaned back against the counter, mug cradled in her hands.

There was danger in anger, too close to the passion that had always flared between them. Today, however, felt different. Her anger ran more cold than hot, and she was able to tamp down the embers that tried to flare up in his presence. Yes, he was gorgeous. Yes, his confidence—arrogance, even—had always been a turn-on. And yes, it would be awfully easy to fall back into lust with him. But she had learned over the past year that she wanted more. She had a new life in the works. She'd bought a house, for chrissakes, and she had a baby on the way. This was much bigger than a little heat between two people who weren't any good for each other. Chemistry was the only thing they had in common.

Luke emerged from the bathroom, a towel around his hips and another around his shoulders, which he was currently using to dry off his hair. He stopped short when he saw Barrett.

"Sorry, I didn't realize we had company."

Dora grinned at him. She could have kissed him, he was that smooth. Actually, she should kiss him. Setting her coffee down on the counter, she walked over to Luke, gave him a sweet kiss on the lips, and said, "Morning, honey. An old friend stopped by to surprise me. Want to throw some clothes on and join us for coffee?"

Last night, Dora had suggested that Luke scoot his backpack into the closet so they didn't trip on it in the morning. Now, as he emerged from the closet with a handful of clothes, it looked an awful lot like he lived here.

Barrett watched Luke like a hawk until he disappeared back into the bathroom to change. It was really the only private place in the apartment. Dora calmly sipped her coffee and ignored Barrett's glare for the minute and a half that it took Luke to get dressed. When he emerged, he looked perfectly at home in her space. Nothing would send a clearer message to Barrett than another man staking his claim.

"Sorry about that," said Luke, walking up to Barrett and offering his hand. "I'm Luke."

Barrett stood and shook his hand, the manners too ingrained to ignore.

"Barrett."

"Please, sit," said Luke. "Enjoy the coffee. I'll grab another chair."

The only other chair in the apartment was the stool she used for painting. It was a bit high, but it worked, and it forced Barrett to look up at Luke, which must be driving him crazy.

"Barrett. Dora has definitely mentioned you before. Are you from New York?"

Barrett nodded curtly.

"What brings you to Chicago?"

"I'm here for the day on business. I had time before my first meeting, so I thought I'd surprise Dora with a visit. My apologies for the intrusion. I didn't realize she would have company."

"Oh, it's no problem," said Luke. "We love visitors."

Barrett missed Luke's wink. She saw it though, and her smile widened. Soon she was going to start giggling, and that would really push Barrett over the edge.

"Why don't I make us all some breakfast," suggested Dora. "We have plenty of eggs."

"Or we could go out," offered Luke. "There's a great breakfast place around the corner."

"No, thank you," said Barrett. "My schedule is tight. I only wanted to stop by to drop off this letter and photos from my wife, Lauren."

He pulled a thick envelope from the inside pocket of his coat, handed it to Dora, and then began to put his coat on.

"Leaving so soon?"

Dora couldn't keep all the amusement out of her voice, but she hoped that it came across as friendly rather than laughter at Barrett's expense. She wanted him to leave, but she didn't actually want to hurt him. Well, only a little.

"I'm afraid so."

He walked toward the door and she followed, opening it for him, and he stepped into the hallway. There were so many things he could have said. The last thing she expected was for him to leave all of it unspoken.

All he said was, "Until we meet again."

Blinking, she wondered if it could possibly be this easy.

"Goodbye, Barrett," she said, and closed the door.

She stared at it for a moment before bolting it again, then walked back to the kitchen. A plate of buttered toast waited beside her mug at the table.

"Thanks, honey."

She gave Luke a big hug, so grateful to have him in her corner. It was sad, really, that only the presence of another man could convince Barrett that she was serious about ending things. This encounter would have been very different without Luke here, so it was also sad that she couldn't be trusted to be alone with Barrett. This time, though, the message had gotten through. Barrett would no longer come looking for her, and she no longer had to worry about whether or not she would be strong enough to resist him. It was over, and she could move on.

CHAPTER FORTY-TWO

Today

ON FRIDAY AFTERNOON, DORA THREW HERSELF INTO
Halloween preparations. She had already decorated outside,
but the cookies wouldn't bake themselves. She had an
assembly line going in the kitchen: baking, cooling, and frosting. While their neighborhood wouldn't be overrun with
trick-or-treaters, enough families would stop by that she
needed to be ready.

Complicating matters, David would arrive soon. He was
curious about Halloween, never having had a chance to experience the American holiday. They celebrated the Day of the
Dead in Ecuador, which was similar to the tradition in Mexico.
But second thoughts had started to trickle in almost as soon as
she had extended the invitation. This thing with David was
new. She wasn't sure of her feelings yet, only that she wanted to
let them develop naturally. Introducing him to the family, especially after this week's emotional upheaval, now seemed like a
singularly bad idea. She had been nervous about taking him
out on the water, but this was ten times worse. If he didn't mesh

with the family, their not-yet-a-relationship would be over before it began.

And then it was too late. David had arrived.

Luke was quick to welcome him. "David, I'm Luke. It's a pleasure to finally meet you."

When David turned away to hand Dora his coat, Luke met her eyes and gave her a thumbs up. She suppressed a smile. No matter how attractive David might be, the real test of compatibility was whether Luke would enjoy hanging out with him for the afternoon.

She needn't have worried. The two basically had a contest to see who could be more charming while she frosted the cookies. David had the international advantage, but Luke had a down-home vibe that more than balanced the scales. The two of them taste-tested the cookies while David shared stories from his travels and Luke responded with stories from his days of touring with the band. David found it fascinating that, like Dora, Luke was also an artist.

David had clearly passed the initial screening, but Dora suspected the true test was still to come. Luke had evaluated plenty of teenage boyfriends, his nice-guy demeanor lulling them into a false sense of success. The tough questions always came as a surprise. Only when David was comfortable did Luke subtly shift into interrogation mode.

"So how long are you in town, David?"

David must have sensed the shift as well, because he looked over at Dora before answering. "I'm not sure," he said. "The decision is not mine to make."

That was very sweet of him, to suggest that she had an influence on his travel plans. She wasn't sure she believed him, but still—very sweet.

"You don't have business or family obligations that will pull you away?"

Dora paused mid-swipe with the frosting. That was an

excellent question. Maybe she should have slipped Luke a list of discussion topics before David arrived. There was a lot she wanted to know.

"I do plan to see my family at Christmas," he said, "but we have not yet decided where to meet."

"What about your business?"

"Each gallery has a very competent director, and I can run the finances from anywhere in the world. There are several artists that I would like to see, but that can wait until the new year."

"And where are those artists located?"

It was a highly specific question and, Dora suspected, not one that David would normally answer, but once again he glanced at Dora and then went out of his way to reassure Luke.

"One of them is in Peru, the other in Chile." It was his next statement that caught her by surprise. "Dora, *querida*, if you are free after the holidays, perhaps you will join me on the trip."

"I...I don't know if I'm free." She ignored Luke's skeptical look. Of course she would be free. She had no responsibilities at the sailing school during the winter. But the idea of traveling with a man she had only just met was both terrifying and thrilling. "I probably am," she said, deciding to ignore the fear and go with "thrilling."

At that moment there was a knock on the back door. She looked at the clock. It was at least an hour before trick-or-treating was due to start. Wiping her hands on the dishcloth draped over her shoulder, she went to open the door.

"Barrett."

He was literally the last person she would have expected to come knocking on her door. Standing on the back steps, he looked like a soft-focus version of his younger self. All the hard edges had blurred. She had carefully avoided him in New York, but she'd seen recent photos on Lauren's bedside table. It was definitely him, and he looked good, all things considered. Thinning hair and a thickening middle, but still attractive in an elder statesman kind of way, and she certainly wasn't in a position to judge someone for having a squishy middle.

Over the years, when she had imagined seeing him again, she had never been quite sure how she would react. Anger had been her first guess, followed by a flare-up of their old chemistry. Less likely, she thought she might feel disappointment, or something like anguish over the lost years, but she hadn't expected indifference. The man before her was a stranger, and he prompted no emotional reaction at all.

"May I come in?" he asked. His voice hadn't changed, but it didn't elicit the same reaction as before.

She thought about his request for a second. Why not? Today was already a weird day. Instead of Scrooge and his serial ghosts, she appeared to be cursed by the ghosts of past, present, and future all at the same time. Happy Halloween?

"Of course," she said. "Come on in."

Stepping back, Dora waved him through the mudroom and into the kitchen, stopping him only long enough to take his coat and hang it on a hook.

"Barrett, you met my husband, Luke, many years ago in Chicago."

"Of course," said Luke, standing up and shaking Barrett's hand. "It's good to see you again."

When Barrett turned his attention to David, Luke gave her a "What the hell?" look behind Barrett's back. She shrugged. Weirdest day ever.

David also stood and offered his hand.

"Barrett, this is David Ignacio Lozano Campoverde." She was quite proud of herself for remembering all of David's names—not that she would ever admit to having practiced until she could say the whole thing without stumbling. She had planned to do a more formal introduction to Luke, but missed her chance. David noticed, however, and gave her a secret smile.

"Barrett Harrington."

"It is a pleasure to meet you," said David.

"David is a friend of mine," said Dora, then wondered how she should characterize Barrett. Lauren had clearly shared her suspicions with him, so there was nothing left to hide. She might as well roll with it. "Barrett is an old friend and the biological father of my children." At David's questioning look, she smiled. "It's a long story. I'll tell you another time."

Barrett seemed taken aback by her frankness, but she couldn't find it within herself to feel bad for him. He was the one who had the harebrained idea of somehow reclaiming her. She gestured for him to join the gentlemen at the kitchen table while she stayed at the counter, adding sprinkles to the Halloween cookies.

"So, Barrett," said Luke, "to what do we owe the pleasure?"

God bless her fearless inquisitor.

Instead of responding to Luke, Barrett spoke to Dora. "You know why I'm here."

Right. He "needed" her. What was that supposed to mean, anyway? He had all the money in the world, two grown children, and she had to assume he filled his time with some kind of meaningful activity. He had built a life with Lauren, seeking out Dora for comfort only after losing his wife. As far as Dora was concerned, there was no clearer way to send the message: "You'll always come second in my heart." Not exactly a compelling case for ditching her current life to follow him like a puppy back to New York. She studied him in a detached kind of way. Had he always been this much of a drama queen?

"The last time we spoke," she said, "you wanted me to come out for the memorial service and meet the children. I declined."

Seeing him in person was almost a let-down. She had

worried for years that their chemistry would still override her good sense, but any chemistry between them had long since faded away. She could remember the effects, but those echoes of the past paled in comparison to her recent, vivid experiences with David. She had been a different person back then, as had Barrett, and their chemistry hadn't survived the changes. If anything, today she could see him clearly for the first time.

"I thought, perhaps, if I made the appeal in person..."

"I'm sorry, but no. While it's wonderful to see you, of course, I haven't changed my mind."

He studied her for a moment, seeming to realize that this was a lost cause.

"I see," he said. "In that case, perhaps I should be on my way." He pushed back from the table and turned toward the mudroom. She stopped him with a hand on his arm.

"You should stay," she said. "The girls will be here soon. You should meet them."

David had been doing a remarkable job of keeping his expression neutral, despite the fact that this must all be very confusing. After her last remark, though, he couldn't hide his surprise. She smiled at him and shook her head, telegraphing many things at once: *Yes, the father of my children has never met them. Long story. I'll tell you later.*

Barrett didn't notice this unspoken exchange between Dora and David because he was frozen in place, one step from the kitchen table.

"Meet them?"

"Yes. The girls. They'll be here any minute."

"I'm not sure that's such a good idea," he said. "There's so much to explain."

Dora wasn't sure it was a great idea either, but it seemed wrong to let the opportunity slip away. She nodded slowly. "I know. They know the basics, though, so you wouldn't be starting from scratch."

"I can't—I'm not ready."

"Okay," said Dora, keeping her voice calm and soothing because Barrett looked like he might panic. "In that case, you probably should be going, or you'll meet them whether you're ready or not."

"Right," said Barrett. He turned back to the table. No matter how freaked out he might be, Barrett would never forget his manners. "It was a pleasure to see you, Luke, and to meet you, David."

He crossed the kitchen to Dora and put a hand on her cheek. She leaned against it, trying to catch the echo of what they once were to each other. As farewells went, it wasn't too bad.

"I'll meet your children whenever they're ready," she said, "not at their mother's funeral. Let them find me in their own time."

He nodded, then left without saying anything else.

Dora walked over to the kitchen sink window and watched him drive away. Then she resumed her sprinkling.

"Well," she said. "That was interesting."

CHAPTER FORTY-THREE

28 years ago, August

DORA KNEW THEY WERE DOING EVERYTHING BACKWARD, BUT SHE didn't care. As far as she was concerned, she was the luckiest girl in the world. Sure, most people choose to date, get married, move in together, and then (maybe) start making some babies. She and Luke had started with the baby, then bought a house, followed by marriage. Dating wasn't really a part of their plan, but friendship certainly was. Dora already counted Luke as her best friend, and she hoped they could hold on to that in the coming years. Standing beside Luke in front of a justice of the peace, with an art school friend by her side and one of Luke's bandmates by his, Dora vowed silently never to take her blessings for granted.

Dora wore a cream silk dress, one that wouldn't fit in another month. Luke wore his one good suit. Their friends had dressed for the occasion as well and, Dora was fairly certain, gotten to know each other by sharing a flask of strong whiskey. She could smell it from three feet away.

From here, they would go to brunch, have some champagne, and celebrate. She planned to nap in the car on the way up to the new house. All their stuff had been taken up by movers, and many unopened boxes awaited them.

Later that afternoon, they parked in the driveway of their new (old) house and looked at each other with a mix of shock and glee.

"Welcome home, Mr. James."

"Likewise, Mrs. James."

"Shall we walk down to the pier to watch the sunset?" asked Luke.

"That sounds amazing, but I don't think the sun is going to set anytime soon."

"Let's go down anyway. I want to get my feet wet."

So they did. And as they sat on the dock with their bare feet dangling in the water, she tilted her head to the side and looked over at her new husband.

"I am seriously lucky."

"Well, obviously," he replied. "You're married to me."

She laughed. "Exactly. Instead of being alone and pregnant with the world's fastest-growing baby, I'm hitched to the best possible dad in the world. Seriously, you're going to be so good at this. You have a kind heart and the patience of a saint."

This time it was Luke who laughed. "Let's hope you're right, because it's a little late to back out now."

Twenty-seven years ago, January

The monthly pilgrimage to the OB/GYN's office had become something of a ritual for Dora and Luke. He would take the afternoon off, and they would go out for coffee afterward, to debate baby names and house rules and all the other things new parents worry about.

At this particular appointment, the doctor did the usual

stuff, measuring her belly and checking her blood pressure and listening to the baby's heartbeat. When he suggested an ultrasound, to find out how big this baby might be, Dora readily agreed. She felt bigger than the last time around, and that had been twins.

He made a call and they were able to do the ultrasound right away. The specialty office was right next door. The exam began much as Dora remembered from her experience with the twins, and wow, the gel was cold on her belly. The tech described what she was doing at each step, but as the exam continued, she spoke less and less. Finally, she frowned, and Dora felt the first twinge of worry.

"Is something wrong?"

"Not exactly," said the tech. "I'm having trouble getting a good angle. Can you excuse me for a moment, please? I have a quick question for the doctor."

"Of course," said Dora, trying to sound calm.

"I know I'm new to this," said Luke, "but something seems off. What do you think?"

"I don't know." Dora couldn't seem to squash her growing panic. "I'm trying not to read anything more into it, but what if the baby is too big? Or worse, what if he's missing something important? What then?"

"You think it's a boy?" asked Luke. He stroked her hair. "Take a deep breath, sweetheart. We're not going to worry until there's something to worry about."

She nodded and took a series of slow breaths. It was a lot harder than it should have been. The tech returned, the doctor trailing behind her, just as Dora was feeling more calm.

"Well, Mama," he said, "I don't think we need to worry about the baby being too big."

She sagged back against the reclined medical bed. "Well, that's a relief."

"In fact," he continued, "I think they'll be on the small side."

Dora stared at him.

Luke recovered first. "They?"

The doctor turned to the tech, who said, "I'm confident that there are two babies in there."

"Oh God," Dora breathed. "Twins again?"

"But," the tech continued, "there may be a third. Let's finish the exam and see if we can get a good angle on that third baby."

Everyone was silent as the tech maneuvered the wand to snap more pictures from different angles.

Finally, she looked at Dora and grinned. "Yep. Three babies."

"Three?" Dora's voice came out as a squeak, and she looked at Luke in a panic.

"Well, honey," he said, "I guess we're very lucky."

CHAPTER FORTY-FOUR

Today

MEL WOKE TO FROST AND SUNSHINE ON SATURDAY MORNING, BUT by the afternoon, the sunshine had warmed things up for the celebration of the finished mural and park. They had finished just in time; snow was forecast for tomorrow, and temperatures were dropping fast. The crowd filling the small park was bundled in winter coats, but nobody wanted to miss the fun, or the free food.

Mel and Fitz had staked out a spot under the old oak on the back side of the park. While Fitz fielded questions from the local newspaper reporter, Mel took the opportunity to photograph the crowd, both wide shots as well as close-ups of the key players on the project. She shamelessly eavesdropped on Fitz and the reporter, glad that he was pointing out some of the subtler features of the mural. If he didn't bring it up, she had planned to brag on his behalf. Not everyone would spot the nod to M.C. Escher, with two-dimensional characters climbing out of the books and becoming three-dimensional. She loved the fact that it echoed his tattoo, although she might be the only person here today who knew that.

The reporter finished up with Fitz and turned to Mel. "Would you be willing to share some of your photos of the mural project? I can take some snapshots today, but I understand you've been keeping a record of the progress."

Mel raised an eyebrow at Fitz. Apparently someone had been bragging on her in much the same way she had planned to brag on him. Great minds and all that.

"Of course. Happy to help," said Mel.

The reporter gave Mel her card with contact information and then headed off to take her snapshots. Taking advantage of the peaceful moment, Fitz gave her a quick but thorough kiss.

"Looks like you two should get a room," said Pippa, interrupting the moment.

Fitz took his time winding up the kiss before turning to his sister. "That's a good idea," he said, keeping an arm around Mel. "Where are the munchkins?"

"Over at story time," said Pippa, gesturing over her shoulder to the willow dome, which was currently overrun with small children. It was also covered with streamers, since the willow whips wouldn't fill in with leaves until springtime. "Nice turnout, by the way. More teenagers than I would have expected."

"A lot of the kids helped on the project," said Mel. "Mostly on the landscaping."

"Do any of them babysit?"

Mel laughed. "You might want to talk to Hannah. She's the one doing story time. She's very protective of her younger sister, and she clearly doesn't mind doing story time, so I imagine she would be a good candidate."

"I will." She gave Fitz a meaningful look. "I'm going to cut back on my hours over the summer so we can spend more time up here with Mom and Dad. A local babysitter would really help to fill the gaps."

"Where are they, by the way? Mom wanted to see the finished mural, and Dad must be happy that the project is over. I thought they'd be here."

"You didn't hear? They got a last-minute appointment with a couples counselor, something about a cancellation. Mom hustled Dad over there before he knew what was happening." Pippa suddenly realized that her kids were leaving story time and heading for the snack table. "Gotta run. Nice job on the mural, little bro. You, too, Mel."

And with that she was off to chase children. Before Mel and Fitz could consider hitting the snack table themselves, Rob and Kat wandered over.

"Congratulations, you two," said Kat. "I was just telling Rob how amazed and impressed I am with the finished project. It's amazing that it all came together so quickly at the end."

Rob and Fitz did a manly handshake / bro hug, and Fitz thanked Kat, who was leaning up against the oak tree. "It was a group effort, as you well know. Thanks for wrangling the teen labor force for us."

"My pleasure."

Mel turned to Rob. "I'm going to sort and edit all the project photos in the next few weeks. I can share the gallery link with you in case you want any of them for your web site or brochure or something."

"That would be great. I need to tackle the website at some point. This is the perfect excuse."

The guys started talking about how the landscaping would change over the seasons, and Mel took the opportunity to pull Kat aside.

"So?" asked Mel, dying of curiosity to know if Kat had actually followed through with her plan.

Kat's sphinx smile told her nothing.

"Did you change Rob's mind?"

"I might have."

"Hah! I knew it. There's a different vibe between the two of you now. Did you have to resort to the plan?"

Kat's eyes rested on Rob, and Mel knew that the two of them were going to make it. "I was very persuasive," she said, and left it at that. "What about you?" asked Kat. "Did you figure things out with your family?"

"It's all good," said Mel. "We have some things to figure out, but it's going to be fine. And I'm sticking with the contract. I leave in a few weeks."

"I'm so glad. Selfishly, I would have loved it if you stayed. I don't have many friends around here, and I'll miss our get-togethers down at the Beach."

"We'll have to keep up the tradition when I'm back in town."

"We will. And in the meantime, I'm going to try to ease off on work and have more of a life—and not only with Rob. I'm planning to go up to Milwaukee once a month to meet up with some school friends."

"That's great. It's a bummer you have to go all the way to Milwaukee to hang out with friends, but you'll be a happier person if you do."

"I agree."

Rob grabbed Kat's hand. "I'm heading over to the snack table. I hear they have Scooby Snacks. Want to come with me?"

She smiled and pushed off the oak tree. "I'll do anything for Scooby Snacks," she said. "See you later."

Dora and Lucy stood near the back door of the library. "Next time you come over, we need to toast to our matchmaking skills," said Lucy. "Fitz and Mel seem to have made a strong connection."

"Yes," mused Dora. "We'll have to see how that connection holds up. I understand he's leaving the country as well."

"I give them a better than fifty-fifty chance," said Lucy, sounding very sure of herself. "We also need to toast to my other success," she said with a smirk.

"Give it some time," said Dora. "I haven't forgiven you yet for the initial bait and switch."

"Yes, you have," countered Lucy. "You got lucky in both business and love, and I expect a detailed report of your progress on both fronts."

"We'll see about that."

David was across the small park, talking intently with Luke. Dora had to stop herself from sighing and going into a sensual daze every time she looked at him. They were moving slowly, which only seemed to make the experience more intense.

"How long is he staying?" asked Lucy.

"I've invited him to join me for Thanksgiving. I actually invited him to stay in the house, but then we both had second thoughts. We're trying to take things slowly, but I can only handle so much temptation. Having him under the same roof would push me over the edge."

"Are you sure you don't want to be pushed?"

"A part of me would love it, but a bigger part of me would like this to be more than a flash in the pan. I think we're wiser to wait."

"Fine," huffed Lucy. "But I still expect to live vicariously through you."

"I'm thinking of traveling with him after Christmas."

"What? Where?"

"We would go to Ecuador where I could meet his family. Then we would go to Chile and Peru to meet with artists."

"That sounds amazing. Any chance you could see Mel while you're traveling? Won't she be in South America somewhere?"

"She'll be all over the place, but I'm hoping we can meet up."

"Will Tessa watch the house for you?"

"She and RJ are planning a trip to California, so I was actually talking with Rob Murray about that. He's interested in building up his off-season business, and he's been thinking about doing property management for vacation homes. As a test he said he'd be happy to keep tabs on the house while I'm away."

"He would be perfect. Good choice."

"Change of topic. What do you know about email?"

"I know how it works. Why?"

"This is embarrassing, but Luke has always done email for the both of us. He lets me know when I have a message. Now that he's moving to Nashville, I'm going to have to figure it out. I was hoping you could teach me."

Lucy slung an arm around Dora's shoulders. "I'm here for you, babe. We'll drink wine and do email and by the end of the night you'll be an expert. Or at least tipsy. No matter what, you win."

Mary Evelyn walked over to Dora and Lucy, saying hello before she turned and tried to wiggle the handle on the back door, which didn't move. She smiled in satisfaction.

"I finally got the door handle fixed," she said. "No more shenanigans in the library."

"I guess they'll have to get a room," said Dora with a laugh.

"Yes, they will."

"What are your plans for the commercial space if Mel's not going to use it?" asked Lucy.

"Well, now that's an interesting question," said Dora. "I could sublet it, of course, but I was also thinking that I might want to teach. It would be a great space to work with young artists."

Mary Evelyn jumped right on that. "I would be happy to

promote your classes. The kids would be lucky to have you as a teacher. Also, you should know that we've had some requests from the wine moms for those 'paint & sip' classes that are so popular these days. I can't host anything like that in the library, but you girls might have fun with it."

Dora and Lucy looked at each other, and the plan formed without either of them saying a word. Hidden Springs was about to get a lot more fun. Mary Evelyn looked back and forth between them, then shook her head. "I'll spread the word at Mom 'n Tots," she said. "I need to talk with them anyway 'bout the tots contributing their footprints to the park. We have a concrete project in mind."

David and Luke started walking in their direction, and all three women paused to soak in the sight. After so many years of living with Luke, Dora had become almost immune to Luke's good looks, but in company with David, their combined masculine appeal merited a moment of silent appreciation. Luke still had his sandy brown hair and boy-next-door vibe, which contrasted nicely with David's silver-shot dark hair and finely chiseled profile. The best thing about the pair of them, though, was that good looks were just the wrapper around two fascinating human beings. Dora took a moment to silently thank Luke for having the good sense to set them on this new path. She couldn't wait to find out what would happen next.

"Does your David have a father?" murmured Mary Evelyn. "Asking for a friend."

"I assume so," said Dora. "Most people do."

David and Luke had drawn close enough to overhear, so David was able to answer for himself.

"I do indeed have a father," said David. "My mother passed away a number of years ago, but my father is still with us."

"And does he look like you?" Mary Evelyn was truly shameless.

David handled the inquiry with grace. "You will have to

decide for yourself when you meet him. He enjoys travel, and I'm sure he will visit Hidden Springs at some point, or perhaps you could visit Ecuador."

"Now that is the best idea I've heard all day," said Mary Evelyn.

CHAPTER FORTY-FIVE

MEL FOUND HERSELF ALONE UNDER THE OAK TREE WHEN FITZ WAS asked to answer some questions over at the mural. She wasn't alone for long. RJ and Tessa walked over to join her, their hands linked.

"Nice job on the mural," said Tessa. "I can't believe you two painted all that in only a few weeks."

"Me either," said Mel. "It helped that Fitz knew what he was doing." She glanced down at their still-linked hands, then back up at their faces. They were so easy with each other now, and Tessa so much more relaxed than she used to be. They were good for each other. "Any decisions on California?"

"We're going out to visit my parents after Christmas," said RJ. "We'll see how we feel about it while we're there. On the one hand, it's a great opportunity. On the other hand, what we have here is pretty great, too. We'll have to see."

"I thought your mom lived in Chicago," said Mel.

"She did," said RJ. "She and my dad are turning over a new leaf. They've been living together for almost five months and they haven't killed each other yet, which has come as a surprise to all of us."

"I wasn't surprised," said Tessa. "I think they're going to make it."

"Well, that makes one of you," said RJ. After Tessa elbowed him in the ribs, he said, "I will try to be supportive and optimistic." The phrase sounded rehearsed, and Mel laughed.

"Maybe we should make it interesting," said Tessa, giving RJ a flirty challenge out of the corner of her eye. "Doughnuts?"

"You're on. Deadline?"

"Our visit."

"Deal," said RJ. "Speaking of doughnuts, I think I saw some on the snack table." He started to back away in that direction.

"Save one for me," called Tessa after him.

"Aye, aye, Captain."

RJ's younger sister Sunny and her husband Will were visiting for the weekend. Mel could see Will over by the snack table. Sunny was headed their way from the willow structure, so Mel assumed her two kids were part of the throng inside. Before Sunny could reach them, though, her children escaped from the dome, splitting up and running in two different directions. Sunny signaled Will, who intercepted little Oscar at the snack table. Sunny trotted after Huck, who was headed straight for the street.

"Wow," said Tessa after watching the scene unfold. "I am so not prepared to have children."

"You and me both, sister," said Mel.

Callie wandered over to join her sisters under the oak tree. "You and Fitz did amazing work on the mural. You should be really proud."

"Thanks," said Mel. She normally wasn't one for public

recognition, but an afternoon full of compliments wasn't all bad. "How long are you in town for?"

"I should be here through Christmas," answered Callie. "The groundwork has been laid in Nashville. All I really need to do now is focus on songwriting, and I can do that anywhere. It will be nice to stay in one place for a while instead of all this back-and-forth."

"Things seem to be going well with Hot Muralist," said Tessa.

Mel winced. "Please, call him Fitz."

Tessa smiled, and Mel knew she had given herself away, but her sisters would have figured it out soon enough.

Apparently story time had ended, because the volume level in the willow dome went up significantly. The oak tree was close enough to the dome that they could hear the kids' conversations quite clearly. The kids were asking lots of questions about the mural, and the newly uncovered cemetery at the far end of the small park. One of Pippa's kids said that their uncle Fitz had a tattoo on his back that was a lot like the people coming out of books in the mural. All the kids decided they wanted to see it, and Mel was half-horrified, half-amused when all three of Pippa's kids ran out of the dome to retrieve Fitz and drag him back over to the crowd of little ones. They invited him inside the dome, then demanded that he take his shirt off. This, of course, prompted a flurry of interest from the mom crowd, who drifted closer in order to admire the view. Not only was Fitz's physique (and tattoo) on full display, but Fitz was forced to explain the tattoo to all the kids. He kept it simple, explaining that—like the illustrated man on his back—he didn't want to live his life inside a box. This somehow prompted a chasing game involving all the kids yelling, "No box for me!"

Callie and Tessa each slung an arm around Mel and gave her a squeeze from opposite sides.

"No box for me," said Mel.

"Me either," said Callie and Tessa at the same time.

After the unveiling, and the cleanup, and all the farewells, Mel and Fitz lingered until they were the last ones on site. The sun had set, lowering the temperature by at least ten degrees, but Mel wasn't ready to leave yet. If she could only extend this moment forever, then her time with Fitz wouldn't need to draw to a close. She zipped up her fleece and sat down on the bench. Fitz silently took a seat beside her.

She would need to come back in the morning to get some shots of the mural when the light was good and nobody was blocking the view. Today had been great for group photos, and close-ups of some of the key players. She was really looking forward to putting together a photo journal of the project. Maybe it would help her close this chapter of her life.

"You know your tattoo is now legend among the ten and under crowd. They're going to be begging for ink of their own."

"My sister gave me the heads up that I was no longer popular among the moms."

"I'm not so sure about that," said Mel, her voice full of humor. "Most of them were staring at your back like they wanted a much closer look."

"I think I'll take angry moms over hungry moms."

With a laugh, Mel said, "Wise choice."

"Are you busy for dinner tonight?" asked Fitz. "I couldn't have done this without you. Seems like a nice dinner out is in order."

"There's no need to thank me. I had a wonderful time. I'm really glad my mom volunteered me for the project."

The last thing she wanted to do was to end their collaboration on a weirdly formal note.

"Work with me here, Mel. I'm trying to ask you out on a date."

"You mean a date date? Or a fake date?" Not that it mattered. She'd be on board for either one.

"I thought we could try a real one, if you're up for it."

She turned to face him on the bench, pulling one foot up and wrapping her arm around her knee.

"I would love to go on a real date with you, but I'm wary. Real dating is going to get complicated fast. How long do we have?"

"Weeks, or possibly days. Now that I'm officially assigned to the project, it's all going to move quickly."

"When do you head back downtown?"

"I was thinking tomorrow morning."

Her heart sank down into her stomach. So little time. Even if she trailed him back to Chicago and crashed at his place, they might only have a few days. And as much as she wanted to follow him, she had a substantial amount of work to complete in the next few weeks, along with all the preparations for the trip. She had spent all her spare time helping him these last few weeks, and now there was none left.

"So tonight is our last chance to hang out for a while."

He nodded. "How would you feel about getting a room and ordering room service?"

The smile started in her heavy heart and floated up to shine on her face. "I would have very friendly feelings about that."

"Good," he said. "Me, too."

She thought about it for a minute. "This is risky, you know. Breaking the rules. We promised each other fake dating, followed by a fake attempt at long-distance."

"This thing between us, whatever we want to call it, is not fake. It's very real, and I'm not prepared to walk away from it. I don't know what your dating life has been like, but I have trouble finding anyone that I want to see after a date or two. We just spent weeks together, all day every day, and I only want to spend more time with you. For me, that's a big deal. So I don't care if our timing is off. I can wait."

Mel swallowed hard. There was no way she would ruin this moment with crying. "We don't need to label this, or put it in a box. Let's be friends who try to spend time together whenever and wherever we can, until we get the timing right."

"Friends with benefits."

"The best kind," she said.

"I'm on board with that plan."

Late that night, tangled up in each other, they made plans for their first international date: coffee in Santiago, Chile, in January. He would be living there. She would be passing through with at least two nights in the city. After three months apart, it would be a great test of their long-distance plan.

EPILOGUE

Three months later

THEY MET AT A SIDEWALK CAFE. SHE HAD ARRIVED IN SANTIAGO earlier that afternoon. He had finished work for the day. The weekend stretched before them, wide open. Both had cleared their schedules. Impatience had her tapping her feet and sipping her coffee too quickly. When she saw him coming down the sidewalk she stood, too excited to be cool and give him a casual wave.

She had worried that it would be awkward, or that he would feel like a stranger, but the opposite was true. After three months of sporadic texts, emails, phone calls, and video chats, depending on her location and quality of internet access, their connection felt stronger than ever, like a rubber band that had been stretched but was now snapping them back together.

Instead of a hesitant greeting, he pulled her in for a long, slow kiss, ignoring their curious and appreciative audience. They took their seats, the sexual tension simmering between them. They wouldn't be here long.

He placed his order in confident Spanish. It seemed they

had both acquired some skills over the last few months. It was a matter of survival, really. If you were immersed in the language all day every day, even the most rudimentary Spanish skills were bound to improve.

"How's the project going," she asked. "Any new crises?"

"This week has been quiet, so I fully expect several things to go wrong next week. The universe will want to balance the scales."

She laughed. "Do you still think the project will finish on time?"

"Hard to say this early in the game, but it's still possible. What about you? Tired of living out of a suitcase yet?"

"The excitement hasn't worn off yet, but I can see how it might get old by the end of the project. A couple of months of life on the road is one thing. Two years will be a whole different deal."

"How's your family?"

"All good. Tessa and RJ are out in California trying to figure out if they want to live there. Callie is still splitting her time between Nashville and home. I got to see Mom and David when I was in Quito. They were there for a few weeks in between visiting artists."

"And how is that going?"

"I'm cautiously optimistic, but it's early days yet."

"You could say the same thing about us."

Wide smile. "For us, I'll have to say I'm very optimistic. But that's just me."

"I find I'm also very optimistic," he said.

"How's your apartment?" she asked. "Is it far?"

"Not far at all. It's around the corner. Would you like to see it?"

"I would love to."

Maybe she wouldn't need a hotel room this weekend after all.

Two years later, Christmas

"Welcome home." Dora pulled Mel into a hug before she made it through the back door. "It's so good to see you. How was your flight? You must be exhausted. What's the time difference with Chile again? Oh, Fitz, there you are. Come in." She didn't stop talking when she hugged him, too. "I'm so glad that you can stay with us over Christmas. We'll be sure to share you with your family. I talked with Margot this morning and your sister and the kids are arriving tomorrow. It will be Christmas at the lake for everyone."

"We're in my room, right?" asked Mel when she could get a word in edgewise.

"Yes, dear. Callie is next door with Adam, of course, and Tessa is with RJ. You and Fitz get your room. Sebastian and Carolina will stay in Callie and Tessa's rooms, and I've turned the study into a guest room, so your dad and Zeke will sleep there."

"Is Callie's room still decked out in *Little Mermaid* decor?"

Dora laughed. "No. She took what she wanted to keep and I did it over a few months ago. Although I don't think Carolina would have minded. Now, I know you'll want to rest, but put your things down for a minute and I'll make you a cup of tea."

"I'll bring in our bags while I still have some adrenaline left," said Fitz. "I'm afraid if I sit down I'll fall asleep in the chair."

He headed back out to the car while Mel slumped gratefully into a kitchen chair.

"Kat asked me to tell you hello," said Dora. "She and Rob are visiting Rob's parents in Arizona, but they should be back before you leave. You'll overlap by at least a few days."

"Cool. When does everybody else get in?"

"Callie and Tessa are already here, of course. Callie has been limiting her time in Nashville so that she can be here with Adam and Danny during the school year. It worked so well going on tour together as a family last summer that they're already planning to do it again next summer. And Tessa and RJ are over at RJ's house. It took forever for her to admit that she was officially living with him. I don't know why. Everyone else knew it was happening. But whatever. I'm so glad they decided to stay here instead of going to California. They're much happier here. Neither one of them would have wanted to work as much as they would have had to work to afford living in California."

None of this was news to Mel, but her mother loved to talk, and right now she didn't really have the energy to keep up her end of the conversation. It was actually kind of soothing to let her mother's words wash over her. She had missed this, time in the kitchen with her mom. Sometimes she wondered how long she would want to live abroad. Two years in, she was still loving it, as was Fitz, and they saw no reason to rush home. She had wrapped up her two-year contract, and was taking a break from suitcase life by living with Fitz in Santiago. His project would finish up in the next six months, so they had some time to figure out what came next. She had enough international contacts now that she should be able to find work anywhere. This gave her the flexibility to follow Fitz to his next project, and to give the bond between them time to deepen and strengthen. Like Tessa, she wasn't in a hurry to make anything official, but in her heart she knew that she and Fitz were in it for the long haul.

"Your father and Zeke are driving up. I expect they'll roll in late tonight, so you'll see them in the morning. Make sure to ask about the rings they're both wearing. They're engaged, but they're shy about sharing the news, so you didn't hear it from me. You just noticed their new rings."

"Got it," said Mel.

"Got it," echoed Fitz, who had come back into the kitchen lugging the suitcases.

"David and his kids arrive tomorrow afternoon. It will be so nice to have everyone together for the holiday."

"Everyone?" asked Mel.

She shouldn't tease her mother, but it was an open secret in the family that she'd like to rope Barrett and his kids into family gatherings as well. The kids had tracked her down a year ago after Christmas, and they had cautiously opened the lines of communication. Mel wasn't sure exactly how much they knew about the unusual surrogacy arrangement, but it was nice that her mother was able to reconnect with them. It helped old wounds to finally heal.

"Actually," said Dora, "there's a chance that Barrett and the kids will join us on Christmas."

"You're kidding."

"I gather the holidays feel hollow without Lauren, so they're looking for a new Christmas tradition. I invited them. We'll see if they show up."

"That would certainly make for an interesting holiday. I'd love to meet them."

Fitz pulled Mel to her feet. "You need to sleep," he said. "I need to sleep. I'm sorry to rush in and then abandon you, but we're not going to be very good company until we recharge."

"Don't worry, you two. Get the sleep you need. If you wake up hungry in the middle of the night, don't be shy about scrounging in the kitchen for food. Nothing is off-limits."

"Thanks, Mom," said Mel, giving her a kiss on the cheek.

As they headed for the stairs, Mel noticed that some new photos had been added to the family photo gallery. There was a shot of herself and Fitz at Machu Picchu, and one of Tessa and RJ down at the pier. The photo of Callie, Adam, and Danny was from the Christmas card they had sent out last year. The snapshot of Luke and Zeke was adorable, probably from the night they got engaged, given their goofy looks and the bottle of champagne on the table in front of them. There was one of Dora and David with Sebastian and Carolina at a landmark of some kind in Ecuador. Maybe the equator? Finally, Dora had added a photo of Barrett, Lauren, and the twins taken shortly before Lauren's death. Mel wondered if this Christmas they would be able to take a giant family photo with all of them together. She hoped so.

At the top of the stairs, Mel paused to peek into her mom's room. Tessa had given her a heads up that not only had their mother redecorated, but she had hung the portrait of David. Sure enough, there it was, and no wonder she had chosen to hang it in the bedroom. David was shirtless, staring intently at the artist, and the painting might as well have had steam rising from it. She wasn't sure she wanted to see David as a hot older guy, so she started backing away, but the small plaque on the bottom of the frame caught her eye. Her mother had titled the painting "Adonis." Definitely too much information.

She found Fitz in her room, suitcases shoved into the corner, and he was heading into the hall to wash up before crashing. She followed his lead, digging out some clean, comfortable pjs and splashing water on her face before crawling into bed beside him.

"It feels good to be home," she said, snuggling into the crook of his arm. "I'm looking forward to seeing everyone."

"Me, too," he said. "It will be great to catch up with everyone."

He was quiet for a minute, and she was drifting off to sleep when he spoke again.

"Home isn't really a place, you know."

"Hmmm?"

"Home is wherever you are."

She lifted her face for a kiss, and then they drifted off to sleep.

Thank you so much for reading *Love Letters*!

If you loved Dora and Mel's stories, go back to the beginning and see how it all began with Callie and Adam in *Love Song (Instrumental)*, followed by Tessa and RJ in *Love Story (Confidential)* and Kat and Rob in *Love Me Not*.

SIGN UP for Lisa McLuckie's eNewsletter (signup link at www.LisaMcLuckie.com) to receive new release alerts, insider information, and bonus content.

THANK YOU for helping to spread the word about *Love Letters*. Reviews help readers discover new authors, so please pay it forward by leaving a review on your favorite book site, and be sure to tell your book-loving friends if you enjoyed the story.

And now, an **EXCERPT** from *Love Song (Instrumental)*.

Love Song (Instrumental)

Callie shut off the car at the top of the hill and looked out across the lake. The sun had yet to crest over the trees on the far shore, but she could see glimmers of it through the screen of bare trunks and branches. The landscape had that ragged, morning-after look of spring. No blanket of snow softened the harsh hangover of winter. Only a few brave buds and shoots dusted the view, hinting at a new beginning. The world was dark, wet, and cold, and Callie wondered if she had made a mistake in coming home.

The sudden silence woke Roscoe, who stretched on the passenger seat, hind leg twitching, then sat up to look around. He shook off his nap and drool splattered around the interior of her ancient Bronco. Callie wiped a few drops off her cheek.

"You're disgusting, hound dog," she said as she scratched behind his ears.

"Arrghuumfp?"

"Yes, you. Truly disgusting."

He didn't seem concerned. Roscoe had seen some hard

times before Callie found him at the shelter, and he knew he had a good gig. He flopped back down, head in her lap, and Callie continued to rub his head while she stared out over the water.

"Well, Roscoe, we made it. Welcome to rock bottom, the place where dreams come to die."

She shifted the car into neutral, eased off the brake, and let the Bronco coast down the long gravel drive until it rolled to a stop in the shadow of the old house.

No curious face appeared at the window over the kitchen sink. Nobody opened the back door. Apparently the old high-school trick still worked: with the engine turned off, they hadn't heard her coming. She couldn't remember who had first thought of it—Mel, probably—but shook her head thinking of all the times it had saved their butts. Given the Bronco's current state of disrepair, she counted herself lucky once again and muscled the gearshift into park. She refused to think about how pathetic it was to be using that trick at the ripe old age of twenty-seven.

Roscoe pawed at the passenger-side door handle.

"Just a sec, Roscoe honey."

She leaned her head back against the headrest. After twelve hours on the road, her legs were stiff, her shoulders sore, and she wanted nothing more than a hot bath and a change of clothes. She looked down at the tabloid under Roscoe's feet, now featuring spatters of his drool, and sighed. She couldn't hide from her parents forever. After several swats in the face with an overactive tail, she gave in.

"Okay, okay. We'll get out. But you keep your voice down."

She shoved her door open and he bounded out, too distracted by all the new sights and smells to waste time barking.

As she climbed out after him, that first breath of icy air cleared her head. The gentle spring of Tennessee had faded into her rear-view mirror more than five hundred miles back. This far north, just into Wisconsin, winter still ruled. She wrapped her long sweater more tightly around her body and crossed her arms, wishing she had thought to pack more sweaters. Maybe some of her old ones were still in her bedroom, if her sisters hadn't appropriated them this past Christmas.

She gently closed the door of the Bronco and followed Roscoe around the side of the house, delaying the inevitable for a few minutes longer. The flagstones on the path were slick with frost, but Callie determinedly picked her way down the hill toward the lake. Roscoe had disappeared, but she didn't worry. He wouldn't venture far without her. When she reached the shore, she breathed deeply, closed her eyes, and listened to the waves breaking on the pebbled beach.

She had missed this. The stillness. The water flowing through her veins. Her roots sinking deep into the earth. Love it or leave it, this was home. And at this moment, the best thing about home was the distance separating it from Nashville. There were no lies here, no roles to play. No photographers or reporters. Best of all, there was no Brian—and no need to stand by her man.

There was only stillness—for the moment, anyway.

She opened her eyes to see her breath on the cold air, echoing the trails of mist rising off the water. She could hear the rhythm of the breaking waves and the branches creaking as the wind passed through them. All around her, the world began to wake up. Two squirrels chattered angrily above her in the trees. An odd assortment of gulls, ducks, and geese gathered in a sheltered inlet nearby, the ducks occasionally turning tail-up to dive beneath the surface of the water. Two chipmunks chased each other through the maze of disassembled docks that had been pulled from the water last fall and stacked on the shore for winter storage. Roscoe explored the beach, overjoyed to discover a dead fish.

She heard the scrape of a shoe on the shore path.

Callie tensed, her fragile peace broken. She turned her head to search for the intruder and found him immediately. Down the path to her left stood a young boy, staring out at the water. He seemed as unaware of her presence as she had been of his. This seemed odd at first, but then she realized he was deep in thought, muttering from time to time under his breath, and punctuating his monologue by kicking a mixture of dirt and gravel from the path into the water. He was awfully young to be down here by himself. Growing up, she and her sisters had known the mantra by heart: Nobody goes down to the water alone.

But where had the boy come from? Most of the cottages along this stretch of the shore belonged to summer people. The arrival of a new family, particularly a year-round family with children, would have been big news, worth at least a mention the last time her mother had called. Then again, maybe not. Callie had been ducking her mother's calls, or cutting them short, for more than a year. Who knew what other news she had missed?

She shot a sharp glance up toward the cottage next door. Had the Reese boys finally sold their grandmother's cottage? Or rented it? Surely her mother would have said something.

"Danny!" A man's voice called out from up the hill—from next door—the sound breaking the stillness of the morning. Roscoe snapped to attention, assessing the threat level. She stiffened as well, every sense on high alert as the implications echoed through her. Somebody was living next door. She had heard enough to sense the tension in the man's voice, the edge of panic, but not enough for her to be sure of his identity.

The boy froze like a startled deer, then darted up the path toward the cottage. Thankfully Roscoe did not give chase. A moment later Callie heard a screen door slam shut. Little Danny was in for a lecture. The question was, from whom?

As far as she knew, Adam was still in Singapore—not that she could be sure of anything anymore. She had cut ties with him years ago. He might as well be on the moon. But his little brother Evan had married Lainey and had a couple of kids. Maybe they had decided to live up here full time. Or maybe they had sold the cottage and nobody had bothered to tell her. Her stomach clenched and she fought a wave of despair. How had she allowed herself to drift so far away? It had been more than two years since she had last been home, and that had been for Christmas. She hadn't been home in the summer, when everyone would be here, since that summer after high school. She sighed, wishing—not for the first time—that life came with at least one do-over.

Callie took one last look across the water. The rising sun made a weak attempt to warm her nose and cheeks, but it didn't help much. She was cold, and like Danny next door, the time had come for her to go inside. There were no answers to be found out here.

She whistled for Roscoe, who scampered behind her as she climbed back up the hill, smelling everything along the way. She grabbed her purse and duffel bag from the car, along with a bag of food for Roscoe, but left the crumpled tabloid on the passenger seat. She would burn it later. The back door didn't open as she approached, and Callie hesitated for a moment, wondering if she should knock. But that seemed too strange, knocking at home, so she just walked in. Her parents sat at the kitchen table, finishing their tea as they shared the morning paper and listened to the news on the radio.

"Hi," said Callie weakly. Too late she realized that she must look a complete mess after driving all night. Her curls straggled down her back, tangled and limp, her clothes felt like she had slept in them, and she hadn't thought to hide the dark smudges under her eyes. This was not going to go well.

By the time she took two steps through the mudroom to the kitchen, they had both jumped up from the table, leaving mugs and newspapers behind. Mom got to her first.

"Callie, sweetie, what in the world are you doing here?" she demanded. Roscoe joined the fun, weaving in and out of all the legs until he found his way into the kitchen and disappeared, exploring again. "And since when do you have a dog?"

Her father neatly grabbed the duffel and set it aside. Her mother pulled her into a huge hug, talking all the while.

"Not that we don't want to see you because of course we do, anytime, you know that. But you didn't call! We had no idea you were coming." Callie found herself suddenly released and held at arms' length. "You didn't send me an email, did you? You know I never check the computer. But your father does." She shot an accusing glance at Luke, keeping hold of Callie. "Luke, did you get an email from Callie and not tell me about it? You know I count on you to tell me about all the emails."

He shook his head, smiling. He knew better than to interrupt before she had a chance to wind down on her own.

"Well then. No call. No email. Oh my God, what's the matter?" her mother asked. "Tell me, quickly. Is it something with the band? What did Brian do this time?"

Her mother's fingers had tightened on her shoulders, so Callie gently pried herself loose while trying to reassure her mother. It was more difficult than usual because her voice was in particularly bad shape this morning. It came out as something between a whisper and a frog.

"I'm fine, Mom," she croaked. "Everything is fine." Callie kept the lie short and sweet, not wanting to trip the parental lie detectors.

At the same time, her father said, "Dora, relax, I'm sure everything is fine."

But then both her parents reacted to the sound of her voice.

Dora planted her hands on her hips. "Everything is certainly not fine, young lady. You have no voice. Running yourself ragged with that band and look what happens! Now you can't even talk. You're pale, you have dark circles under your eyes and your hair looks like it hasn't been brushed in weeks. And why do you need to dress like a hippie? There's a reason it all went out of fashion, you know. You're not even wearing a coat! Are you sick? You don't have throat cancer, do you? Oh my God. I'll call the doctor."

By this time Callie was laughing, hoarsely, which turned into a coughing fit. With her voice gone, she couldn't talk over her mother as she normally would. Luke looked concerned as well, but he put his arm around Dora and drew her back toward the kitchen table.

"Now, Dora, let's give Callie a chance to explain why she's here. Sit down," he said more firmly as she tried to walk around him to get back to her daughter. "Callie, would you like some tea? Might help that throat, and the kettle's still hot."

She nodded, giving her father a quick hug. She took a seat across the table from her mother, who was muttering something under her breath about how she had always known that the band would be trouble even before they had chosen the name Deep Trouble. Callie didn't feel like arguing the point.

She waited until her father joined them with the hot tea and took a slow sip, easing the roughness in her throat while she thought about how much to say. Her father took a seat next to her mother, mostly so he could anchor her to her chair.

The seating arrangement gave Callie a disorienting sense of déjà vu. This was not a press interview. There were no TV cameras to capture every slip of the tongue or any tell-tale body language, but she couldn't help feeling the similarities. As if he could sense her unease, Roscoe chose that moment to return to the kitchen and curl up on her feet. Before her mother could freak out about the dog, Callie took a deep breath and began.

"You can hear that I have no voice," she whisper-croaked.

"Yes, but why?" asked Dora, as Luke simultaneously said, "Hush, let her finish." They both smiled at her in encouragement.

"It's not cancer," she said as firmly as she could. "It's not even a virus. I'm not sick, exactly."

Callie paused to clear her throat, even though the doctor had told her repeatedly that throat-clearing would only make the problem worse. She just couldn't help it.

"The doctor calls it vocal fatigue, and he said the only cure is to rest both myself and my voice for at least a month. Maybe longer."

It was the 'longer' that really scared her. Callie intended to follow the doctor's advice, but she needed to get back to Nashville by the end of May to prepare for the summer tour. No matter how bad things might be with the band right now, the tour was her only path forward—unless she abandoned her career completely. Hopefully four weeks of rest would be enough. It had to be enough.

Callie continued before her parents could ask more detailed questions.

"So of course I came home. Things are just too crazy in Nashville. Even if I'm not singing, there's so much work to do.... I needed to get away—really away. So I came here."

Callie stopped and took another sip of the tea, bracing herself for the follow-up questions. But they never came. Luke spoke first, while simultaneously giving Dora a warning squeeze.

"Of course you came home," said Luke. "This is the perfect place to get the rest you need, and we're so glad that you knew you would be welcome"—he gave Dora a pat on the shoulder —"no questions asked."

Dora shot him a dark look. Callie knew the questions were simply on hold, but she appreciated the reprieve.

"Did you drive all night?" her father asked.

Callie nodded.

"Are you hungry?"

Callie shook her head.

"Then it's off to bed with you. Don't show your face back downstairs until noon at the earliest. Got it?"

Callie nodded again and smiled with relief. Yes-no questions were easy.

"I have to go to work, but I'll see you ladies later today." He turned to Dora as he stood up. "And don't pester her with questions. You'll get your answers soon enough."

Dora crossed her arms like a petulant child, but she nodded curtly. Callie stifled a smile as she stood up, wiggling her feet out from under Roscoe. She grabbed her bags, then gave her dad a peck on the cheek and her mom a hug.

"Thanks," she whispered. "It's good to be home."

She turned quickly, blinking back tears, and headed for the stairs with Roscoe padding after her. She could hear her parents arguing in whispers as she turned the corner on the landing, but the bathtub was calling, and the bed after that. Everything else could wait.

Want to read more? Find *Love Song (Instrumental)* at your favorite bookseller.

ACKNOWLEDGMENTS

Most people think of writing as a solitary affair, but in reality it takes a village. I'd like to take a moment to acknowledge all the people in my village who helped to make this book happen.

In addition to all the people who have helped shape the world of Hidden Springs through the first three books, I'd like to extend a special thank you to Julie Sarton, who shared her insight into the business of art. Melissa Frain and and Darlene Johnson lent their editorial and proofreading skills to this project, and once again Sue Giroux designed a beautiful cover. As always, thanks to my family for their patience with the mysterious "work" that is writing.

With love and gratitude,
Lisa

ABOUT THE AUTHOR

Lisa McLuckie was born a wanderer. She has lived in four states and two foreign countries, had twenty-four different addresses, and explored five of the seven continents. Her debut novel, *Love Song (Instrumental),* earned two honors from the Independent Book Publishers Association in 2015: the Benjamin Franklin Gold Award for Romance Fiction, and the Bill Fisher Silver Award for Best First Book (Fiction).

She currently lives on the fringes of Chicagoland with her husband, three sons, and a ridiculously adorable dog named Daisy. Learn more at LisaMcLuckie.com.

Books by Lisa McLuckie
Love Song (Instrumental)
Love Story (Confidential)
Love Me Not
Love Letters

ABOUT HIDDEN SPRINGS

Growing up, I spent a lot of time in the lake country of south-eastern Wisconsin. This area may not be quite as famous as the Finger Lakes region in upstate New York, or Lake Tahoe out west, but for me that makes it better. A little more down-to-earth. A little less crowded. The fictional town of Hidden Springs is a wonderful mash-up of all the different lake towns I love, past and present, large (relatively speaking) and small.

If you want to know more about the real-world lakes of southeastern Wisconsin, these websites provide a great starting point.

- http://www.travelwisconsin.com/southeast/walworth-county
- http://www.visitwalworthcounty.com/
- https://www.visitlakegeneva.com/
- http://www.discoverwhitewater.org/
- http://www.cruiselakegeneva.com/
- http://www.atthelakemagazine.com/

I'll see you at the lake!
Lisa

Made in the USA
Middletown, DE
03 July 2022